AMBUSH!

Smoke slipped the hammer thongs from his Colts, then put his hand on the butt of the Henry rifle in the scabbard next to his saddle and shook it a little to make sure it was loose and ready to be pulled.

He tugged gently on the reins to slow Horse from a trot to a walk and settled back in the saddle, hands hanging next to his pistols.

Even with his precautions, he was surprised when a man jumped out of the brush into the middle of the trail in front of him. It was George Hampton, and he was pointing a Colt Navy pistol at Smoke.

"Get down off that horse, you bastard."

Smoke spread his hands wide and swung his leg over the cantle and dropped, cat-like, to the ground. "Hampton, I thought you'd be halfway home by now."

"I ain't gonna go home 'til I've put a bullet between the eyes of the famous Smoke Jensen."

BOOK YOUR PLACE ON OUR WEBSITE AND MAKE THE READING CONNECTION!

We've created a customized website just for our very special readers, where you can get the inside scoop on everything that's going on with Zebra, Pinnacle and Kensington books.

When you come online, you'll have the exciting opportunity to:

- View covers of upcoming books
- Read sample chapters
- Learn about our future publishing schedule (listed by publication month *and author*)
- Find out when your favorite authors will be visiting a city near you
- Search for and order backlist books from our online catalog
- Check out author bios and background information
- Send e-mail to your favorite authors
- Meet the Kensington staff online
- Join us in weekly chats with authors, readers and other guests
- Get writing guidelines
- AND MUCH MORE!

**Visit our website at
http://www.zebrabooks.com**

GUNS OF THE MOUNTAIN MAN

William W. Johnstone

Zebra Books
Kensington Publishing Corp.
http://www.zebrabooks.com

ZEBRA BOOKS are published by

Kensington Publishing Corp.
850 Third Avenue
New York, NY 10022

First Printing: November, 1999
10 9 8 7 6 5 4 3 2 1

Printed in the United States of America

One

Calvin Woods was talking to himself as he rode out to the northern section of the Sugarloaf Ranch. He and Pearlie, the foreman, had been stringing fence earlier, and Cal had forgotten to load up the extra wire and tools when it came time to head back to the ranch house. Now he was having to ride all the way back out there to pick up the tools, and was giving Pearlie first shot at the bearsign donuts Miss Sally was sure to have cooling in the kitchen.

"Darn it all, by the time I get back Pearlie'll have 'bout near all them bearsign eaten up, Dusty," Cal said bitterly to the back of his horse's head. "I'll be lucky if'n I get more'n one or two."

Cal's horse was the offspring of a cross between Joey Wells's big strawberry roan named Red and one of the Palouse mares Sally had given to him and his wife a couple of years ago. The horse, called a quicksilver gray, was actually almost pure white, differing from a true white albino by having blue eyes instead of pink. The bronc was a pale gray in front with snow-white hips, without the typical Palouse spots on its hindquarters. Cal had named him Dusty, and had formed a deep bond with the animal the first time he'd ridden him.

He found the tools where he'd left them and loaded them in a burlap sack, which he tied to the back of his saddle. As he stood next to his horse, he built himself a cigarette. He figured he'd smoke it out here, since Smoke Jensen's wife, Sally, didn't much care for him smoking. She said he was too young, and he'd have plenty of time to smoke and drink all he wanted when he got older.

Heck, he thought, *I'm old enough to smoke or drink if'n I want to. I'm dang sure old enough to string ten miles of fence 'round this here pasture an' work 'til I'm sore all over.*

As he puffed, he looked out over the herd of Hereford and shorthorn mixes. *Smoke was really smart to get those Herefords from Mr. Chisum an' breed 'em with the shorthorns last year,* he thought. *They sure do throw off some good lookin' calves.*

He remembered what Miss Sally had said when she proposed the crossbreeding—that the crosses would be more hardy, give more and better tasting meat, and be more resistant to disease than either of the parent breeds.

Just as he stubbed out his cigarette, he heard the sound of horses, lots of them, coming from just over a nearby ridge.

Wonder who that could be? he thought. *This pasture is smack in the middle of the Sugarloaf, and there shouldn't be nobody riding across it unless they're up to no good.*

He swung into the saddle and loosened the rawhide hammer thong on his Colt as he rode toward the ridge. Lately, he'd taken to imitating his hero, Smoke Jensen, and carried both a Winchester in his left saddle boot and a Greener 10-gauge double-barreled express gun in his right boot.

Cresting the ridge, he pulled the shotgun from its scabbard and eared back the hammers as he reined his horse to a halt.

Down the hill, he saw a group of about fifteen or twenty men on horseback. Several of the riders were cutting a fat steer out of the herd while the others sat in their saddles, watching.

Cal was trying to decide whether he should ride down and brace the men alone or hightail it back to the ranch house and get some help. He didn't particularly like the odds of twenty to one, but he knew if he took the time to go for backup the men might be gone by the time they got back here.

His decision was made for him when one of the rustlers looked up and saw him sitting on the ridge. He leaned over and spoke to a tall man wearing a black frock coat, who turned to stare at Cal.

"Heck," Cal mumbled to his horse, "in for a penny, in for a pound, as they say."

He spurred his bronc down the hill and rode up to the group.

"Howdy, gents," he said, speaking to the tall man who appeared to be in charge.

Up close, the galoot was even stranger looking than he had been from a distance. He appeared to be over six and a half feet tall, was skinny to the point of being gaunt, and had a scraggly goatee covering his lips and chin. His eyes had a wild, haunted look as if there was nothing behind them, and he was dressed all in black, from his coat and vest to his pants and boots. His boiled shirt was the only spot of lightness about him. As he turned in the saddle, Cal could see he wore a Colt on each hip, and a Henry Yellow Boy rifle was resting across his thighs.

All in all, he reminded Cal of the man named Ichabod Crane in the story "The Legend of Sleepy Hollow" Miss Sally had read to him when he was taking his schooling.

"You men are aware you're trespassin' on private property, aren't you?" Cal asked when he got no response to his greeting.

"What is your name, boy?" the man in black asked.

"My name's Cal. What's yours?"

"Lazarus. Lazarus Cain," the man answered, acting as if the name should mean something to Cal.

It didn't.

"Have you been saved, Cal?" Lazarus asked.

Cal snorted. The man's eyes didn't lie. He *was* crazy.

"Saved from what?" Cal asked, his eyebrows raised.

"Why, from hell and damnation, of course."

"What's all this got to do with the fact you men are stealin' my boss's cattle?"

"I don't like this young pup calling me a thief, boss," a young Mexican said, kicking his horse to ride up in front of Cal. He put his hand on his pistol butt and added, "Why don't I just kill him?"

Lazarus turned his head to look at Cal, his eyebrows raised, as if waiting to see how Cal would handle the challenge.

"Anytime you think you're ready, *cabrón*," Cal said, easing the barrel of the express gun toward the Mexican.

Cabrón being about the worst thing a Mexican could be called, the man went for his pistol.

Cal let the hammer down on his shotgun, firing from the hip, and splattered the Mexican all over the men behind him, blowing him out of the saddle to land in several pieces on the ground.

As the explosion echoed across the hilly landscape and the horses jumped and crow-hopped at the noise, Cal pulled the barrel around until it pointed at Lazarus.

"We got you outnumbered twenty to one, boy," Lazarus said, staring at Cal with an appraising stare.

Cal inclined his head toward the body on the ground. "Nineteen to one now, Mr. Cain, an' if'n any more of your men get itchy trigger fingers, you'll be the next one I kill."

"You're pretty brave sitting behind that shotgun, boy."

Cal showed his teeth, but he wasn't smiling. "Like Mr. Colt said, God created all men equal, only this here express gun makes some more equal than others." He inclined his head. "Now, I'd suggest you gentlemen ride on outta here, leavin' the beeves you've cut outta the herd behind."

As he finished speaking, Cal saw out of the corner of his eye a man start to raise a pistol.

He swiveled in his saddle and fired the second barrel of the Greener, blowing the man's right arm off at the shoulder and slamming him out of the saddle.

Before he could turn back, Lazarus drew his pistol and fired twice, one slug taking Cal in the left shoulder and the other in the right chest, shattering a rib and imbedding itself deep within his chest.

Cal was catapulted off his horse to land flat on his back, staring at a cloudless, blue sky.

Lazarus got off his mount and walked over to stand looking down at Cal.

"You got a lot of sand—I'll say that for you boy."

Cal's vision blurred, then focused in time to see Lazarus do the strangest thing . . . He pulled out a Bible and held it up, spreading his hands wide toward heaven. Then he began to pray for Cal's soul in a loud, harsh voice.

As the crazy man prayed, Cal noticed blackness creeping across the sky until it became a large, dark hole which swallowed him up.

After Cal lapsed into unconsciousness, Lazarus continued to pray for a few moments. He had started to walk back toward his horse when he noticed Dusty standing a short distance away from Cal.

He pursed his lips, thinking. Then his eyes widened and a joyful expression came over his face. He walked over and picked up Dusty's reins, calming the horse with a low, soothing voice when he tried to shy away from the stranger.

Lazarus pulled the reins and led Dusty over to the group of men waiting to see what he would do next.

He grinned and pointed at the white horse with one hand, held up his Bible, and began to speak in low, sonorous tones,

"So I looked, and behold, a pale horse. And the name of him who sat on it was Death, and Hades followed with him. And power was given to them over a fourth of the earth, to kill with sword, with hunger, with death, and by the beasts of the earth."

"What the hell is that supposed to mean, Lazarus?" asked Blackie Jackson, who sat leaning forward in his saddle with his arms crossed over his saddle horn.

Lazarus cut his eyes toward Blackie. "That, Blackie, for your information, is from the Bible, the Book of Revelation, chapter six, verse eight."

"Yeah, boss, but what's it mean?" asked Curly Joe Ventrillo as he upended a small bottle of whiskey and drained it dry.

"Coming upon this young man, with his pale horse, is another sign from God that I . . . that is *we,* are on the correct path. That we are indeed doing his bidding and will be rewarded with his blessings."

"So, you intend to take that white hoss, or what?" asked another of Lazarus's gang members—Tom "Behind the Deuces" Cartwright.

Lazarus bent and released the belly cinch on Cal's saddle and let it drop to the ground. "Yes, I intend to ride this pale horse, as the Bible said, and I will ride across a fourth of the country, like Death followed by Hades, killing and doing God's work until he calls us home."

Blackie Jackson covered a prodigious yawn with a ham-like hand. "Well, whatever the hell you're gonna do, you better hurry up and do it. Them shots are liable to bring some more punchers on the run."

"If anyone else comes, we will deal with them the same way we did this young man," Lazarus said, as he tightened down his saddle on Cal's bronc.

"I for one do not mind fighting, old chap," said Jeremy Brett, the Englishman, "but personally, I would rather save my energies for when there might be a possibility of profit in the matter."

Lazarus climbed into the saddle. "Well said, Jeremy." He put the spurs to Dusty's flanks and called out, "Let's ride!"

Two

Smoke Jensen, legendary gunfighter, leaned against the wall of his cabin with his arms folded and watched his ranch foreman, Pearlie, devour Sally's bearsign donuts as if he hadn't eaten for months. Sally, standing next to the kitchen table, wiped flour off her nose and shook her head. As many times as she'd seen Pearlie eat, it still amazed her how much food the cowboy could put away.

Standing just under six feet tall, Pearlie weighed no more than a hundred and fifty pounds and hadn't an ounce of fat on his body. His face was brown as mahogany and wrinkled from twenty years riding in the sun, and one could usually tell what he'd had for his last meal from the crumbs that accumulated in his handlebar mustache. He was a good foreman, and his hands were intensely loyal in spite of the many practical jokes he played on them.

"Pearlie," Smoke asked, "didn't you just have breakfast a few hours ago?"

Pearlie mumbled something, but his mouth was so full Smoke couldn't understand him.

"Come again?"

Pearlie swallowed with an audible gulp, then washed the donuts down with a tall glass of fresh cow's milk. "I said, I was runnin' late this mornin' an' I only got to eat three or four hen's eggs and a handful of bacon and three or four biscuits. Wasn't hardly enough to keep a body alive 'til noon-time."

"Oh, I see what you mean," Smoke said. "I guess I'm going to have to talk to Cookie about keeping you men on starvation rations."

Pearlie nodded, then took the platter of bearsign and put them in the cabinet, out of sight. He broke off a small piece of one and placed it in the middle of the table on a plate.

"Pearlie, what are you doing?" Sally asked.

Pearlie grinned. "When Cal gets back here, all he's gonna see is that little bitty piece of bearsign, an' he's gonna think I ate 'em all up." He laughed. "Boy, is he gonna be mad."

Pearlie, like most of the Sugarloaf hired hands, thought of Cal as a little brother, and was continually teasing him about one thing or another. Cal had even complained that he was getting calluses on his back from Pearlie riding him so much.

Smoke walked out on the porch to light a cigar and finish his coffee, as Sally didn't allow smoking in the cabin. He smiled to himself, thinking back on how Pearlie had come to work for him and the changes in the young man since that day.

Pearlie had come to work for Smoke in a rather roundabout way. He was hiring his gun out to Tilden Franklin in Fontana when Franklin went crazy and tried to take over Sugarloaf, Smoke and Sally's spread. After Franklin's men raped and killed a young girl in the fracas, Pearlie had sided with Smoke and the aging gunfighters he had called in to help put an end to Franklin's reign of terror.*

Pearlie was now honorary foreman of Smoke's ranch, though he was only a shade over twenty years old himself—boys grew to be men early in the mountains of Colorado.

*Trail of the Mountain Man

As Smoke emptied his coffee cup, he heard a distant boom-ing, followed by two sharp cracks which echoed off nearby mountain peaks. He jerked his head around to look toward the area the sounds came from.

"Pearlie!" he called, stepping off the porch to get a better look.

Pearlie, recognizing the urgency in Smoke's voice, came running out the door.

"Yes sir?"

"I just heard what sounded like shots from the direction you and Cal were working in this morning. Is anybody else out in that section?"

"No sir," Pearlie answered, a worried look on his face. "The rest of the hands were over to the west, worming the new calves."

"What's wrong, Smoke?" Sally asked, wiping her hands on her apron as she followed Pearlie out the door.

"I don't know, but I'm afraid Cal is in some trouble. Gun-shots from the pasture where he's working."

Smoke hesitated just a moment, then said to Sally, "You get a buckboard and head on out to the north pasture, where we have the Hereford crosses. Pearlie and I'll ride on ahead to see what's happening."

"All right," she said, jerking her apron off.

"And Sally, bring your medical kit and your pistol."

Smoke ran to the hitching post in front of the cabin where he and Pearlie had their horses tied. He was riding a new two-year-old stud Joey Wells had sent over from Pueblo, Colorado. Joey and his wife had bought the old Rocking C Ranch after killing Murdock, the man who owned it, and Smoke and Sally gave them some Palouse mares to breed with Joey's big roan, which he called Red.*

*Honor of the Mountain Man

Smoke's stud was a blanket-hipped Palouse, roan-colored in the front with hips of snow white, without the usual spots of a Palouse. He'd named him Joker because of his odd coloring.

Pearlie also had one of the offspring of Red, a gray-and-white Palouse he'd named Cold. When Smoke asked him why he'd named him that, Pearlie said it was because the sucker was cold-backed in the morning and bucked for the first ten minutes every day when Pearlie saddled him up.

In spite of this, both studs were beautiful animals and had inherited their father's big size and extreme strength and endurance, along with the Palouse's legendary quickness and intelligence.

Smoke and Pearlie leaned over the necks of their mounts and rode hell-bent-for-leather toward the pasture where Cal was.

A short time later, Smoke was leaning over Cal's still body, holding a bandanna soaked in water from his canteen pressed tight against the boy's chest wound when Sally arrived in the buckboard. Pearlie's bandanna was tied as a tourniquet around Cal's arm just below the shoulder, and had slowed the bleeding there to a trickle.

Sally grabbed her medical bag from the seat next to her and jumped to the ground. After ripping Cal's shirt open to get a better look at his wound, she took a deep breath and glanced at Smoke with a worried frown on her face.

"It's a lung wound. See how the blood on his lips is frothy, and bright red?"

Smoke nodded. No stranger to gunshot wounds himself, he'd come to the same conclusion. "Do you think there's any chance?"

Sally frowned. "If we can stop the air from his lungs from coming out of the wound, it might allow his lung to re-expand and keep him alive until Doc Spalding can operate on him."

She glanced over her shoulder at the wagon she'd ridden in on. Pulling a clean, white cloth from her medical kit, she handed it to Smoke. "Here, take this rag over to the wagon and smear axle grease from around the wheel bearings all over it. Put on a thick coat."

Smoke did what she said, then handed her the grease-covered cloth.

Sally opened it up and slapped it over Cal's sucking chest wound, plugging the hole and stopping air from hissing in and out every time he tried to breathe.

The grease had the added effect of slowing the blood from the wound, but even so, Cal was the color of flour.

"He's lost a lot of blood," Sally said.

"Do you think he's able to make the trip into Big Rock?" Pearlie asked.

"We don't have any choice. If he's going to have any chance of survival at all, Doc's going to have to operate as soon as possible."

"Smoke, looky here," Pearlie called.

Smoke walked over and saw Pearlie standing over Cal's saddle, lying on the ground. Nearby were two large pools of blood, soaking into the soil.

"It appears Cal put lead into at least two of 'em," Pearlie said, pointing to the bloodstains.

"Yeah, and the bastards stole Dusty after they shot Cal," Smoke added, his face as dark as clouds fronting a thunderstorm.

As soon as Cal was breathing more normally, Smoke and Pearlie lifted him up and put him in the back of the wagon.

Pearlie grabbed the reins and drove while Sally and Smoke sat in the back, trying to keep Cal from rolling around too much as they traveled over rough terrain.

Once, Cal's eyes flicked open for a second. They were vacant, as if he really wasn't fully conscious.

Smoke leaned close to his ear. "Cal, it's Smoke. Who did this to you?"

"Ichabod . . . Ichabod Crane," Cal croaked through dry, blood-covered lips.

Smoke sat back, wondering what the hell he meant. As he watched the young man fight for his life in the back of a bouncing wagon, Smoke thought back to the day the boy had come to work for him. . . .

Calvin Woods, going on nineteen years old now, had been just fourteen when Smoke and Sally had taken him in as a hired hand. It was during the spring branding, and Sally was on her way back from Big Rock to the Sugarloaf. The buckboard was piled high with supplies, because branding hundreds of calves made for hungry punchers.

As Sally slowed the team to make a bend in the trail, a rail-thin young man stepped from the bushes at the side of the road with a pistol in his hand.

"Hold it right there, miss."

Applying the brake with her right foot, Sally slipped her hand under a pile of gingham cloth on the seat. She grasped the handle of her short-barreled Colt .44 and eared back the hammer, letting the sound of the horses' hooves and the squealing of the brake pad on the wheel mask the sound. "What can I do for you, young man?" she asked, her voice firm and without fear. She knew she could draw and drill the young highwayman before he could raise his pistol to fire.

"Well, uh, you can throw some of those beans and a cut of that fatback over here, and maybe a portion of that Arbuckle's coffee, too."

Sally's eyebrows raised. "Don't you want my money?"

The boy frowned and shook his head. "Why, no ma'am. I ain't no thief. I'm just hungry."

"And if I don't give you my food, are you going to shoot me with that big Navy Colt?"

He hesitated a moment, then grinned ruefully. "No ma'am, I guess not." He twirled the pistol around his finger and slipped it into his belt, turned, and began to walk down the road toward Big Rock.

Sally watched the youngster amble off, noting his tattered shirt, dirty pants with holes in the knees and torn pockets, and boots that looked as if they had been salvaged from a garbage dump. "Young man," she called, "come back here, please."

He turned, a smirk on his face, spreading his hands, "Look lady, you don't have to worry. I don't even have any bullets." With a lightning-fast move he drew the gun from his pants, aimed away from Sally and pulled the trigger. There was a click but no explosion as the hammer fell on an empty cylinder.

Sally smiled. "Oh, I'm not worried." In a movement every bit as fast as his she whipped her .44 out and fired, clipping a pine cone from a branch, causing it to fall and bounce off his head.

The boy's knees buckled and he ducked, saying, "Jiminy Christmas!"

Mimicking him, Sally twirled her Colt and stuck it in the waistband of her britches. "What's your name, boy?"

The boy blushed and looked down at his feet. "Calvin, ma'am. Calvin Woods."

She leaned forward, elbows on knees, and stared into the boy's eyes. "Calvin, no one has to go hungry in this country, not if they're willing to work."

He looked up at her through narrowed eyes, as if he'd found life a little different than she described it.

"If you're willing to put in an honest day's work, I'll see that you get an honest day's pay, and all the food you can eat."

Calvin stood a little straighter, shoulders back and head held high. "Ma'am, I've got to be straight with you. I ain't no experienced cowhand. I come from a hardscrabble farm, and we only had us one milk cow and a couple of goats and chickens, and lots of dirt that weren't worth nothing for growin' things. My Ma and Pa and me never had nothin', but we never begged and we never stooped to takin' hand-outs."

Sally thought, *I like this boy. Proud, and not willing to take charity if he can help it.* "Calvin, if you're willing to work, and don't mind getting your hands dirty and your muscles sore, I've got some hands that'll have you punching beeves like you were born to it in no time at all."

A smile lit up his face, making him seem even younger than his years. "Even if I don't have no saddle, nor a horse to put it on?"

She laughed out loud. "Yes. We've got plenty of ponies and saddles." She glanced down at his raggedy boots. "We can probably even round up some boots and spurs that'll fit you."

He walked over and jumped in the back of the buckboard. "Ma'am, I don't know who you are, but you just hired you the hardest workin' hand you've ever seen."

Back at the Sugarloaf, she sent him in to Cookie and told him to eat his fill. When Smoke and the other punchers rode into the cabin yard at the end of the day, she introduced Calvin around. As Cal was shaking hands with the men, Smoke looked over at her and winked. He knew she could never resist a stray dog or cat, that her heart was as large as the Big Lonesome itself.

Smoke walked up to Cal and cleared his throat. "Son, I hear you drew down on my wife."

Cal gulped. "Yes sir, Mr. Jensen. I did." He squared his shoulders and looked Smoke in the eye, not flinching though he was obviously frightened of the tall man with the incredibly wide shoulders standing before him.

Smoke smiled and clapped the boy on the back. "Just

wanted you to know you stared death in the eye, boy. Not many galoots are still walking upright who ever pulled a gun on Sally. She's a better shot than any man I've ever seen except me, and sometimes I wonder about me."

The boy laughed with relief as Smoke turned and called out, "Pearlie, get your lazy butt over here."

A tall, lanky cowboy ambled over to Smoke and Cal, munching on a biscuit stuffed with roast beef. His face was lined with wrinkles and tanned a dark brown from hours under the sun, and his eyes were sky-blue and twinkled with good-natured humor.

"Yes sir, boss," he mumbled around a mouthful of food.

Smoke put his hand on Pearlie's shoulder. "Cal, this here chow hound is Pearlie. He eats more'n any two hands, and he's never been known to do a lick of work he could get out of, but he knows beeves and horses as well as any puncher I have. I want you to follow him around and let him teach you what you need to know."

Cal nodded, "Yes sir, Mr. Smoke."

"Now let me see that iron you have in your pants."

Cal pulled the ancient Navy Colt and handed it to Smoke. When Smoke opened the loading gate, the rusted cylinder fell to the ground, causing Pearlie and Smoke to laugh and Cal's face to flame red. "This is the piece you pulled on Sally?"

The boy nodded, looking at the ground.

Pearlie shook his head. "Cal, you're one lucky pup. Hell, if'n you'd tried to fire that thing it'd of blown your hand clean off."

Smoke inclined his head toward the bunkhouse. "Pearlie, take Cal and get him fixed up with what he needs, including a gun belt and a Colt that won't fall apart the first time he pulls it. You might also help pick him out a shavetail to ride. I'll expect him to start earning his keep tomorrow."

"Yes sir, Smoke." Pearlie put his arm around Cal's shoulders and led him off toward the bunkhouse. "Now, the first thing you gotta learn, Cal, is how to get on Cookie's good side. A puncher rides on his belly, and it 'pears to me that you need some fattin' up 'fore you can begin to punch cows."

Smoke glanced up from his reverie to see Sally staring at Cal, too, tears in her eyes. He figured she was remembering the same things he was.

He reached across and took her hand in his, squeezing it to show he was as worried about Cal—a young man they'd both come to look upon as a son—as she was.

"We can't let him die, Smoke," she said, her voice husky with worry.

"Cal's too tough to die, Sally. He'll make it through this, I promise."

As the buckboard bounced and rocked over the uneven road toward Big Rock, Colorado, both Sally and Smoke prayed silently for their friend.

Pearlie, on the hurricane deck fighting the reins, was too busy to pray, but not too busy to cuss the men who'd had the gall to shoot his best friend, a man he considered closer than a brother.

In between hollering at the horse team pulling the wagon to run faster, Pearlie pledged he'd repay those who had done this to Cal if it was the last thing he ever did.

Three

As he rode, Lazarus enjoyed the feel of the pale horse underneath him. The animal was long through the croup, and thus had an easy, rocking chair gait. It was truly another sign from God that he was a chosen one, picked out of all the men on earth to spread God's word, and more importantly, to punish those evildoers who didn't obey His commandants.

The easy motion of the bronc lulled Lazarus into a dream-like state, and his mind roamed back to the day the Lord took him under His wing. . . .

It was just one of thousands of dirty little battles in the War Between the States, not even important enough to have a name. The Sixth Confederate Brigade from Arkansas was pinned down in a copse of woods—live oaks, maples, and birch mainly. It was the tail end of winter, and there were ragged patches of snow still on the ground in areas shadowed by trees or rocks.

The young boy from Lizard Lick, Arkansas, was more frightened than he'd ever been in his life. Laz, as he was called by his friends, lay on his stomach in the soggy, frigid mud and prayed that God would let him live through this terrible day. Over half the men in his troop had been killed or wounded, and the fire from the Yanks on the hills above them was devastating and showed no signs of stopping.

Another kid from his neck of the woods, Johnny Slater, was lying next to him in the muck, mumbling over and over how he wanted his mom and how he didn't want to die. Laz, whose father was a lay preacher in the Blood of the Sacred Lamb Pentecostal church back home, planned to follow his father into the preacherhood. He scrabbled over to Johnny on his hands and knees, pulling out his Bible.

"Johnny, pray with me for a minute, an' God will get us through this," Laz said, holding up the palm-sized Bible his dad had given him when he marched off to do battle for the Confederacy.

Johnny had raised wide, bulging eyes to stare at Laz. Then he'd broken out in maniacal laughter, his voice rising to levels that would have made a choirmaster proud. "Git away from me, Laz. Yore gonna draw their fire, you crazy bastard!" he screeched, waving Laz back with his hand.

"But, Johnny, you've got to take the Lord by the hand or we'll never survive this battle," Laz pleaded.

Just as he finished talking, a ball from a Yankee musket sang as it passed over their heads, making an evil-sounding thump as it buried itself in a tree trunk next to them.

"See, see?" Johnny screamed, rolling over to get farther away from Laz. "I tole you ya' was gonna bring their fire down on us with yore damn yappin' an' Bible-thumpin'."

"But—" Laz started to say.

"But nothin'," Johnny yelled, scrambling to his feet and lifting his musket out of the mud. He eared back the hammer and held the long rifle in front of him as he started running, low and bent over, toward a thicker group of trees fifty yards away.

"Johnny," Laz called, holding up his Bible, "trust in the Lord!"

Johnny paused and stood up to look back over his shoulder

at Laz, and his eyes widened and his mouth opened in surprise as a bullet passed into his back and erupted out of his chest, taking a good part of his ragged gray tunic with it.

The boy stood there a moment, looking down at the hole in his chest as if he couldn't believe it. Then he glanced up reproachfully at Laz, just before he tumbled to lie facedown in the soggy grass of the field.

At the sight of the death of his friend from home something snapped in Laz, and he jumped to his feet. He jammed his Bible into his breast pocket, where his dad had told him to wear it over his heart, and picked up his rifle. He began to yell and scream, urging his friends and fellow troops to get off their bellies and attack the Yankee dogs.

Unmindful of the withering fire from the slopes and hillocks around them, Laz walked out of the woods and began to fire and reload, fire and reload, all the while remaining miraculously unhit by musket balls and pistol bullets that flew around his head like angry bees.

Both shamed and inspired by this act of bravery, the men in Laz's troop jumped up and began to run at the Yankee troops dug in on the hills around them. As they ran they gave rebel yells and screams, terrifyingly loud and eerie in the foggy, misty morning air, ghostly tendrils of fog coming from their mouths.

Men around Laz began to fall from the fire above, but he remained unhit, firing his musket until the barrel glowed a ruddy red and steam poured off it. The sight of the rebel troops—advancing into hellish fire, screaming and yelling like madmen—unnerved the Yanks, and one by one they began to leave their positions and run away, looking back over their shoulders to see if those crazy rebs were still coming.

One of the last to leave took aim on the man leading the charge and fired. His ball took Laz in the chest and slammed him backward to land spread-eagled on his back in a patch of snow.

Some of the men nearby walked over to stare down at Laz, and almost fainted when he shook his head and sat up, a look of wonder on his face.

"Laz, boy, you awright?" Billy Manright asked around a plug of tobacco in his cheek.

Laz put his hand to his chest and pulled his father's Bible out of his pocket. Imbedded in it was the bullet meant to take Laz's life. At that moment, surrounded by dead and dying men, inhaling the stink of cordite and sulphur and blood and excrement, Lazarus Cain knew he'd been chosen by God for some important purpose.

"God saved me, boys!" Laz shouted. "He wants me to kill some more Yanks 'fore I die!"

The men gathered around him shouted and yelled, and they all turned to finish their attack, completely routing the superior Yankee forces that had them pinned down.

After the battle, Lazarus Cain received a promotion and a commendation. Before the war was to end, he would make colonel and lead his own troops into battle, always carrying his Bible with the bullet in it.

After that traitor to the cause, Robert E. Lee, surrendered, Lazarus and his band of men continued to fight, raiding towns sympathetic to the Yankees, killing and pillaging, looting and burning, until there was no place in the country they could go without being hunted. They were wanted in virtually every state and yet they continued to fight, even after forgetting what they were fighting for and who their enemy was. It became a way of life for them, and as his men got killed or captured Lazarus replaced them with men equally bloodthirsty and dangerous. . . .

This thought brought him fully awake, and he looked around him at the men riding with him. On his right hand was his second in command, Blackie Jackson. Five feet ten inches in height and weighing over two hundred and fifty pounds of solid muscle, Blackie had hands like hams and arms thicker than most men's necks. He was an ex-blacksmith from a small town in Texas. He had come to ride with Lazarus after catching his wife with another man. He'd worked on the man's head like it was a horseshoe, and when he finished with him had turned to his wife, sticking her head in his coal pit until it had burned to ashes. He was a man who liked to fight with his hands, and had never in his life been beaten.

On Lazarus's left rode Tom "Behind the Deuces" Cartwright. An ex-gambler, Tom got his nickname from his habit of betting heavily at faro whenever he was dealt two deuces. Physically, he was a small man with a rat-like face and a pencil mustache, skinny of frame with greasy, black hair that was thinning on top. Sensitive about his balding head, thinking he was a ladies' man, he rarely took his hat off. His favorite weapons were a derringer two-shot .44 he carried in his vest and a knife hidden in his boot. Though for long range he used a Winchester rifle, he much preferred the derringer, stating he liked to see the look in a man's eyes when life left him.

Behind Cartwright rode Curly Joe Ventrillo. Of Italian descent with dark, curly hair, he was twenty years old and a favorite with girls and women of all ages, having a baby face that was very handsome. His good looks hid his propensity for heavy drinking and violence toward women. This began on the owlhoot trail after cutting up a prostitute's face when he couldn't perform one night after getting drunk. He soon discovered he liked rough sex and hurting females, and repeated the act every chance he got.

On the other side of the group was Pig Iron Carlton, ex-professional fisticuffs champion. He had been running from the law since beating two men to death in a barroom brawl. Tall, muscular, he had hands and knuckles covered with scar tissue from his many bare-knuckled fights, so he couldn't hold a pistol very well. He favored a Winchester .44/.40 rifle and a sawed-off 10-gauge shotgun for close-in work. He wasn't particularly mean, and only killed when forced to by circumstances. His cauliflower ears and the scar tissue around his eyes and his oft-broken nose made him look frightful— and no man dared laugh at his appearance.

Riding next to Carlton was Jeremy Brett, an Englishman relatively new to America. Jeremy talked with a heavy British accent, and his dress was very dapper—a bowler hat and dark suit covered with a black duster while on the trail. Soft-spoken, he used a shoulder holster with a Smith and Wesson American sheriff's model .44 caliber pistol. No one knew why he'd chosen to ride the owlhoot trail, as he wouldn't speak of it and became extremely violent if pushed on the matter.

The last of Lazarus's lieutenants was King Johannson. A big, fair-haired, blue-eyed Swede farmer from up in Minnesota, he was borderline mentally retarded. Though his mind was slow he was very quick with his guns and could be very mean when he was upset, going into violent rages if crossed. At other times he was like a small child, sweet and mild-tempered. He carried a shotgun on a sling around his shoulders and a long, machete-type knife in a scabbard on his belt, the blade of which was rusty from the blood of his victims. He never wiped the sword-like instrument off after using it.

There were another fifteen or so men at any one time riding with Lazarus, each and every one as mean and dangerous as the next. They had no real plan and no real destination. The gang rode wherever they wanted and took whatever they needed. So far there hadn't been anyone brave enough, or good enough, to stand against them.

Lazarus had no compunction about killing anyone who crossed him. In his mind he could do no wrong, since he'd been personally chosen by God. If by chance he happened to kill an innocent man or woman, he felt they would be rewarded by God and taken to heaven. He didn't have to feel guilt since he was sending them to a better place. On the other hand, if someone deserved to die God would send them to hell, and Lazarus was just doing God's work for Him.

"Hey, boss, looks like there's a town up ahead," Blackie said, interrupting Lazarus's reverie.

Lazarus glanced down at the weather-beaten sign next to the road. "Fontana?" he said. "I don't remember a town by that name on the map."

"Me neither, Lazarus," said Tom "Behind the Deuces."

Lazarus shrugged. "Well, boys, let's ride on in and see what this Fontana's like."

As they rode down the center of the town's main street, they were greeted by broken-down, rotting buildings and boardwalks that'd seen better days.

"Damn, looks like a ghost town," said Curly Joe.

"Nope," answered Pig Iron Carlton. He pointed up ahead. "There's some hosses outside that saloon."

Sure enough, there were three horses reined to a post in front of a saloon with a faded, hand-lettered sign hanging askew over the door—DOG HOLE.

"Sounds like my kind of place," said Tom "Behind the Deuces." "Wonder if they got a faro game."

"Hell, I wonder if they got any whiskey," said Blackie. "Place looks pretty rundown."

The gang dismounted and walked into the saloon. A man behind the counter had a silver star on his chest and a dark top hat on his head.

Lazarus, upon seeing the badge, placed his hand on his pistol butt. "Are you the local sheriff?" he asked the man.

The man laughed, pointing at his badge. "Hell, yes. I'm the sheriff, the mayor, the dogcatcher, and the bartender. In fact, I'm just about the whole damn town."

Lazarus relaxed, seeing the man was no real lawman. "What's your name?"

"I'm Bob Blanchard. You men come on in and have a seat. There's plenty of whiskey and beer, though not much food."

"You got any women?" asked Curly Joe, a lecherous gleam in his eyes.

Blanchard smiled. "Oh yes. I've got a couple." He looked over his shoulder and then leaned forward and whispered, "They ain't much to look at, but they'll get the job done, if you know what I mean."

As he spoke, a woman walked out of a room upstairs and leaned over the railing, smiling a gap-toothed smile. She weighed at least two hundred pounds, and her hair looked as if someone had pulled part of it out of her scalp.

"They'll get the job done, all right," Tom "Behind the Deuces" said, "after about a quart of whiskey, maybe."

Curly Joe grinned. "I don't need no whiskey, at least not first . . . maybe later." He started up the stairs.

"Curly Joe," Lazarus said, his voice hard.

"Yeah, boss?"

"I don't want any trouble, not until we're ready to leave. You understand me?"

Curly Joe, a disappointed look on his face, shrugged. "All right."

Lazarus turned to Blanchard. "Set up whiskey for all my men. Then you can tell me what happened to this town."

After Blanchard had set out bottles of whiskey on each of the tables he leaned on the bar, absentmindedly wiping it with a dirty rag as he talked.

"Town was founded by a man named Tilden Franklin a number of years ago after gold was discovered here. He named it after a Mexican girl he once knowed."

Lazarus's interest was piqued. "Gold? They discovered gold here?"

"Yeah, only most of this valley belonged to a man named Jensen, Smoke Jensen. And he didn't particularly care to have a bunch of miners running around on his land lookin' for gold."

"So what happened?"

Blanchard shrugged. "Franklin brought in a gang of toughs. Some of the meanest men in several states came here to help him take the valley away from Jensen."

"And did they?"

Blanchard shook his head. "Naw. Jensen called in a bunch of old gunfighters, men most people thought were long dead, an' they had one of the biggest gunfights in history right here in Fontana. Streets ran red with blood, I'm told."

"Must have been something to see."

"I guess. I weren't here myself, but those who survived either left town, or were carried out on boards."*

"Where did the ones who left go?"

Blanchard pointed south. "On down the road a ways, to a town Jensen started, called Big Rock, Colorado."

"And the gold?"

Blanchard leaned forward, speaking in a hoarse whisper. "Still here, I reckon. Since then, no one's had the courage to try and dig it outta the ground, 'cause they know Jensen'd be on 'em like ticks on a hound dog if'n they did."

Lazarus turned and leaned back, his elbows on the bar. "You don't say? Mr. Blanchard, do you have a telegraph in this town?"

"Yes sir. I forgot to mention, I'm also the chief telegraph operator."

*Trail of the Mountain Man

Four

Sally felt Cal's pulse, a worried look on her face.

"I don't like the way Cal looks, Smoke. I have a feeling you'd better ride on ahead and have Doc Spalding ready to operate as soon as we get there."

Smoke didn't question Sally's expertise. She'd treated more bullet wounds than most doctors, a good many of them on him.

He grabbed Joker's reins, which were tied to the rear of the wagon, and pulled the animal alongside. He didn't dare take the time to stop their progress toward Big Rock, so he jumped into the saddle from the rear of the buckboard. He gave Sally a smile for encouragement, then leaned over Joker's head and spurred him into a full gallop toward town.

Smoke rode into Big Rock as fast as his horse could run. As he passed the sheriff's office, Monte Carson stepped out the door and pushed his hat back on his head, watching Smoke race by, a quizzical look on his face.

When Smoke reined up in front of Dr. Cotton Spalding's office, Monte came running, knowing something bad had happened.

Smoke jerked the door open, startling several women and two children who were waiting to see the doctor.

He touched his hat, mumbled a quick apology, then stepped to the consulting room door. Restraining his first impulse to burst through the door, Smoke tapped lightly instead.

After a moment, Cotton opened the door, his sleeves rolled up and a frown on his face.

"What is it?" he asked, then noticed it was Smoke knocking on the door, and the anxious look on his face.

"Oh, I'm sorry, Smoke. Didn't know it was you."

"That's all right, Doc. But Cal's been hurt real bad, took a bullet in the chest and the shoulder."

"Oh!"

"Sally says to tell you it's in his lung, an' he's lost a lot of blood. She says you need to operate as soon as they get here."

"Well, if Sally says it, then it must be serious."

He stepped into the waiting room and said, "I'm sorry, ladies. I have an emergency coming in that's going to need surgery. There's no need for you to wait here. Why don't you come back in a couple of hours?"

As the women and children left, he turned back into his consulting room. Smoke looked over his shoulder and saw a man bent over the table, his buttocks exposed and showing a bright red lump on one cheek.

"Earl, I'm afraid I'm going to have to lance that boil later. I've got an emergency coming in."

Earl straightened up, looking angry. "Look here, Doc. I'm in pain, and I want this boil cut now! The other can wait his turn."

Cotton put his hand in front of Smoke, who'd started through the door with his fists clenched.

"Earl, I've got a young boy with two bullets in him, one in his chest," Cotton said in a low, even tone, not a trace of anger or annoyance in it. "He's gonna die if I don't operate right away. Do you really want me to make him wait his turn?"

Shamefaced, Earl lowered his gaze, his expression softening. "No, of course not, Doc. It's just that this damned carbuncle is driving me crazy."

Cotton walked to the medicine cabinet and took out a small bottle. "Here, Earl. Take this laudanum. Two sips every hour or so and you won't feel the pain. Come back in a couple of hours and I'll fix you up permanently."

Earl pulled up his pants and took the bottle. "Thanks, Doc, and I'm awful sorry 'bout your friend, mister. I didn't mean nothing by what I said before."

Smoke nodded, tempted to smile in spite of the circumstances.

Just then, Sheriff Monte Carson came into the office. "Hey, Smoke. What's going on?" he asked, a concerned look on his face.

Smoke and Monte Carson had become very good friends over the past few years. Carson had once been a well-known gunfighter, though he had never ridden the owlhoot trail.

When Tilden Franklin hatched his plan to take over the county and dig up most of the gold that had recently been discovered for himself, he'd hired Carson to be the sheriff of Fontana, a town just down the road from Smoke's Sugarloaf spread. Carson went along with the man's plans for a while, 'til he couldn't stomach the rapings and killings any longer. Then he'd put his foot down and let it be known that Fontana was going to be run in a law-abiding manner from then on.

Franklin sent a bunch of riders in to teach the upstart sheriff a lesson. The men killed Carson's two deputies and seriously wounded him, taking over the town. In retaliation, Smoke had founded the town of Big Rock, and he and his band of aging gunfighters cleaned house in Fontana.

When the fracas was over, Smoke offered the job of sheriff of Big Rock to Monte Carson. Monte married a grass widow and settled into the job as if born to it. Neither Smoke nor the citizens of Big Rock ever had cause to regret his taking the job.

"Cal's been shot, Monte."

"Is it bad?"

"About as bad as it can be and him still be alive."

"Any idea who did it?"

Smoke shook his head. "He woke up long enough to say it was Ichabod Crane, but I don't know what he meant by that."

"Ichabod Crane?"

"A character in a story by Washington Irving," Cotton called from the next room. "Tall, skinny, with a prominent Adam's apple, as I recall."

Monte pursed his lips. "You think that's what he meant, Smoke? Tryin' to describe the fellow for us?"

"Possibly, but I'm more concerned with saving his life right now. I'll get to the man who did this after it's over, one way or another."

Monte nodded. He knew Smoke didn't let anyone harm a friend of his, not without making them pay dearly for it.

"Come on, Smoke," Cotton called from his consulting room. "You can help me set up for the surgery."

"I'll talk to you later, Monte."

"Sure, come on by the office. Meanwhile, I'll be goin' through some posters, see if I can find the galoot who did this."

Smoke walked into the consulting room, and Cotton led him through a rear door into his operating room—surgery, as he called it.

There were windows on every side of the room to let as much light in as possible, and two large lanterns in sconces on each wall. In the middle of the room was a long table with a pad on it. There were straps for arms and legs, for those occasions when it wasn't possible to give an anesthetic.

"Smoke, fill that basin with carbolic acid and dump that tray of instruments into it, will you?"

"Carbolic acid? What's that for?"

"There's this man in Austria, named Semmelweis, who says the reason wounds get infected is due to contamination with small organisms, called bacteria."

Smoke didn't look up as he filled the basin from a large bottle of liquid, turning up his nose at the strong astringent smell. "Uh huh. I've never seen any small animals in wounds with pus, unless you're talking about maggots."

"No, these organisms are too small to be seen with the naked eye. You need a microscope. Anyway, Semmelweis says if doctors would wash their hands and instruments in carbolic acid, and wash wounds with soap and water, it would cut down on the number of infections and save a lot of lives."

"And you believe him?"

Cotton shrugged as he laid out dressings and sutures in preparation for the operation.

"I don't know. Some of the other doctors in Austria say the man is crazy. But my feeling is it can't hurt, so why not give it a try? I do know that since I've been doing it I haven't had a single wound suppuration following surgery."

Smoke heard the buckboard pulling up outside the office. "Better get your hands washed, Doc. Here they are."

Smoke and Pearlie carried the unconscious Cal into the surgery and laid him on the table. Sally began stripping his clothes off. "You men go on outside. I'll stay and help Cotton with Cal."

"Put the closed sign on the door, will you, Smoke? That way we won't be interrupted."

"All right. We'll get Monte and go on over to Longmont's for some coffee. You can reach us there if . . . if anything happens or you need us," Smoke said, his voice breaking as he realized it might be the last time he saw Cal alive.

As soon as they left, Cotton washed his hands in the weak solution of carbolic acid and had Sally do the same. Then he laid out his instruments on a side table next to where Cal lay unconscious, his breathing labored, bloody froth on his lips.

Sally had stripped him to his waist and positioned herself next to the instruments, ready to assist in the surgery.

"Scalpel, please," Cotton said, holding out his hand.

After Sally placed the razor-sharp knife in his hand, Cotton bent low over the table and made an incision horizontally over the entrance wound of the bullet in his chest.

"I'll work on the chest wound first," he said, "since that's the most dangerous."

After opening the incision wider, he took a long, blunt-tipped probe and used it to follow the path of the slug, being gentle so as not to cause any more bleeding than was necessary.

Cal was so deeply asleep that he didn't move when the probe was inserted.

After a few moments of this, Cotton looked up. "It's as I feared when I saw the froth on his lips. The slug is imbedded in his right lung. Luckily, from the depth the probe went in, it doesn't appear to be deep in the lung but just on the edge. I suspect hitting the rib slowed the bullet up enough so it couldn't penetrate any farther."

Taking the scalpel again, he lengthened the incision even more and used a clawlike tool to spread Cal's ribs apart. Using blunt dissection, he followed the path of the bullet to where it lay against the lining of the right lung. After about an hour of painstaking dissection, he felt the metal object with the tip of his scissors, doing most of his work by touch since he couldn't see the bottom of the wound.

Sally handed him some long, narrow-tipped forceps and he plucked the bullet out, placing it in a metal basin with a clank.

Using gauze he first dipped in the carbolic acid, he stuffed the wound full and used bandages to hold it tight and compress it so as to stop the bleeding and close the hole in the lung, allowing it to re-expand.

Next, he gave his attention to the shoulder wound and was happy to find the bullet had passed cleanly through flesh, missing Cal's arm bone. Cleansing the wound as best he could, he packed it with gauze and wrapped a tight bandage around the entire arm.

Finally, exhausted and dripping with perspiration, he stepped back from the table and sleeved sweat off his face and forehead.

"Now it's in God's hands. I've done all I can."

Sally slumped against the table, as tired as Cotton was.

"You did a great job, Cotton. No one could have done more," she said.

Louis Longmont was sitting at his usual table, playing solitaire, when he saw Smoke and Pearlie and Monte walk through the batwings. Noticing the serious expressions on their faces, he signaled a waiter.

"Johnny, bring a pot of coffee and three more cups to the table."

"Yes sir, Mr. Longmont," the young black man answered.

Louis got to his feet and held out his hand to Smoke. They'd been friends for a long time.

Louis was a lean, hawk-faced man with strong, slender hands and long fingers, the nails carefully manicured and hands clean. He had jet-black hair and a black, pencil-thin mustache. He was, as usual, dressed in a black suit with a white shirt and dark ascot—something he'd picked up on a trip to England some years back. He wore low-heeled boots, and a pistol hung in tied-down leather on his right side. It was not for show, for Louis was snake-quick with a short gun and was a feared, deadly gunhand when pushed.

Louis was not an evil man. He had never hired his gun

out for money, and while he could make a deck of cards do almost anything, he did not cheat at poker. He did not have to cheat. He was possessed of a phenomenal memory, could tell the odds of filling any type of poker hand, and was one of the first to use the new method of card counting.

He was just past forty years of age. He had come to the West as a very small boy, with his parents, arriving from Louisiana. His parents had died in a shantytown fire, leaving the boy to cope as best he could.

He had coped quite well, parlaying his innate intelligence and willingness to take a chance into a fortune. He owned a large ranch up in Wyoming Territory, several businesses in San Francisco, and a hefty chunk of a railroad.

Though it was a mystery to many why Longmont stayed with the hard life he had chosen, Smoke thought he understood. Once Louis had said to him, "Smoke, I would miss my life every bit as much as you would miss the dry-mouthed moment before the draw, the challenge of facing and besting those miscreants who would kill you or others, and the so-called loneliness of the owlhoot trail."

Sometimes Louis joked that he would like to draw against Smoke someday, just to see who was faster. Smoke allowed as how it would be close, but that he would win. "You see, Louis, you're just too civilized," he had told him on many occasions. "Your mind is distracted by visions of operas, fine foods and wines, and the odds of your winning the match. Also, your fatal flaw is that you can almost always see the good in the lowest creatures God ever made, and you refuse to believe that anyone is pure evil and without hope of redemption."

When Louis laughed at this description of himself, Smoke would continue. "Me, on the other hand, when some snakescum draws down on me and wants to dance, the only thing I have on my mind is teaching him that when you dance, someone has to pay the band. My mind is clear and focused on only one problem, how to put that stump-sucker across his horse, toes down."

Smoke took Louis's hand.

"You look worried, my friend," Louis said.

"Cal's been shot, Louis. Bad shot."

"Is he—"

"No. Doc and Sally are working on him right now."

Louis sat them at his table and poured coffee all around while Pearlie and Smoke built cigarettes and Monte fired up his pipe. Louis took a long, black cigar from his vest pocket and joined them in smoking.

"I offered Smoke and Pearlie some coffee at my office," Monte said, "but for some reason they wanted to come over here."

"Has that pot in your office ever been cleaned, Monsieur Monte?" Louis asked, trying to lighten the mood of their two friends, like Monte.

Monte nodded. "Of course. Two year ago, I believe it was."

"Did you find any papers on the man Cal described?" Smoke asked, not in the mood for their usual banter.

"Well, there were several it could have been, but none have been reported in this neck of the woods. 'Bout the nearest one I saw was a man name of Lazarus Cain. He and his gang did some raiding down in Arkansas recently, but there was no mention of his heading this way."

"Well, if this Cain has decided to pay us a visit and did this to Cal, he's gonna wish he'd never left Arkansas," Smoke said through gritted teeth.

Five

It was over two hours before the solemn group gathered in Longmont's saloon heard any news from the doctor. Longmont had tried cheering them up by ordering a special meal from his French chef, Andre, but in spite of the wonderful food they all just picked at their plates with no real enthusiasm. Even Pearlie, who could normally eat his weight in foodstuffs, barely tasted the roasted duck with orange sauce and fried potatoes with sliced tomatoes and peach halves.

When Sally walked through the batwings they were all on their feet asking questions at the same time. Exhausted, and looking as if she hadn't slept for days, she flopped down at the table and requested coffee, and lots of it.

After drinking half her first cup in one long swallow, she leaned back and pushed stray wisps of hair out of her face. "Cal made it through the surgery, though it was scary going for a while. Dr. Spalding says it's in God's hands, but that Cal is young and healthy and has a lot going for him."

"He's gonna make it!" Pearlie said with conviction, his eyes wet with unshed tears. "That boy's had plenty of experience with gittin' shot, an' he's tough as an old boot. He'll be all right, I just know it."

"Did he wake up at all, Sally? Was he able to say any more about who shot him?" asked Monte.

She shook her head. "No, he didn't even move when Doc

made his incision. Doc says he's in a coma from shock and loss of blood."

Seeing she was on the verge of breaking down, Smoke put his hand over hers on the table. "Come on, Sally. Let's go home. Doc'll let us know how he does."

Pearlie stood up. "If it's all right with you, Smoke, I'll just hang around here for a while. Make sure Doc don't need nothin'. I can watch Cal while he tends to his other patients."

"Sure thing, Pearlie. That'd be very nice, and I know that when Cal wakes up he'll be glad to see a friendly face by his side."

"Friendly, hell! I'm gonna box his ears for lettin' hisself get shot up without me there to take care of him," Pearlie said with mock ferocity. "If I've said it once, I've said it a dozen times—that boy's a magnet for lead."

As Pearlie left to go over to Doc's, Monte said, "I'm going to wire the surrounding sheriffs and see if anyone's had any trouble lately with any tall, skinny galoots, or if they've heard of this Cain feller. I'll get in touch with you at the Sugarloaf if I hear anything."

"Don't bother, Monte," Sally said. "As soon as we get the ranch house shut up, Smoke and I'll be back to town to sit with Cal until he's better."

"Yes, we'll take a room at the hotel," Smoke added.

"Nonsense, I won't hear of it," Louis said with some heat. "You and Sally will stay at my place on the edge of town. I have a spare bedroom, and the food is guaranteed to be better than the hotel's."

A year or so back, tired of living in hotels, Louis had bought a widow's house on the outskirts of town. It was bigger than he needed, but he said he was tired of looking at the same four walls all the time. He wanted some room to roam around in when he wasn't at the saloon. Since then, he'd fixed it up really nicely, with an extra bedroom for guests and a place in the back where his cook lived.

Smoke showed up at Louis's house around nine that night. "Sally's going to sit with Cal for a while. I'm supposed to pick her up at ten o'clock," he told Louis when he opened the door.

"Come in and make yourself at home, Smoke. Would you like some coffee?"

"Sure. It's been a hell of a long day."

As they drank coffee and smoked, Louis one of his ever-present black cigars and Smoke a handmade cigarette, Smoke asked, "Did Monte hear anything back on his wires?"

Louis wagged his head. "Not as far as I've heard. He said he probably wouldn't hear anything for a day or two."

Noticing the worry in Smoke's eyes, Louis asked, "How are you doing, pal?"

Smoke looked up. "Not too well, Louis. Since our children have been over in Europe for the past two years with Sally's father, Cal and Pearlie have been like sons to us. Now, with the prospect of maybe losing one, Sally and I are really worried."

"Like the doc said, Cal's young and tough. I'm sure he'll pull through."

"But I keep blaming myself for letting him go out there alone. Someone should have been with him."

"Nonsense, Smoke. Cal is a grown man, and this is a tough country. Like you always say, a man's got to saddle his own horse and kill his own snakes."

"You're right, of course. Whatever Cal got into out there on the Sugarloaf, he was ready and willing to do it. I figure the first shots I heard were his."

"Did you find any bodies?"

"No, but there was a hell of a lot of blood, and it was

scattered over too large an area to be all Cal's. I think he got at least one, maybe two, before they took him down."

"So there must have been several men he was facing, if there were enough left after losing two for the others to cart off the bodies."

"That's the way I figure it."

Louis shook his head, admiration in his eyes. "If that's true, then Cal must've drawn on them knowing the odds were heavily against him."

Smoke nodded. "There never was any back up in Cal. That boy would bow his back and face down the devil himself if it ever came to that."

"Kind of like someone else I know," Louis added with a smile at his friend.

Six

Lazarus Cain was sitting at the table he'd appropriated as his own in the Dog Hole Saloon. His chair was in a corner, so he had walls on both sides at his back and an unobstructed view of the batwings that served as the entrance to the bar.

It had been two weeks since he and his gang had settled in Fontana, and he was now the acknowledged leader of the town that was only a few citizens away from being a ghost town. Bob Blanchard, the man who'd been top dog here until Lazarus arrived, had accepted his new role as servant to Lazarus and his men without complaint, figuring it was the smart thing to do, and necessary if he were to go on breathing.

"Bob," Lazarus called, "bring me and the boys another round over here."

As Bob brought another bottle of whiskey to the table, he stopped for a moment.

"Mr. Cain, one thing I can't figure out."

"What's that, Bob?" Lazarus asked as he filled his glass to the brim with the amber-colored liquid.

"Well, the boys all say you're a holy man of sorts, having been called by the Lord to do his work."

"Yes?"

"Well, how is it you drink so much whiskey and beer? Doesn't the Good Book speak out against such things?"

Blackie Jackson cast a worried glance at his boss, wondering just how he would take this question. Lazarus's moods were hard to predict. One time he'd laugh and throw his arm around someone. The next, he was as likely to draw his Colt and put a bullet in the offending man's head.

This time, Blanchard was lucky. Lazarus was in a forgiving mood.

"Bob, I refer you to the Good Book, First Timothy, chapter five, verse twenty-three."

Bob pursed his lips. "Uh . . . Mr. Cain, I ain't exactly on speakin' terms with the Bible. I'm not familiar with that particular verse."

"It says, 'No longer drink only water, but use a little wine for your stomach's sake and your frequent infirmities'," Lazarus quoted with a benign smile.

"Oh," Blanchard said, "wine."

"Yes, and since they didn't have Kentucky bourbon in those days, I'm sure the Lord would have included it if there'd been any around to drink. The point is, the Lord recognized a man sometimes needs a little alcohol to soothe him when life begins to get too much to handle."

"Thanks for clearing that up," Blanchard said, grinning. "I'll have to remember that particular verse so's I can quote it if'n someone ever tries to make me quit drinkin'."

Lazarus took a deep swallow of his whiskey and wiped his mouth with the back of his sleeve. "Perish the thought, Bob, perish the thought."

After Blanchard walked off to stand behind the bar and await further orders, Blackie leaned back in his chair and gave Lazarus an appraising glance. Since he seemed to be in one of his good moods today, he figured he'd ask him again about what the rest of the boys had been wondering.

"Say, Lazarus, when are you gonna tell us what you got planned, an' why we been stuck here in this two-bit excuse for a town for the past two weeks?"

Lazarus pursed his lips as if thinking it over, then nodded and leaned forward on his elbows.

"I've decided to stay around here and do a little gold mining."

"Gold mining?"

Lazarus nodded. "From what I hear, that Jensen fellow's land is absolutely brimming with gold. Word is it's so thick over there you don't even have to dig in some places. It's just lying around on the ground waiting to be picked up."

"But boss, we ain't miners. What made you decide to do this?"

Lazarus leaned back, a look of smug self-satisfaction on his face. "Spreading the Lord's word is expensive, Blackie. That's why we've been having to spend too much of our time raising money by rustling and robbing the occasional bank. If I can make one big score, get me enough money to last the rest of my life, then I can devote all my energies to doing the Lord's work. I might even open me up a church somewhere, one like my pappy used to preach at."

Blackie nodded, knowing it would do no good to try to talk Lazarus out of his scheme once his mind was made up. But there were other things to worry about.

"What about this Jensen fellow? Blanchard said the last guy that tried to take that gold had twenty or thirty men and got plumb wiped out."

Lazarus grinned, as if he had a secret. "I know. It won't be easy, especially since Jensen's built that town of Big Rock and has all the citizens in it behind him."

"So, you think the twenty of us can pull it off, tree the town, and get the gold before the U.S. Marshals or the army finds out about it and sends in the troops?"

"No, twenty of us can't, so I've wired for some help."

"Oh?"

"Yes. I've sent for some . . . special men who once rode for the Yellow and Gray, men who didn't quit when that traitor

General Lee surrendered. Men who kept fighting the good fight."

"Who's that, boss?"

"Men who rode with Bloody Bill Anderson and Quantrill's Raiders and Merrill's Marauders."

"I heard Bloody Bill an' his men got pretty well shot up a year or so back. Word is that Bloody Bill was shot in the head by Marshal Wyatt Earp and some other galoots over in Dodge City."

Lazarus grinned again. "Yes, and do you know who was mixed up right in the middle of that little fracas?"

"No."

"It was this same Jensen, Smoke Jensen, that practically wiped out Bloody Bill and his men. The ones that survived are thirsty for revenge."

"But I heared they was all put in jail in Dodge, and due to be hanged," Blackie said, his chubby cheeks screwed up in an expression of puzzlement.

Lazarus gave a slow grin. "They were, 'til one of their other gang members snuck into town one night while Wyatt was busy dealing faro over at the Oriental Saloon and broke 'em out."

"Oh."

"Yeah. They hightailed it up into a little town a couple of hundred miles from here, called Sweetwater, Colorado."

"How'd you know all this?"

"I heard it from a man at that last tradin' post where we took on supplies. He was run out of town by some of the outlaws, and was pretty mad about it. Said he was going to tell the first marshal he ran across where they were hidin' out."

"So, them're the ones you sent the wires to?"

"Yes, and a few others scattered around the territory who might be interested in some gold that's just lyin' around for the takin'."

"When do you think they'll be gettin' here?"

Lazarus peered over Blackie's shoulder, and then drained the last of his whiskey in one long swallow.

He pointed out the window. "Right about now, I suspect."

Blackie looked over his shoulder and saw a group of four men riding up. They were wearing dusters and hats that were covered with trail dust.

Lazarus stood up and stretched. "Time to meet our new partners, boys."

Four men walked through the batwings, hands on pistol butts as they surveyed the room.

One of the men, a youngster who looked no older than seventeen or so, walked with a pronounced limp. His face lit up with a smile when he saw Lazarus, and he hobbled over to shake his hand.

"Howdy, Lazarus."

"Hello, Floyd. How's the leg?"

"Stiff, an' it hurts like hell when the northers come through."

Lazarus shook his head in sympathy, then shook hands with the other men.

"It's sure good to see you boys," he said. "It's been a long time since we all rode with Quantrill."

He turned to his men, seated at several tables in the corner of the room. "Men, let me introduce you to some boys that know how to fight."

He pointed to the young one with the limp. "This here is Floyd Devers. He's still carrying a bullet Smoke Jensen put in his right leg. The others are Walter Blackwell, Tad Younger—Cole's cousin—and Johnny Sampson. These are the last of Bloody Bill's gang."

Lazarus's men crowded close and shook hands all around with the outlaws.

"Mr. Blanchard, more whiskey for these men. They need something to wash the trail dust outta their throats," Lazarus called to the bartender.

Seven

After Floyd and the others all had bottles and glasses full in front of them, Lazarus sat at their table.

"Floyd, tell me about what happened that day Bloody Bill got killed."

Floyd took a long drink of his whiskey and wiped his mouth with the back of his sleeve, then began to talk in a low tone, as if he didn't particularly like to relive those hours. . . .

Bill stood on a rock ledge just before dusk, watching their backtrail with his field glasses. He and Buster Young talked as Bill studied the horizon from the highest point they could find while the men waited in a draw, resting and drinking whiskey to pass time or dress a few minor flesh wounds that three of his gang had taken during the robbery. It had been a hard push to cover so much ground—hard on horses as well as men. And there was a problem of another sort—a man, or several men, who kept following them, who had killed Dewey and Sammy with a knife in a spot where they should have been able to see someone stalking them. Bill had watched closely for dust sign to the rear, and he'd seen nothing all day—not so much as a wisp of trail dust. What was happening didn't make a hell of a lot of sense. He'd been

running from lawmen and Union cavalry for so many years
that he'd been sure he knew all the tricks of the game—until
then. For reasons he couldn't explain, he felt it was the work
of just one man, and that was even more puzzling. Who
would go alone after a gang the size of his? Only a madman,
or one crazy son of a bitch.

"Joe an' Shorty ain't comin'," Buster said. "The guy who
got Dewey an' Sammy got them, too."

"Not Joe Lucas," Bill answered. "He's too damn careful
to get bushwhacked. It's just takin' 'em more time than they
figgered."

"This gent's slippery," Buster argued. "He could even be
the feller who got Scar Face. Maybe he's got some others
with him . . . a posse. That'd explain why it's takin' Joe and
Shorty so long to git back. They coulda run into a whole
bunch of guns back yonder."

"We'd've seen some dust if it was a posse," Bill said, passing his glasses along the crests of hills, then along the low
places between them. "It's that sumbitch who flung Homer
off the roof who's responsible. I've got this feelin' about it,
about how it's him."

"It can't be no good feelin', if it's just one man," Buster
told him, frowning. "It just don't figger why some tough son
of a bitch would be in Dodge this time of year. The gent
who got Homer wasn't no lawman. Big feller . . . real tall,
from what I seen of him. I remember one more thing. He
yelled real loud when he throwed Homer's body, like he
wanted us to know it was him an' that he was up there. Damn
near like he was darin' somebody to shoot at him. Could be
he's crazy."

"Crazy like a fox," Bill replied angrily, still reading the
horizon through his lenses. "A genuine crazy man woulda
showed hisself by now. I seen a few crazies durin' the war,
when they seen too much blood, too much dyin'. They'd come
runnin' at our lines like they was bulletproof, screamin' their

damn fool heads off 'til a bullet shot 'em down. Some of 'em would get right back up an' come chargin' at us again whilst they was dyin'. It was a helluva sight to see. This bastard who's followin' us ain't that kind of crazy. Somehow, he's able to sneak up on us without showin' hisself . . . which is damn hard to do in this open country. But I still don't figger he got Joe. Shorty, maybe, but not Joe Lucas."

"Ain't no man bulletproof, not even Joe," Buster said after a pause.

Bill's glasses found movement on a distant hill. A pair of horses came trotting into view. Bill let out a sigh. "Yonder they come, both of 'em," he told Buster. "I can see both their horses—a sorrel an' Joe's big buckskin."

"Let's hope they killed the sumbitch," Buster remarked. "If they did, we can quit worryin'."

Bill watched the horses a little longer, because something about them seemed wrong, yet he couldn't put a finger on just what it was. Dusky darkness made it hard to see detail. Long black shadows fell away from the hills in places, preventing him from seeing Joe and Shorty clearly.

He waited while the horses came closer, holding a slow trot along a trail of horse droppings and hoofprints his gang had left in their wake. Bill was in too much of a hurry to make the alabaster caves west of old Fort Supply, where they could hide out, and there hadn't been time to be careful about leaving a trail to follow until they crossed over the Kansas line at the Cimarron River. In the river, they could ride downstream in the shallows and lose any possemen or cavalry when the current washed out their horse tracks.

"I can see 'em now," Buster said, squinting. "Two horses, only they sure as hell are comin' real slow. Looks like they'd be in a hurry to bring good news. Maybe they couldn't find the sneaky son of a bitch."

The pair of horses rounded a low hill, and Bill could now see them plainly enough. His jaw muscles went taut when his teeth were gritted in anger. "Damn!" he said, taking one last look before he lowered his field glasses, hands gripping them so tightly his knuckles were white.

"What the hell's wrong, Bill?" Buster asked, unable to see all of what Bill had seen, without magnification.

"He got 'em," Bill snapped.

"What the hell're you talkin' about?" Buster wanted to know, glancing back to the horses that were approaching the ledge where they stood. "Yonder they come. That's Joe's yeller dun, an' that's Shorty's sorrel, ain't it?"

Bill's rage almost prevented him from answering Buster. A moment passed before he could control himself. "It's the horses," he growled. "Shorty an' Joe are tied across their saddles. Means they're dead."

"Dead? Why would the bastard take the time to tie Shorty an' Joe to their saddles?"

"He's sendin' us a warnin'," was all Bill could say right then, fuming.

Buster frowned at the horses a third time. "Son of a bitch," he said softly, unconsciously touching the butt of his pistol when he said it. "They *are* dead. I can see their arms danglin' loose." He turned to Bill. "What kind of crazy son of a bitch would do that?"

Bill tried to cool his anger long enough to think. "A man who don't give up easy. He aims to dog our trail all the way to the Nations. Can't figure why, only it's real clear he ain't in no mood to give up."

"I ain't so sure it's one man, Bill. One man couldn't have handled Joe and Shorty so quick. I say there's a bunch of 'em back yonder. Damn near has to be."

"I've got this feelin' you're wrong," Bill said, swinging off the ledge, taking long, purposeful strides down to the spot where his men rested. "But there's eleven of us left, an' we'll be more careful from here on," he added.

"We've lost some of our best shooters," Buster reminded him when he saw the men waiting for them in the draw.

Bill was in the wrong humor to discuss it. "Send a couple of men out to fetch Joe an' Shorty back here. Their horses're comin' too slow, followin' the scent of these others. I'll have everybody get mounted. Maybe we can lose that bastard when we come to the river."

Pete Woods and Stormy Sommers led the horses, with bodies lashed to saddles, over to Bill. Stormy's face wasn't the right color.

"Joe's got a hole blowed plumb through his neck," Pete said while jerking a thumb in Joe Lucas's direction. "Shorty caught one in the chest right near his heart."

Bill paid no attention to the swarm of blowflies that were clinging to both bodies, wondering how anyone could have taken Joe Lucas by surprise. "Cut 'em down an' leave 'em here. We'll use their horses for fresh mounts. See if there's any money in their pants pockets. Don't leave nothin' valuable behind."

"Whew, but they sure do stink!" Pete said, climbing down to cut pieces of rope that were holding the corpses in place. Shorty's body fell limply to the dirt. Joe slid out of his blood-soaked saddle to the ground with a sickening thump. "Goddamn flies been eatin' on 'em, on the blood."

Bill didn't care to hear about the smell. "Search their pockets like I told you," he said. "Time we cleared outta here quick. Been here too long. We oughta hit the river close to midnight."

"Who you reckon done this?" Charlie Walker asked, fingering his rifle in a nervous way.

"A crazy man," Buster answered when Bill said nothing. "He has to be outta his goddamn mind."

Bill wheeled his horse, heading south onto a darkening

prairie, leading ten men and four pack animals loaded with bags of money toward the Cimarron.

In the back of his mind he wondered what kind of man was following them. Unlike Buster, Bill wasn't quite so sure the stalker was crazy. Deadly might be a better word.

And to make matters worse, the man on their trail seemed to be enjoying himself, in a way. Why else would he have sent the bodies back, unless he wanted fear to cause Bill and his gang to make another careless mistake?

The clatter of horseshoes on rock announced their arrival at the Cimarron River. Beyond the sluggish, late fall current, trees grew in abundance, which suited Bill Anderson just fine—more places to hide in the all-but-total darkness of a night without a moon.

Buster rode up next to him while they halted on the riverbank to look things over.

"Seems quiet enough," Buster observed.

Bill wasn't satisfied. He gave the far bank a close look, listening.

"Yore actin' real edgy, Bill," Buster said. "That bastard can't get ahead of us, hard as we been pushin' these horses. I say we get across quick."

Bill had been thinking about what had happened to Joe, Shorty, Dewey, and Sammy for the last few hours. "I've done give up on tryin' to predict what he'll do. But once we get in the river, we're gonna ride down it maybe a mile or two. It'll make it harder for him to find out where we came out. We'll look for a stretch of rock north of them alabaster caves to ride out. Can't no man track a horse on them hard rocks."

"This ain't like you, Bill, to act worried 'bout one or two men, however many there is. We used to ride off like we was in a damn parade every time we pulled a job. Seems like we're runnin' with our tails tucked between our legs now, an' all on account of one or two gents chasin' us."

Bill scowled at the forests beyond the Cimarron. "Things have started to change, Buster. This land ain't empty like it was before. An' the sumbitch behind us—maybe it is two or three—has proved to be pretty damn good."

"That ol' fort is abandoned. We could ride for it hard an' be there by daylight. No matter who's behind us, we can stand 'em off there real easy."

"It's gettin' across this river that's got me playin' things safe. Send a couple of men down to the water ahead of us. If nobody shoots at 'em, we'll bring the money down."

Buster turned back in the saddle, picking out men newer to the gang. "Floyd, you an' Chuck ride down to the river, an' keep your rifles handy."

Two younger members of the gang spurred their trail-weary horses past the others to ride down a rocky embankment to the water's edge. Both men approached cautiously, slowing their mounts to a walk.

Bill waited until no shots were fired at his men. "Let's go," he said, sending his horse downslope.

Floyd Devers turned to Chuck Mabry. Beads of sweat glistened on Floyd's face. "Looks safe enough," he said to his cousin from Fort Smith.

As Chuck was about to speak, a rifle cracked from the opposite bank, accompanied by a blossom of white light from a muzzle flash.

Mabry, the newest member of Bill Anderson's gang at the tender age of nineteen, fell off his horse as if he'd been poleaxed. Floyd's horse bolted away from the shallows when it was spooked by the explosion.

Floyd was clinging to his saddle horn when a bullet struck him in the right hip. "Yee-oow!" he cried, letting his rifle slip from his fingers. Pain like nothing he'd ever known raced down his leg, causing him to let go of the saddle and to slide slowly off to one side.

Floyd landed in the water with a splash, thrashing about, making a terrible racket, yelling his head off about the pain.

From Bill Anderson's men, half-a-dozen guns opened up on the muzzle flash. The banging of guns rattled on for several seconds more, until the shooting slowed, then stopped.

Bill turned his horse quickly to ride back behind the bank of the river, out of the line of fire.

"Goddamn!" Buster yelled, trying to calm his plunging, rearing horse. "How'd that bastard get across ahead of us?" he wondered at the top of his voice.

Bill was furious. He knew he should have sent an advance scouting party ahead to get the lay of things at the river, but with fatigue tugging at his eyelids he'd forgotten to do it until it was too late.

He could hear Floyd thrashing about in the water, making all manner of noise. The kid, Chuck, fell down like he was dead the moment the bullet hit him.

"This don't make no sense," Bill said when Buster got his horse stilled. "We've been ridin' as hard as these damn horses could carry us an' he still beat us to the river."

"Give me two men," Buster said, "an' I'll ride upstream an' cross over so we can get behind him. He won't be expectin' that from us."

Bill knew men as well as he knew anything on earth. "This son of a bitch, whoever he is, has got us outguessed with every move we make."

"We can't just sit here all night, Bill."

"Wasn't aimin' to," Bill replied. "We'll swing to the east and ride as hard as we can. Let's test his horse, see if he can stay up."

"He sure as hell ain't had no trouble so far," Buster said before he reined his mount around.

"Make sure you stay close to the money," Bill added in a

quiet voice. "If one of our own decides to get rich while all this is goin' on, shoot him."

"I'll stand by you, Bill. Always have. But this gent we got shootin' us a few at a time is smart. You'll have to hand him that. We need to stay together. It's when we split up that he cuts some of us down."

"Numbers don't appear to make no difference to this son of a bitch," Bill answered. "Just do like I say. Stay close to the packhorses. We'll ride the riverbank for a ways an' see what he does next."

"We need to make it over to them trees, Bill," Buster told him. "Out here in the open, he's got a clear shot at us damn near every time. We'll be a helluva lot safer on the other side. We keep on this way, he's gonna bushwhack us all."

"I've got eyes, Buster, an' I don't need no help countin' the men he's killed. Start ridin'.'"

"Hold on a minute, Bill!" Pete Woods cried, pointing down the river. "Listen to Floyd yonder. He's hurt real bad, an' he needs somebody to go an' fetch him outta that water."

Bill aimed a hard-eyed look at Pete. "You go fetch him out, if you want," he said. "I ain't gonna make no target out of myself. Floyd can figure his own way out."

"He's just shot in the leg!" Pete protested.

Bill had grown tired of the useless banter. "You could get shot in the head if you run down there, Pete. This was a chance every one of us took when we decided to rob them banks. Men get bullet holes in 'em sometimes when they take what ain't theirs. But if you're so damn softhearted, you ride right on down to that river an' lend Floyd a hand."

"Sure seems hard," Pete said, quieter.

"Robbin' folks of their money ain't no church picnic," Bill said.

Pete lowered his head, unwilling to challenge Bill over it any longer.

Bill rode off in the lead, and beyond the lip of the riverbank he could hear Floyd crying out for help. It reminded him of the war, when no one had been there to save all the brave soldiers from Missouri or Tennessee when they begged for assistance.

Someone near the loaded pack animals began to gag, and Bill knew it was the kid, Stormy Sommers. He ignored the sound, and spoke to Buster. "High time some of the little boys learned a thing or two about robbery. If it was easy, every son of a bitch who owned a gun would take up the profession."

Buster sounded a touch worried. "Don't leave us with but nine men, Bill."

"Nine?" Bill asked, his voice rising. "You don't think nine men stack up right?"

"Whoever's doin' the shootin' at us has been real good, or real lucky, today," Buster answered.

"Luck is all it is," Bill said.

Another rifle shot boomed from across the river, and Bill pulled his horse to a stop, turning his head to listen. He heard another painful cry coming from the Cimarron.

"Damn! Damn!"

It was Pete Woods's voice.

"Pete was dumb to ride down there so soon," Buster said with his head turned toward the sound. "He shoulda waited for a spell to see if things was clear."

"We don't need no careless men," Bill announced to the men around him. "Pete wasn't thinkin' straight, or he'd've knowed to wait, like Buster said."

Stormy continued to gag, gripping his sides. Bill's nerves were on edge, and he had to do something to calm them. "Shut the hell up, Stormy, or I'll kill you myself. If you ain't got the stomach for robbin' banks, then ride the hell away from here—an' do it now!" Bill's right hand was on the grips of one revolver when he said it.

"We're all gonna die," Stormy whimpered. "That feller who's followin' us ain't no ordinary man."

Bill didn't want Stormy's fear to infect the others. He took out his Colt .44, cocked it, and fired directly at Stormy's head.

Stormy's horse bolted away from the banging noise as he went off one side of it. He landed with a grunt, falling on his back, staring up at the stars.

"Anybody else don't like the way I'm runnin' things?" Bill asked defiantly.

When not another word was said, he reined his horse to ride east, spurring his horse to a trot. He hadn't wanted to kill any more of his own men, like he'd had to do when Lee Wollard pulled that damn fool stunt inside the bank, hitting the banker so hard it knocked him out. But there were important things for men to learn if they aimed to stay outside the law, and one was when to take orders and follow them to the letter. A leader couldn't run a military outfit any other way.

Keeping his men and their precious cargo well out of rifle range from the far side of the Cimarron, Bill led his men east at a gallop, determined to make a crossing into the Nations as soon as he felt it was safe. . . .*

"What happened next, Floyd?" Lazarus asked.

"Well, when I saw Pete Woods hit whilst tryin' to get me outta the water, an' then Bill an' the others ride off into the darkness, I knew I was done for. I managed to crawl an' swim to the bank, and put my leg up on a rock so's the bleedin' would slow down."

*Pride of the Mountain Man

He paused to refill his whiskey glass, his voice hoarse from all the talking.

"After about ten minutes or so, this real tall galoot ridin' with another, younger man, 'bout my age, comes crossin' the Cimarron as cool an' unconcerned as if he were out for a ride to enjoy the evenin' air. He says his name's Smoke Jensen, an' he proceeds to take his bandanna off and wrap it around my leg, tyin' it down real tight."

"Why didn't he just finish you off right then?" Blackie Jackson asked, his head cocked to the side.

Floyd shrugged. "Don't rightly know. It's sure what Bill woulda done. Anyways, he tells me to get on over to Dodge City and give myself up to Marshal Wyatt Earp, 'cause he's gonna go on after Bill an' the others."

"And he expected you to do that?" Lazarus asked.

Floyd nodded. "Yep. He said if'n he got back to Dodge an' I wasn't there, he'd hunt me down an' kill me."

"Did you believe him?"

"Damn straight! That's why I agreed to join this little party of yours. I've been lookin' over my back ever since I broke outta jail, just knowin' he was gonna be standin' there some day, lookin' down at me over the sights of his Colt."

Floyd shook his head. "I gotta finish this with Jensen, one way or another, so I can quit watchin' my backtrail."

"I can't believe you just waltzed on back to Dodge City and asked Marshal Earp to put you in jail 'cause you was afraid of Jensen," Blackie said, his expression looking as if he'd tasted something bitter.

Floyd gave the big man a look. "Just wait, big mouth. Soon you'll be facing Jensen, with those eyes that look like they're made of ice, an' we'll see how big you talk then."

Eight

When Smoke walked into the hotel room where Cal was being nursed back to health, he found Pearlie standing next to the bed with his hands on his hips, arguing.

"Dammit, Cal! Doc says you got to eat or you ain't gonna make up for all that blood you lost. Now I'm tellin' you for the last time, either eat that stew or I'm gonna get a tube and stick it down your gullet and pour it in there myself."

Cal cast worried eyes over Pearlie's shoulder to stare at Smoke, as if asking for some help dealing with this mother hen he was facing.

"Take it easy, Pearlie," Smoke said as he walked over to the bed. "Just because Cal can't shovel grub in like you do doesn't mean he's not eating enough. Doc says he's doing just fine."

"Well, he needs to eat more. That boy don't eat enough to keep a bird alive."

Cal grimaced with pain as he pushed himself up to a sitting position against a pile of pillows. "Now, if Miz Sally would cook up some bearsign, then I'd probably feel a whole lot better about eatin'. Might perk up my flaggin' spirits a mite, too."

Smoke laughed. "Cal, I can see you're learning real fast how to take full advantage of being wounded."

"Trouble is, if Miz Sally did make those bearsign," Cal

said mournfully, glancing at Pearlie out of the corner of his eye, "I have a feelin' somebody else'd eat 'em up 'fore they got here."

Pearlie's eyes got big and he looked astonished that Cal would say such a thing. "Well that's a fine howdy do. I sit up here day an' night for two weeks spoonfeedin' this young'un so he can get well, an' he accuses me of eatin' his bearsign."

"Seems to me Sally did bring a platter of donuts up here last week. Didn't Cal get any of those?" Smoke asked.

Pearlie blushed a bright red. "Uh . . . not exactly. At the time Miz Sally brought those, Doc still had Cal on liquids only, so naturally—"

"See! I tole you he'd eat 'em up 'fore I got any," Cal said, pointing his finger at Pearlie. He turned his head to look at Smoke. "From now on, if you don't mind, Smoke, would you ask Miz Sally if'n she'd bring me those bearsign personally? That's the only way I'm ever gonna get any."

"All right, Cal, I'll tell her myself to cook up a fresh batch for tomorrow. Now, we need to talk about what happened out there the day you got shot. Doc said you're feeling up to discussing it now."

"Yes sir."

Pearlie walked to the corner of the room and pulled two chairs over for him and Smoke to sit on while Cal told his story.

After Cal finished telling them about Lazarus Cain and about the two men he'd shot before they got him, Smoke nodded his head.

"That's about how we had it figured, only we didn't know how many men you were facing that day. You say there were about fifteen or twenty?"

"Yes sir, minus the two I shot."

"And this man told you his name was Lazarus Cain?"

"Yes sir."

"Sheriff Carson has some paper on him, but it didn't say anything about him being headed this way."

"Smoke, that man is plumb crazy," Cal said, his face paling a little as he thought back on the shooting incident.

"What do you mean, Cal?"

"Well, I seem to remember, after he shot me an' I was lyin' there, feelin' my life sorta ebbin' away, he stood over me and began to pray for my soul."

"Pray? Like to Jesus an' everthing?" Pearlie asked, astonishment on his face.

"Yeah. He even had this old raggedy Bible with a bullet stuck right in the middle of it."

Smoke nodded but didn't say anything, seeing that thinking about it was making Cal feel bad.

"Has anybody reported any problems or seein' these galoots since they shot Cal, Smoke?" Pearlie asked.

Smoke wagged his head. "No, and that's the strange thing. You'd think with a group that big someone would have run into them, or they'd have robbed or shot someone else by now. They don't exactly seem the kind of men to move quietly through an area without attracting any notice."

"Maybe some of the outlying ranchers have seen 'em an' just haven't been to town to tell anybody yet," Cal said.

"That's a good thought, Cal." Smoke stood up and grabbed his hat off the dresser. "I think I'll ride on a little circuit around the area and see if anyone's heard or seen anything. It might be good to warn them to stay away from this gang if they can, so no one else will get hurt," Smoke said.

"I think I'll come with you, Smoke, if it's all right. I'm gettin' cabin fever cooped up here with this ungrateful pup," Pearlie said, casting a hurt look at Cal.

Cal laughed. "You know I'm grateful to you, Pearlie. You're about the best friend a man could ever have, long as they ain't no bearsign to come betwixt us."

Pearlie smiled. "Since you put it that way, I'll make sure

to bring those bearsign out to you myself, first thing in the mornin'."

"Try an' leave at least one or two out of the whole bunch, Pearlie," Cal said, a grin on his face.

Smoke and Pearlie began to ride a wide circuit around Big Rock. The first ranch they came to belonged to Johnny and Belle North. Johnny North was an ex-gunfighter who'd come to town a few years back to settle an old score with Monte Carson. Seems they'd both loved the same woman for a time. Instead of fighting, the two men had sat down and eaten a meal together, and found neither one could much remember what they were supposed to be mad at each other about.

Later on, Johnny decided to settle down when Belle Colby's husband got himself shot to death in a gunfight with the men who'd raped their daughter and killed their son. Johnny moved in to help her with their ranch and teenage daughter, and before long they were married. He'd hung up his guns for good that day.

As Smoke and Pearlie approached the North ranch, Belle appeared on the porch, cradling a shotgun in her arms.

Smoke raised his hands as he walked Joker closer to the cabin. "Don't shoot, Belle. It's me, Smoke Jensen."

"I know who you are, Smoke. I'm not so old I can't see. At least, not yet. How are you doing, boys?"

Smoke crossed his arms on his saddle horn and leaned forward. "We're doing fine, Belle. Where's Johnny?"

She inclined her head. "He's off with the hands, brandin' some of the new calves. By the way, thanks for those Hereford bulls. They sure do make a good cross with our shorthorns."

Smoke nodded. "They sure do. By the way, Belle, where is George Hampton? Doesn't he work for you anymore?"

Belle smiled. "Not exactly. Johnny and I gave him a hundred acres up to the north. He and my daughter Velvet are plannin' to get hitched this spring, so we figgered we'd make him a rancher 'stead of a hired hand."

Smoke and Pearlie both smiled. "Congratulations, Belle. And give Velvet my best wishes. George is a good man."

Belle pointed to the east. "Johnny's just over that rise there, 'bout four or five miles, if you need to see him."

Smoke and Pearlie tipped their hats and reined their horses around and headed east.

"I can't hardly believe Velvet's gettin' married," Pearlie said.

Smoke glanced at him out of the corner of his eye. "That's right. Didn't I see you dancing with her quite a bit at the last Fourth of July picnic?"

Pearlie blushed a bright red. "Well, maybe one or two dances, is all. She is a right smart lookin' woman, though."

"About your age, I believe?"

Pearlie looked at Smoke. "Now, don't you go gettin' no ideas. I ain't near old enough to be thinkin' 'bout gettin' hitched."

"You aren't getting any younger, Pearlie, and there aren't that many eligible women around."

"Smoke, you heard Miss Belle. Velvet's engaged to George Hampton, an' he's a good man."

"Yes, he is," Smoke said with a grin, thinking back to the day he'd first met George Hampton. He and Pearlie and Cal had been out in the forest cutting wood for the upcoming winter. Smoke had gone to take a nap while the younger men finished loading the buckboard with their morning's work. . . .

The sound of a gunshot brought Smoke instantly awake and alert. Years in the mountains with the first mountain man, Preacher, had taught Smoke many things. Two of the most important were how to sleep with one ear listening, and never to be without one of his big Colt .44s nearby. The gun was in his hand with the hammer drawn back before echoes from the shot had died.

"Sh-h-h, Horse," he whispered, not wanting the big Appaloosa to nicker and give away his position. He buckled his gun belt on, holstered his .44, and slipped a sawed-off 10-gauge American Arms shotgun out of his saddle scabbard. Glancing at the sun, he figured he had been asleep about two hours. Cal and Pearlie were nowhere in sight.

Raising his nose, Smoke sniffed the breeze. The faint smell of gunpowder came from upwind. He turned and began to trot through the dense undergrowth of the mountain woods, not making a sound.

Smoke peered around a pine tree and saw Cal bending over Pearlie, trying to stanch the blood running down his left arm. Four men on horseback were arrayed in front of them, one still holding a smoking pistol in his right hand. "Okay, now I'm not gonna ask you boys again. Where is Smoke Jensen's spread? We know it's up in these hills somewheres."

Cal looked up, and if looks could kill the men would have been blown out of their saddles. "You didn't have to shoot him. We're not even armed."

"You going to talk, boy? Or do you want the same as your friend there?" The man pointed the gun at Cal, scowling in anger.

Cal squared his shoulders and faced the man full on, fists balled at his sides. "Get off that horse, mister, and I'll show you who's a boy!"

The man's scowl turned to a grin. His lips pulled back from crooked teeth as he cocked the hammer of his weapon. "Say good-bye, banty rooster."

Smoke stepped into the clearing and fired one barrel of the shotgun, blowing the man's hand and forearm off up to the elbow, to the accompaniment of a deafening roar.

The men's horses reared and shied as the big gun boomed,

while the riders clawed at their guns. Smoke flipped Cal one of his Colts with his left hand as he drew the other with his right.

Cal cocked, aimed, and fired the .44 almost simultaneously with Smoke. Smoke's bullet hit one rider in the middle of his chest, blowing a fist-sized hole clear through to his back. Cal's shot took the top of another man's head off down to his ears. The remaining gunman dropped his weapon and held his hands high, sweating and cursing as his horse whirled and stomped and crow-hopped in fear.

Smoke nodded at Cal, indicating he should keep the man covered. Then he walked over to Pearlie. He bent down and examined the wound, which had stopped bleeding. "You okay, cowboy?"

Pearlie smiled a lopsided grin. "Yeah, boss. No problem." He reached in his back pocket and pulled out a plug of Bull Durham, biting off a large chunk. "I'll just wet me some of this here tabaccy and stuff it in the hole. That'll take care of it until I can get Doc Spalding to look at it."

Smoke nodded. He remembered Preacher had used tobacco in one form or another to treat almost all of the many injuries he endured living in the mountains. And Preacher had to be in his eighties, if he was still alive, that is.

With Pearlie's wound seen to, Smoke turned his attention to the man Cal held at bay. He walked over to stand before him. "Get off that horse, scum."

The man dismounted, casting an eye toward his friend writhing on the ground and trying to stop the bleeding from his stump.

"Ain't ya gonna hep Larry? He's might near bled to death over there."

Smoke walked over to the moaning man, stood over him, and casually spat in his face as he took his last breath and died, open eyes staring at eternity. With eyes that had turned ice-gray, Smoke turned to look at the only one of the men still alive. "What's your name, skunk-breath?"

"George. George Hampton."

"Who are you, and what're you doin' here looking for me?"

"Why, uh, we was lookin' fer Smoke Jensen."

Smoke sighed, shaking his head. "I *am* Smoke Jensen, you fool. Now you found me, what do you want?"

Hampton's eyes shifted rapidly back and forth from Cal to Smoke. "You can't hardly be Smoke Jensen. You're too danged young. Jensen's been out here in the mountains killing people for nigh on ten, fifteen years."

"I started young." He drew his .44 and eared the hammer back, the sear notches making a loud click. "And I'm not used to asking questions more than once."

Hampton held up his hands. "Uh, look Mr. Jensen, it was all Larry's idea. He said some gunhawk gave him two hundred dollars to come up here and kill you." He started speaking faster at the look on Smoke's face. "He said he'd share it with we'uns if we'd back his play."

"What was this gunhawk's name?"

Hampton shook his head. "I don't know. Larry never told us."

Smoke looked at Hampton over the sights of his .44. "You sold your life cheap, mister."

Cal cried out, "Smoke! No!"

Smoke lowered his gun, sighing. "Cal's right. I've gone this long without ever killing an unarmed man. No need to change now, even though you sorely need it." He stopped talking, an odd expression on his face. He sniffed a couple of times, then looked at Hampton through narrowed eyes. "That smell coming from you, mister?"

Hampton's face flared red and he looked down. "Uh, yes sir. My bowels kinda let loose when you cocked that big pistol of yours."

Pearlie let out a guffaw. "Hell, Smoke. You don't want to kill this 'un. Let him go, and if he's any kind of man he'll die of shame 'fore the day's over."

Smoke holstered his gun and turned to walk away. Cal nodded at Hampton. "Get out of here while the gettin's good."

As Hampton stepped in his saddle and took off looking for a hole, Pearlie called out, "And you can tell your kids you once looked over the barrel of a gun at Smoke Jensen and lived to tell about it. Damn few men can say that!"

Later that afternoon, Smoke was halfway to Big Rock when Horse began to act up. First the horse snorted, pricked his ears and looked back toward Smoke with eyes wide. Smoke had been lost in thought about who might be gunning for him, letting Horse find his own way to town. He came fully awake and alert when the animal began to nicker softly.

Leaning forward in the saddle, he patted Horse's neck and whispered, "Thanks, old friend. I hear you." Mountain-bred ponies were better than guard dogs when it came to sensing danger. Smoke shook his head, thinking Preacher would be disgusted with him. If there was one thing the old mountain man had stressed it was that the mountains were a dangerous world, and not to be taken lightly. Riding around with your head in the clouds, especially when you knew someone was trying to nail your hide to the wall, was downright stupid, if not suicidal.

Smoke slipped the hammer thongs from his Colts, then put his hand on the butt of the Henry rifle in the scabbard next to his saddle and shook it a little to make sure it was loose and ready to be pulled.

He tugged gently on the reins to slow Horse from a trot to a walk and settled back in the saddle, hands hanging next to his pistols.

Even with his precautions, he was surprised when a man jumped out of the brush into the middle of the trail in front of him. It was George Hampton, and he was pointing a Colt Navy pistol at Smoke.

"Get down off that horse, you bastard."

Smoke spread his hands wide and swung his leg over the cantle and dropped, cat-like, to the ground. "Hampton, I thought you'd be halfway home by now."

"I ain't gonna go home 'til I've put a bullet between the eyes of the famous Smoke Jensen."

Smoke glanced at the revolver Hampton was holding, smiled, and shook his head. "Hampton, I really don't want to kill you. Why don't you just put that gun down and head on home?" He spread his hands wider, stepping closer to him. "And just where is your home, anyway? You never got around to telling me yesterday."

Hampton licked his lips, the gun trembling a little in his hand. "Just keep yore distance, Jensen. I'll admit I ain't no expert with the six-gun like you are, but I can't hardly miss at this distance."

Smoke kept his hands in front of him. "Okay, okay, don't get nervous. I'll stay back. But it seems to me a man ought'a know just why he's bein' killed."

Hampton nodded. "Well, yore right. I can see the justice in that, 'cept I don't rightly know. Larry, the man you kilt, he made me and the other boys the offer down on the Rio Bravo in Texas. Seems that gunhawk met him in a saloon in Laredo, and told him he wanted you dead in the worst way . . . somethin' about how you had humiliated him a while back, and he wanted you in the ground because of it."

Smoke's eyes narrowed and turned slate gray. "So you and the other boys decided to pick up some easy money on the owlhoot trail, huh?"

Sweat was beading on Hampton's forehead in spite of the cool mountain air. "Naw, it wasn't like that. We're just cowboys, not gunslicks. There's an outbreak of Mexican fever in the cattle down Texas way, and there ain't much work for wranglers, leastways not unless you're hooked up with one of the big spreads." He shook his head, gun barrel dropping a little. "Hell, it was this or learn to eat dirt."

Smoke relaxed, his muscles loosening. "I'll tell you what, Hampton. There's always work for an honest cowboy in the high country. If you're willing to give an honest day's labor, you'll get an honest day's pay."

The pistol came back up and Hampton scowled. "Yore just sayin' that cause I got the drop on you."

Smoke smiled. Then, quick as a rattlesnake's strike he reached out and grabbed Hampton's gun while drawing his own Colt .44 and sticking the barrel under Hampton's nose. "No, George, you're wrong. You never had the drop on me." He nodded at Hampton's pistol. "That there is a Colt Navy model, a single action revolver. You have to cock the hammer 'fore it'll shoot, and I can draw and fire twice before you can cock that pistol."

Hampton's shoulders slumped and he let go of his gun and raised his hands. "Okay, Jensen, it's yore play."

Smoke holstered his Colt and handed the other one back to Hampton. "I told you, George, you got two choices. You can get on that pony there and head on back to Texas, or I can give you a note and send you up to one of the spreads hereabouts and you can start working and feeling like a man again. It's all up to you."

Hampton looked down at his worn and shabby boots and britches, then back to Smoke. "That's no choice, Mr. Jensen. You give me that note and I promise I'll not make you sorry you trusted me."

Smoke walked to Horse and took a scrap of paper and a pencil stub out of his saddlebags. After a moment, he handed the paper to Hampton. "Take this note to the next place you see up to the north of mine. It belongs to the Norths. They can always use an extra hand, and Johnny pays fair wages."

Hampton held out his hand. "I don't know how to thank you, Mr. Jensen, but . . . thanks."

Smoke grinned, knowing Hampton was a friend for life. In the rough-hewn country of the West, favors, or slights, were not soon forgotten. Help a man who was down on his luck, and he was honor-bound to repay you, even at the cost of his life if it came to that . . .*

Vengeance of the Mountain Man

Nine

Smoke and Pearlie found Johnny North just where Belle said he would be. He was bending over a tied-down calf with a branding iron in his hand while two of his men held the struggling animal down.

After the red-hot iron seared the North brand into the calf, sending smoke smelling of burned flesh into the air, Johnny stepped back and sleeved sweat off his forehead.

One of his men pointed over his shoulder and he looked, smiling widely when he saw Smoke and Pearlie approaching.

"You boys keep on workin'. I'm gonna take a short break an' talk to Smoke," he said, handing the still smoking iron to his foreman.

He walked over to the campfire nearby and squatted, pouring three mugs of coffee as Smoke and Pearlie got down off their horses.

"You men look like you could use some *cafécito*," Johnny said.

"Thanks, Johnny," Smoke said, taking a cup.

"Much obliged," Pearlie said, nodding his hello.

Johnny took a sack of Bull Durham out of his shirt pocket and began to build a cigarette. "What brings you boys way out here on a workday?"

"Cal was shot a couple of weeks back while working on the Sugarloaf," Smoke said.

"Damn!" Johnny exclaimed. "Is he gonna be all right?"

"Looks like he's going to make it."

"Who did it? Somebody local?"

Smoke shook his head. "No. Cal says there were about twenty men, give or take. He shot two before they got him. I was wondering if you or any of your hands had seen anything of a bunch like that lately."

Johnny stuck the cigarette in his mouth and lighted it, shaking his head. "Not that I've heard of. I'll ask around to make sure, but I'm certain they'd've mentioned it if they'd seen a group of men that big."

Smoke finished his coffee and put the cup next to the fire. "Well, ride with your guns loose, partner. These are bad men, and they're up to no good if they're still around. Tell Belle to be careful too, all right?"

"Sure thing, Smoke. I'll keep an eye out. Thanks for the warning."

"Oh, and congratulations on George and Velvet's engagement. We're all mighty proud of her around here."

"Thanks, Smoke. I'll tell her and George both you said hi."

Smoke and Pearlie got on their horses and rode toward the next ranch, hoping to find some sign Cain and his men had been spotted. . . .

Back in Fontana, Lazarus turned to Walter Blackwell. "Walt, tell us what happened out there after Floyd was shot and you and Bloody Bill and the others rode off."

Walter nodded and leaned forward, his elbows on the table as he started to talk. . . .

Four men sat huddled around a small fire, deep within a rock cavern with curious, glistening walls of solid alabaster. Bloody Bill Anderson was chewing a mouthful of jerky, washing it down with whiskey. Deeper into the cave, their horses and pack animals were hobbled and fed what little grain the gang had left in towsacks. Bags of money lay near the fire, and piles of currency, along with gleaming gold and silver coins, were stacked in neat rows. Bill watched Walter Blackwell count the money.

"More'n forty thousand so far, Bill," said Walter, a quiet, retiring man who was a remarkably good shot with a pistol.

"We're rich," Bill said, cocking an ear toward the entrance where Buster, Billy Riley, and Cletus Miller were standing guard. "Best of all, we gave that sneaky bastard the slip, so our troubles're over. He'll never find us here. Hell, the cavalry an' dozens of U.S. Marshals from Fort Smith've been ridin' past these caves for years. Hardly nobody knows they're here. We lay low for a little while, maybe five or six weeks, an' then we ride out free as birds." He gave Walter a stare. "Keep on countin'. You ain't hardly more'n half done. There's gonna be sixty thousand dollars, way I figure."

Tad Younger, the cousin of Cole and his famous outlaw bunch, was frowning. "Sure do hope whoever's been behind us don't show up. He's made a habit out of showin' up when he ain't supposed to."

Bill wagged his head. "We lost him. Can't no Indian or white man find a horse's tracks where we just rode. Slabs of rock don't leave no horse sign."

"Here's ten thousand more," Walter said, adding a stack of banknotes to the counted money.

Bill grinned. "Maybe there's gonna be seventy thousand, after all—" He abruptly ended his remark when a series of loud explosions came from the mouth of the cave.

Bill leapt to his feet, clawing both six-guns out of his holsters, shattering the bottle of whiskey he'd been holding.

A scream of agony came from the tunnel, followed by a much louder bellowing string of cusswords in Buster Young's voice.

Bill took off in a run for the entrance, leveling his pistols in front of him, almost tripping in the dark. Then two more heavy gun blasts sounded, and he recognized Cletus Miller's cry of pain.

Racing up to the opening, caught in a wild fury beyond his control when he knew the man who'd been tracking them had showed up at the cave in spite of all his precautions, he stopped when he saw three dark shapes lying behind a pile of boulders where his guards had been hiding. Big Buster Young was writhing and rocking back and forth, holding his belly, gasping for air, his face twisted in a grimace.

Billy Riley lay facedown on the rocks in a pool of blood, and he wasn't moving. Cletus sat against a big stone, a shotgun resting on his lap, arms dangling limply at his sides while his mouth hung open, drooling blood on his shirt.

And when Bill saw this—all three of his men dead or dying from three, well-placed shots—he tasted fear for the first time in his life. Gazing out at the darkness, where only dim light from the stars showed any detail of his surroundings, something inside him stirred—a knot of terror forming in his chest that had never been there before. And he noticed that the hands holding his pistols were shaking so much he knew his aim would be way off target . . . if he could find anything to shoot at.

"Come on out, Anderson!" a deep voice shouted. "Got you cornered! There ain't gonna be no escape!"

Bill crouched down. In spite of the night chill, sweat poured from his hatband into his eyes. "You're gonna have to kill us!" he yelled back. "You ain't takin' none of us alive!"

"Suits the hell outta me!" the voice answered.

Bill heard soft footsteps coming up behind him. He didn't bother to turn around to see who it was. "Get your rifles," he said in a whisper. "We'll gather up the money an' shoot our way out of here."

"He'll kill us!" Walter Blackwell said.

"Like hell he will," Bill snapped. "Just do like I say, an' get rifles ready. Tell the others to saddle our horses an' put the money on them packsaddles."

Walter, always soft-spoken, said, "I've never disobeyed an order from you, Bill, but this is different. It'll be like we killed ourselves if we try to ride out. Whoever that feller is, he don't miss."

Bill's fear turned to anger. "Shut the hell up, Walter, an' do what I ordered!"

"I won't do it," Walter said very quietly.

Bill turned an angry glance over his shoulder, staring up at Walter's dark shape standing right behind him. "You what?" he demanded.

Bill heard a soft click while Walter spoke. "I won't let you get the rest of us killed," he whispered.

The sudden realization of what Walter meant to do struck Bill Anderson a split second before the hammer fell on a Mason Colt .44/.40 conversion. A roar filled the cave mouth, and then Bill's ears, when it felt as if a sledgehammer had hit him squarely in the middle of his forehead.

He was slammed against a cavern wall, with his ears ringing, until the noise made by the gunshot died away. He stood there, leaning against the wall with blood streaming down his face and into his eyes for a moment. Then he slumped limply to the ground. . . .*

Lazarus leaned back in his chair, his eyes hard. "So, you shot Bill, huh?"

"That's right. He didn't leave me no choice in the matter," Walter said quietly.

"What happened next?"

*Pride of the Mountain Man

Walter shrugged. "We gave ourselves up. Smoke Jensen took us and the money back to Dodge City and turned us over to Marshal Earp."

Lazarus looked skeptical. "You mean Jensen had the drop on you men, and there was over seventy thousand dollars on those packhorses?"

"That's right."

"A man'd have to be crazy to pass up a fortune like that when all he had to do was finish you boys off and no one would ever know he'd taken it," Lazarus said, staring at Walter.

Walter shook his head, a small smile on his face. "Jensen ain't like no ordinary man. Money don't seem to mean nothin' to him."

"I need to find out more about this man if we're gonna go up against him," Lazarus said.

He glanced at the table where some of his men were sitting, drinking whiskey and playing poker.

"Pig Iron, you and Curly Joe come on over here. I got a job for you to do."

When they got to his table, Lazarus said, "I want you two to ride on over to Big Rock an' get the lay of the land. See what the people are sayin' 'bout that runt we killed, and see if you can size up Smoke Jensen. I want to know if he's got as much sand as Walter and Floyd here say he does."

Ten

As they rode into Big Rock, Curly Joe gave a low whistle. "Damn, Pig Iron, we been holed up in that ghost town so long I've almost forgot what a real town looks like."

Pig Iron nodded. "Yes. It's kind'a nice to see people on the street instead of tumbleweeds."

When they came to a buckboard parked in front of the general store with a man loading sacks of flour in it, Curly Joe reined his horse to a halt.

"Say, mister, you happen to know Smoke Jensen?"

The man looked up with a smile. "Sure, everybody in Big Rock knows Smoke. Why?"

"You know where he might be found?"

"Well, if he's in town he's usually over at the sheriff's office or at Longmont's saloon."

"Thank you kindly," Curly Joe said, tipping his hat as they rode on down the street.

As they passed the sheriff's office a man in the doorway, leaning against the wall drinking a cup of coffee, gave them a long look.

"Appears the sheriff don't much cotton to havin' a pair of strangers ridin' into town," Curly Joe said with a grin, as if to show he didn't much care what any hick town sheriff thought.

Pig Iron nodded, but he wasn't as carefree about it as Curly

Joe. He realized from what the citizen back there had said that the sheriff and Jensen were good friends, and that was going to make it that much harder to try to take Jensen out—now or later.

At the Longmont Saloon they dismounted and tied their mounts to the hitching rail in front. Curly Joe, as usual, swaggered through the batwings first, trying to impress Pig Iron with his bravado.

Pig Iron shook his head, knowing better. He'd always figured Curly Joe was a coward deep inside, like all braggarts and showoffs, and he didn't intend to count on him for any backup.

They walked to the bar and ordered whiskey, and were glad to see that the bottle the bartender placed in front of them actually had a label on it.

"This has got to be better than that rotgut we been drinkin' over at—" Curly Joe started to say. Pig Iron interrupted him with a sharp jab in the shoulder with his elbow.

"Sh-h-h," Pig Iron whispered. "There ain't no need in advertising where we been stayin', you fool."

Curly Joe assumed a hurt look, as if he wouldn't have been that stupid. "I know that," he said. "I was just gonna say that *other place.*"

Pig Iron turned around and leaned back, his elbows on the bar, and surveyed the room. It was a nice saloon, furnished much better than most such places he'd been in. Almost all the tables were full, indicating it was a popular place to eat and drink. He noticed most of the people at tables were eating, not just sitting around drinking.

"Food must be pretty good here, too," he said.

"Huh?" Curly Joe asked, pouring himself another glass of whiskey.

"Never mind," Pig Iron said, realizing he'd been right—Curly Joe wasn't going to be much help to him today. The man was dumber than a post.

Pig Iron turned back around and asked the bartender, "Say, is Smoke Jensen around today?"

The barman glanced around the crowded room for a moment, then shrugged his shoulders. "Nope. Don't see 'im."

"A friend told us to look him up and say howdy, but he didn't tell us what the man looked like."

"You can't miss Smoke Jensen. He's 'bout the biggest man in town, couple'a inches over six feet, with shoulders wide as an ax handle, sandy-colored hair, an' he's usually wearin' buckskins."

"Thanks," Pig Iron said with a smile. "We'll keep an eye out."

Smoke and Pearlie eased out of their saddles in front of Longmont's.

"Damn, I'm stiff as leather been sittin' in the sun fer too long," Pearlie said, putting his hands in the small of his back and leaning back, trying to stretch muscles grown sore from too long in the saddle.

Smoke rubbed his butt cheeks with a sigh. "I can see we've both been having it much too soft lately. I can remember the time when I could sit a saddle from dawn to dusk and not feel this sore."

Pearlie chuckled. "Yeah, but that was back when you was a lot younger, Smoke. You got to realize yore gettin' older now, got to take it a mite easier than you used to."

"Old?" Smoke said as they pushed through the batwings. "What do you mean by that, you young whippersnapper?"

They saw Louis Longmont sitting at his table drinking coffee and walked over to join him.

"I mean it, Smoke. It's 'bout time for you to get a rockin' chair and sit on the porch all day an' let young'uns like me an' Cal do the hard work."

Louis arched an eyebrow. "What is this I hear? The redoubtable Smoke Jensen, mountain man extraordinaire, being told to seek early retirement?"

Smoke flopped in a chair, glaring at Pearlie with mock anger. "Can you believe it, Louis? This young pup thinks I'm getting old just because I got a little saddle-sore after riding around the mountains all day."

Pearlie grinned. "Say, Louis. Have you got in your shipment of sarsaparilla yet?"

"Yes, Pearlie. It arrived yesterday. Would you like some?"

"Sure, an' some food too, if'n you don't mind."

"What is the house special today, Louis?" Smoke asked. "I'm hungry enough to eat raw bear meat."

"I'm sorry, Smoke. We are fresh out of bear meat. Today's special is Steak *Louie*. That is a tender fillet of young beef, cut thin and marinated in white wine for twelve hours, then cooked over a low flame until it is barely seared on the outside, but still red and moist on the inside. It is served with asparagus spears, fresh corn on the cob, and a salad of assorted greens."

"I'll take an order of that," Pearlie said, licking his lips, "'cept you can leave off that asparagus. It makes my pee turn green an' smell funny."

"And that bothers you, *mon ami?*" Louis asked, smiling.

"Naw, it don't bother me, but it does kind'a give me a start the next mornin' to look down and see a green stream comin' out."

"How about you, Smoke?"

"I'll have the lunch special also, Louis, and you can give me Pearlie's asparagus. I'm so hungry my stomach thinks my throat's been cut."

As Louis turned to call out the order to the waiter, he saw two men approaching the table. Their expressions were hard, and so were their eyes.

He turned back to face Smoke, reaching down and unhooking the rawhide hammer thong on the Colt at his side. "Looks like trouble approaching, Smoke."

"I see 'em, Louis," Smoke said, his hand at his side undoing his hammer thong at the same time.

As the two men approached the table, Smoke examined them closely with an appraising eye. One was tall, over six feet, and looked to be built well, all muscle and no fat. From the scar tissue on his cheeks and his flattened, misshapen ears and gnarled knuckles, Smoke knew he'd been a professional fighter. His eyes were intelligent, and Smoke could see the man was sizing him up at the same time.

The other man was shorter, about five feet eleven, with dark, curly hair and a face that was handsome in a weak sort of way. His eyes were cold and vacant, and it was plain he was a man who wouldn't hesitate to kill—but only if he had an edge. He had the look of a coward about him.

When they stopped in front of the table Smoke leaned back in his chair, extending his right leg a bit to make it easier to reach for his Colt should the need arise.

"Good afternoon, gentlemen," Smoke said, since they were both staring at him.

"Are you Smoke Jensen?" the tall one asked, his voice firm, with no animosity in it.

"Yes, I am."

"My name is Carlton, Pig Iron Carlton. I ran into an old acquaintance of yours the other day, and he said to look you up and say hello."

"And who was that?" Smoke asked.

"Floyd Devers."

"Devers, huh? Last I heard he was in jail, waiting to be hanged for robbery and murder over in Dodge City."

"Not anymore. He's out now, and he says he can't wait to see you. He says you're a lying, cheating, back-shooting bastard."

Smoke's eyes narrowed, and the room grew quiet at the

sound of those words, which in the West were almost always followed by gunfire.

"Oh, so that's what he says? What do you say, Mr. Carlton?"

"I say I believe him. You look like a coward to me, Jensen. Like a man with a yellow streak down his back a mile wide."

Smoke sighed and stood up, knowing there was no way to avoid a confrontation now. The man had come looking to pick a fight, and that was what he was going to get.

Smoke walked toward the door, pulling a pair of thick, black leather gloves from his waistband and putting them on.

"Are you running away, Jensen?" the shorter, curly-haired man called out, a smirky grin on his face.

"Nope. Just taking it outside so your friend doesn't bleed all over Mr. Longmont's furniture."

"You're the one that's going to bleed, Jensen," Pig Iron said, following Smoke through the batwings.

Smoke stopped in the street and turned to face Pig Iron. "Oh, I suspect we're both going to bleed, Mr. Carlton, but I've been bloody before, and I've always been the last one standing when it was over."

Pig Iron stripped his shirt off, revealing rows of well-sculpted muscles.

"Jesus," Pearlie whispered from the boardwalk, where he and Louis and the rest of the patrons of Longmont's had gathered to watch the fight. "He looks hard as a rock."

"Where do you think he got the name Pig Iron?" Louis asked. "He was the fisticuffs champion of the United States for a few years."

"What happened? Did someone beat him?" Pearlie asked.

"Not that I know of. He got in some trouble with the law and just disappeared."

"Do you think Smoke knows that?"

Louis shrugged. "Wouldn't make any difference to Smoke.

He knew the man wanted to pick a fight, so there was no way out other than to oblige him."

In the street, the two men circled each other, Pig Iron's hands up in the classic pugilist's stance.

"I see you used to be a professional fighter," Smoke said, moving his head around and swinging his arms to loosen his neck and shoulder muscles.

"That's right," Pig Iron said. "Over a hundred professional fights, and never lost one."

"Well, out here, we don't go by the Marquis of Queensberry's rules of fisticuffs. There's only one rule in the West."

"What's that?" asked Pig Iron.

"There aren't any rules," Smoke said, leaning to the side and lashing out with his right foot.

The toe of his boot caught Pig Iron in the solar plexus, doubling him over as his breath escaped with a whoosh.

Smoke stepped in and swung a short left jab to Pig Iron's head, flattening his right ear and tearing it partially off.

Pig Iron, after two blows that would have knocked a lesser man out, stood up and danced toward Smoke, his hands in the air.

Pig Iron's eyes were watering, but they remained clear and focused, showing the punches hadn't addled his brain any. It was evident he'd been hit before, and was used to taking punishment. Smoke realized he needed to end the fight as soon as possible or he was going to be in trouble.

As Pig Iron swung a sharp, right jab, Smoke leaned back, using his momentum to soften the blow to his cheek, then hunched his right shoulder as Pig Iron swung a roundhouse left hook into him.

The force of the blow staggered Smoke and almost knocked him off his feet. He thought again that he couldn't afford to mess around with this man. He was much too dangerous an adversary. He had to end the fight quickly, in any way he could.

Pig Iron danced in, trying to follow up his advantage while Smoke was still off-balance, but Smoke stepped nimbly to the left and kicked out with his right foot into the side of Pig Iron's knee.

There was a loud crack as the cartilage in the knee snapped and gave way. Pig Iron yelped in pain and went down on one knee, while Smoke stepped in and swung a right upper cut to his chin. The blow lifted Pig Iron up onto both feet again, snapping his head back.

Smoke quickly stepped in close and, almost faster than the eye could follow, peppered Pig Iron's stomach with rapid-fire blow after blow.

Pig Iron doubled over, blood streaming from his smashed lips and torn ear, both hands holding his abdomen. He was completely defenseless, and looked up out of the corner of his eye with his head tilted, waiting for Smoke to finish it.

Instead, Smoke took off his bandanna and dipped it in a nearby horse trough. He handed it to Pig Iron, saying, "Better put some pressure on your mouth 'fore you bleed to death."

On the boardwalk, Curly Joe, seeing Pig Iron was beaten, put his hand on the butt of his pistol.

He froze when he felt a gun barrel pressed against his temple and heard the hammer eared back. A soft voice said in his ear, "Unless you want your brains spread all over the street, you'd better unhand that pistol."

He glanced around and saw the gambler, Louis Longmont, smiling over the sights of his Colt. "I would dearly love for you to give me a reason to fire this. I haven't had to kill a man for over a month now, and I am getting out of practice," Louis said, the hardness in his eyes belying the grin on his lips.

Curly Joe pulled his hand away from his pistol and crossed his arms over his chest, fear-sweat springing out on his forehead while a fine tremor made his hands shake.

Monte Carson walked up to Smoke, where he stood breathing hard next to Pig Iron.

"What's goin' on here, Smoke?"

"A small difference of opinion, Monte. Nothing to get excited about."

"All right," Monte called, waving his hands. "All you people, break it up. The fight's over, so go on about your business."

Curly Joe wasted no time and rushed over and grabbed Pig Iron by the shoulder, having to help him walk on his ruined knee toward their horses. After he helped him get in the saddle, he jerked his horse's head around and pointed at Smoke.

"You haven't heard the last of this, Jensen," Curly Joe snarled with mock bravado.

Smoke gave him a lazy smile. "I suspect not, mister. But you can tell Devers something for me."

"What's that?"

"The last time I saw him, I told him if I ever laid eyes on him again I was going to kill him. That still stands."

As the two gunmen galloped out of town, Smoke looked at Louis. "You think our food's ready yet, Louis? I'm still mighty hungry."

Pearlie pointed to Smoke's cheek, which was cut and leaking a fine trail of blood down his face. "Maybe you ought'a have Doc take a look at that, Smoke."

Smoke sleeved the blood off. "It'll heal, Pearlie. I've bled before, and I'll probably bleed again. Let's go eat."

Eleven

In the hotel room where Cal was recuperating, Sally looked up as Smoke and Pearlie walked in. Her eyebrows raised, she stared at Smoke's cheek for a moment before getting up and crossing to him.

She gave him a kiss on the other cheek and gazed into his eyes. "What's that I see on your face, Smoke Jensen?"

Smoke reached up and fingered the cut, which was already scabbing over. "Nothing, dear."

She put her hands on her hips. "Have you been fighting again?"

Smoke grinned sheepishly, like a small boy caught stealing cookies. "Well, maybe a little."

Sally turned to Pearlie, who was standing nearby trying to look innocent. "Pearlie, I'm ashamed of you! You're supposed to keep Smoke out of trouble when I'm not around."

"I'm sorry, Miz Sally, but there weren't nothin' I could do 'bout it. The man was spoilin' fer a fight, an' he didn't give Smoke no chance to avoid it at all."

Cal moved as if to get out of bed, but Sally rushed over to push him back against the pillows.

"Just where do you think you're going, young man?" she asked.

He grinned at her as he cut his eyes to Smoke and Pearlie. "It's clear to me, Miss Sally, that those two can't manage to stay out of trouble without me around. I need to get out of this bed and get back to work."

"Oh no, you don't, Calvin Woods," Sally said firmly. "Dr. Spalding says you have to stay in bed at least another week, and it's going to be at least three weeks before you can sit a horse, so no arguments."

Smoke approached the bed. "Cal, I was braced by a couple of men today who said they'd been in touch with Floyd Devers. Do you remember him?"

Cal nodded. "Sure, he was the one you shot in the leg durin' that fracas with Bloody Bill Anderson a while back. I was there with you."

"Did you happen to notice if Devers was with that bunch that shot you?"

Cal wagged his head. "No, sir. He weren't there, I'm sure of that. I'd've noticed him for sure."

"How about a big, tall man with scars on his face and funny lookin' ears?" Pearlie asked.

Cal shrugged. "Nope, can't say for sure 'bout him. There were so many of 'em that I only really noticed the two I shot an' the leader—the tall, skinny galoot dressed all in black."

"Smoke, did you have any luck with the surrounding ranchers?" Sally asked.

"No. Either the gang has left the area or they're holed up somewhere where nobody can see them. Not one person we spoke to had even seen them riding by."

"That's strange."

He shrugged. "Not really, not if they want to stay out of sight. There's thousands of acres around here where a group of that size could make a camp without being seen."

"But why would they want to stay out of sight, Smoke?" Pearlie asked. "Fer all they know, they kilt Cal deader'n yesterday's news, so if'n the only person who could tell anybody they done it wasn't around no more, why hide out?"

"You're right, Pearlie, it doesn't make sense." He shrugged, puzzled by it.

"Maybe they just rode on out of the county on their way somewhere else," Pearlie offered.

Sally looked worried. "Smoke, I have a bad feeling about all this. I don't think those men have left the area."

"I agree, Sally. I think they're up to something, but I'm hanged if I know what it is."

"You think they might be after the bank in Big Rock?"

He shook his head. "If they were, they would have already hit it. There wouldn't be any reason for them to hang around cooling their heels for two weeks after shooting Cal."

"Well, I just know they're up to something no good."

"You can bet on it, dear, but I'm afraid we're just going to have to wait and see what it is. If they have gone somewhere else, we'll find out about it. Monte Carson has wired all the neighboring towns to be on the lookout and let us know if they're spotted."

"And if they are?" she asked, although she knew the answer already. She'd lived with Smoke too many years not to know what he had in mind.

"Then I'm going to ride to wherever they are and teach them a lesson about minding their manners when they're on my property," he answered, his face serious.

In Fontana, more men were arriving every day, in groups of two, three, and four so as not to attract too much attention from the surrounding towns and ranches.

There were already over forty hard men, most wanted one place or another, who had come seeking easy money. Just the mention of the word gold could make normal men do strange things, and these men were by no stretch of the imagination normal to begin with.

Things were getting so hectic with all the new residents

that Bob Blanchard had to send for supplies and reopen the general store, as well as the hotel. Lazarus had also ordered a large amount of ammunition and extra weapons, including two small cannons. He figured if he was going to try to tree a town, he needed all the help he could get.

Mickey O'Donnel, a man small in stature and mean as a snake, had arrived two days ago and was busy trying to drink up the entire supply of whiskey in Fontana all by himself. The more he drank, the meaner he got. Even the other hard cases in town moved across the room when he was in one of his dark moods.

"Hey, Lazarus," he shouted just after noon, while most of the men were in the saloon eating lunch.

"Yes, Mickey. What is it you want?" Lazarus asked, looking up from his beans and enchiladas—about the only things the Mexican cook Blanchard had hired could cook that were worth eating.

"Tell me again why it is that you're plannin' to go up against this entire town when it's just the one man who's stoppin' us from gettin' our hands on all that gold."

Lazarus used the tip of his knife to pick a piece of stringy beef from between his teeth, then looked across the room at Mickey. He noticed the shanty Irishman hadn't eaten, but had drunk his lunch, as usual.

"Well, Mickey me boy, it's like this. First of all, Jensen has quite a reputation as a gunfighter, so he won't be all that easy to kill. Second, word is he is quite popular in the town, and anyone who does manage to kill him certainly won't be allowed to hang around mining for gold on his property."

"What if several of us could manage to catch him alone someplace? Then, we could hide his body so it'd be some time 'fore anybody even knew he was dead. That ranch of his is a big place, an' we could be gettin' the gold off the more isolated parts while his hands were lookin' for him."

Lazarus stroked his goatee and mustache. The man's idea

did make some sense, assuming of course any of the riffraff in this town was good enough to take Jensen, even if they outnumbered him four to one. Still, it was worth a try, and he had nothing to lose except men who were easily replaced should Jensen manage to kill them.

Lazarus stood up and addressed the room. "Men, Mickey O'Donnel has come up with an idea. While we're waiting for the rest of our supplies to get here, he thinks a team of four men should try and kill Smoke Jensen. I've got five gold twenty dollar pieces for anyone willing to give it a try. That's more'n a year's wages for most cowboys."

Mickey stepped away from the bar, a pugnacious sneer on his face. "It were my idea, so I'm goin'."

Lazarus nodded. "All right, that's one. I need three more men who're good with a gun."

Two men at a corner table stood up. They were obviously brothers, for they looked alike, both tall, with dark, curly hair and prominent noses on narrow faces. "Tom and me'll go, Mr. Cain," said Joe Blakely.

"Ah, the Blakely brothers," Lazarus said. "Anyone else?"

A very young-looking boy of about eighteen years stood up. He was dressed like the gunfighters in the dime novels— with black pants tucked into knee-high, black leather boots, a black leather vest over a white shirt with a black bow tie— and carried Colts on both hips, tied down low on his leg. "How about if one man could get the job done by himself, Cain? Would he get all the money?"

Lazarus recognized the boy. He called himself the Arizona Kid, and claimed to have bested eleven men in gunfights so far. Lazarus had seen him practicing his draw, and he was cat-quick with a handgun, but was he quick enough to beat Smoke Jensen?

"No, Arizona. This is too important to risk it that way. The plan is for four men to go."

"What if I don't like your plan, Cain? You fast enough to

make me do it your way?" the Kid said, loosening the rawhide hammer thongs on his Colts and squaring off to face Lazarus from across the room.

Lazarus's lips curled in a half-smile. He'd known this would happen sooner or later—one of the miscreants he'd summoned would challenge him for leadership of the group. Might as well get this over with.

Lazarus pulled his coat open and tucked the tail in the back of his pants out of the way, letting his hand hang next to the Colt on his right hip.

As he squared to face the Arizona Kid, Blackie Jackson and King Johannson stood up, ready to back his play. "Hold on, boys," Lazarus said. "I'll handle this young pup alone."

"All right, boss," Blackie said, and he and King sat down.

"Arizona, have you been saved?" Lazarus asked, his voice low, his eyes hard and black as flint.

The Kid laughed. "Saved? You mean like in church an' all?"

"That's right. Have you given your soul to God, son?"

"No, old man. Why?"

" 'Cause in the final reckoning, your soul belongs to God, but your butt belongs to me," Lazarus said as his hand flashed toward his gun.

The boy was quick, and he managed to get his pistol out of his holster and cocked before Lazarus's first shot hit him in the breastbone, shattering it and driving him back against the wall.

He leaned there, an astonished look on his face, as blood ran down the wall behind him to pool at his feet. "But . . . but . . . I'm the Arizona Kid," he mumbled, still trying to raise his pistol.

As he managed to get it waist high, Lazarus casually aimed and let the hammer down on his Colt, putting his slug directly between the Kid's eyes, blowing brains and bits of scalp and skull all over the wall.

The Kid hit the floor about the same time Lazarus returned to his meal. "Let me know if anyone else wants to try and take command of this operation," he said, as he shoveled some beans into his mouth.

When no one spoke up, he glanced at Mickey O'Donnel. "Mickey, I'm going to let you pick your fourth man. Meet with me later this afternoon and we'll go over the plan."

"What do you want us to do with Arizona, boss?" Blackie Jackson asked.

Lazarus said around an enchilada he was chewing, "Drag his carcass out back and let the coyotes take care of it."

"But it's gonna stink somethin' fierce," said Curly Joe.

"Good," Lazarus said. "Every time the men smell it, they'll be reminded of the consequences of going up against me."

Twelve

Smoke Jensen stood next to the buckboard and tucked in the edges of the quilt covering Cal in the back. "Looks like they got you pretty well set up, Cal," Smoke said.

"Yes sir. Pearlie piled enough hay in here to feed half the horses on the Sugarloaf, and then Miz Sally fixed up all these quilts so I feel snug as a bug in a rug."

"I may need to add another couple of hosses to this rig, Smoke," Pearlie said from the driver's seat of the buckboard. "Cal's fattened up so much from all this babyin' we been doin' to him that I don't know if only two animals can handle the load."

"You think maybe we need a couple of Percheron draft horses?" Smoke asked.

"Two could probably handle it if'n we was goin' downhill all the way."

"Perhaps we should stop off at the general store and get him some new pants to wear," Smoke said, grinning.

Cal raised his head, an indignant look on his face. "Hey, fellows, I ain't gained all that much weight."

"Oh, it must be table muscle then," Pearlie said sarcastically.

Just then, Sally appeared from the doctor's office, carrying a brown bottle in her hands. "Doc Spalding sent this laudanum in case the pain gets too bad on the trip back, Cal."

Pearlie rolled his eyes and shook his head. "I swear to goodness, Miz Sally, you're gonna plumb ruin that boy by spoilin' him like that. I ain't never gonna get no work outta him in the future."

Cal winked at Smoke and called out, "Yeah, Pearlie, you're right. The doc told me not to do any heavy liftin' for at least six months."

"What?" Pearlie said, half turning in his seat, until he saw Smoke and Cal laughing at him.

"Huh! I'm gonna take pains to remind that boy just who the ramrod is on the Sugarloaf, an' he won't never forget again."

Smoke helped Sally up onto the seat next to Pearlie.

"Are you coming with us, Smoke?" she asked.

"Not just yet. I'm going to go meet with Monte and see if he's heard anything on the whereabouts of the gang that shot Cal. Then I'll be coming home."

"All right, dear. We'll see you later," Sally said.

After the buckboard was out of sight, Smoke walked along the boardwalk toward Monte Carson's office. Out of a habit that had been with him so long he no longer noticed it, his eyes flicked back and forth as he walked, analyzing and checking everything he saw for possible danger. Having been a gunfighter and sometimes wanted man for most of his adult life, Smoke had learned the hard way that life was dangerous and the only way to survive it was to be ever vigilant.

More than once his life had been saved because he'd noticed a shadow where it shouldn't have been, a furtive movement in an alleyway, or someone's eyes hastily averted when he looked at them.

On the way to the sheriff's office, his habit of watchfulness paid off. He noticed several things that weren't quite right.

Down the street, a man was standing next to a pair of horses, and he was wearing a long duster. That struck Smoke as odd because the day was mild and the temperatures were in the low eighties, much too warm for standing around in a duster doing nothing. If the man had been standing in front of the bank, Smoke would have worried about a robbery about to take place. There was a feeling about the scene of the man waiting for something to happen.

Just as he was about to tell himself he was being foolish and overly suspicious, Smoke noticed something else out of kilter.

Two other men whose faces he didn't recognize were climbing up on their horses fifty yards ahead. Both had long guns in their hands, one a short-barreled shotgun and the other a Winchester Yellow Boy, the brass-plated rifle that'd been made a few years before. The funny thing was, Smoke could see empty saddle boots on both animals, so there wasn't any need for the men to be carrying the long guns unless they expected to be using them shortly.

When Smoke came to Monte's office, he went in the door without looking back over his shoulder at the three strangers who were acting suspiciously.

"Hey, Smoke. What's up?" Monte asked from his usual position—sitting in his chair with his boots up on the desk and a coffee cup in his hand.

Smoke walked over to the stove in the corner and took a cup off a peg on the wall. He poured himself a cup of coffee from the pot that had been cooking there as long as he could remember. The thick black liquid looked to be the consistency of syrup as it flowed slowly into Smoke's cup.

"Damn, Monte. This stuff'd float a horseshoe," Smoke said.

"Remember what your old mountain man friend Puma Buck used to say about makin' good coffee? It don't take near as much water as you think it do," Monte said, raising the pitch of his voice to do a credible imitation of Smoke's old friend.

"Well I can tell you didn't make too many trips to the well

for this pot," Smoke said, grimacing as he took a tentative sip.

"You come all this way just to gripe about my coffee?"

"No. I was just wondering if you'd had any answers to your wires asking about Lazarus Cain and his men."

"Some. I heard from Earp over at Dodge City. He said Floyd Devers, Walter Blackwell, Tad Younger, and Johnny Sampson all broke jail while he was out of town serving a warrant. He also said to tell you hello, and to let him know if we spotted 'em."

Smoke nodded. "Anything else?"

"Yeah, now that you mention it. Several sheriffs and marshals in surrounding towns wired back that they hadn't seen anything of Cain, but that some other hard cases had passed through their towns over the past couple of weeks."

Smoke shrugged. "What's so strange about that? There are a lot of hard men in this territory, and they often have to move around 'cause no one wants them in their counties."

"The strange thing is, they all seemed to be headed in this direction. The sheriffs to the south said the men were headed north, and the ones to the north said the gunslicks were headed south."

Smoke looked at Monte over the rim of his cup. "I see what you mean. You think it's connected somehow with Lazarus Cain?"

Monte wagged his head. "I don't know what to think, but I don't much like the idea that a bunch of men on the edge of the law are on their way in our direction. This is a good town, an' I don't want it to change. Hell, I ain't even had to draw my gun in nigh on two weeks."

Smoke edged over to glance out of the window on the front wall of the office, standing to the side so he couldn't be seen from outside.

"Well, dust the cobwebs off your Colt, Monte. I have a feeling you're gonna get to use it before long."

"What do you mean?" Monte asked as his feet hit the floor and he came out of his chair in a quick, clean movement, his hand already on the butt of his pistol.

"Stand off to one side and peek out the window."

As Monte looked, Smoke pointed out the three men he'd noticed on his way into the office. "At first I just thought I was being overly suspicious, but they still haven't moved or changed position. And see how every few minutes they glance over here? I think they're waiting to ambush someone, either you or me, when we come out of the door."

"I know the two men on the horses," Monte said. "I remember them from my days when I used to hire out my gun."

"Who are they?"

"Tom and Joe Blakely. Tom ain't so bad, but Joe is mean as a snake, an' twice as slippery. Tom's pretty good in a fight, but Joe plumb enjoys killin', an' he's done plenty of it to my certain knowledge."

"You know the other galoot, the short man over there with the duster on?"

"No, I don't think I've ever seen that one before."

"Any reason the Blakelys would be after you?"

"No, not that I know of. We parted on good terms last time I worked with 'em."

Smoke glanced at Monte out of the corner of his eye. His friend had been a noted gunman years ago, though he'd never been wanted by the law as far as Smoke knew.

"I won't ask about that," Smoke said, grinning.

Monte gave a half-smile. "That's a story for some winter sittin' around your fireplace up on the Sugarloaf."

"How do you want to handle this?" Monte asked, stepping over to the gunrack on the wall and pulling down a double-barreled 10-gauge express gun. He broke open the barrel and shoved two shells in and snapped it shut, adding a handful of shells to his vest pockets.

"Give me about five minutes to get in position, then come out the front door," Smoke said. "While their attention is on you, I'll brace 'em from behind."

It was a long five minutes, and by the time the hand on the wall clock had ticked five times Monte was sweating. As brave as Monte was, and as experienced at gunplay, he knew that luck played a big part in who lived and who died when lead started flying. It'd been a lot of years since he'd made his living holding a pistol. He hoped when push came to shove, as he knew it would, he wouldn't be so rusty that he got himself or his friend Smoke killed.

Finally, it was time. Monte hitched up his pants, eared back the hammers on the shotgun, and ambled out the door, looking a lot more calm than he was.

He stepped out on the boardwalk and stretched and yawned, looking around as if he had nothing more on his mind than a stroll through town.

He glanced across the street and acted as if he'd just noticed Tom and Joe Blakely sitting on their horses.

He walked casually toward them, the shotgun over his shoulder. "Hey boys, long time no see," Monte called, a fake grin on his face.

Tom looked at Joe and spoke in a low tone. "Did you know Monte Carson was involved in this?"

"Naw, but it don't make no difference, does it?"

Tom glanced at Monte ambling toward them as if he hadn't a care in the world. "Yeah, it does. Monte was always good to us, an' he never did us no hurt."

"Well, if he keeps his nose outta it he'll be all right. We're here to put lead in Smoke Jensen, not Monte."

"Hey, Monte," Tom called, his voice a little shaky with nerves. "What're you doin' here?"

Monte pointed to his left chest, where he had a star pinned to his vest. "I'm the sheriff of Big Rock, boys," he said, stopping about twenty feet from the two men.

"That's a hoot," Joe Blakely said with a smirk. "The famous Monte Carson a sheriff."

Monte smiled a lazy, half-smile. "Yeah, I can see where you'd think that. But boys, I want you to know I take my job very seriously. I don't allow nobody, even old friends, any slack when it comes to this town."

Tom shifted nervously in his saddle, while Joe glared at Monte through narrowed eyes. "Monte, this ain't no concern of your'n. Why don't you just go on back in that nice, safe office and tell Jensen he's got to come out sometime, an' we're waitin' here 'til he does."

Monte nodded, his face set, his eyes serious. "Oh, you men waitin' on Smoke Jensen?"

"That's right. We got some business with him," Joe replied, holding up the rifle in his hand.

"Well, here I am," Smoke called from fifteen feet behind the men. He was standing partially hidden in shadows in the alley behind the two men, just off the street.

As the Blakelys whirled around—Tom trying to bring his shotgun up and Joe thumbing back the hammer on his Winchester as he pointed it—Smoke made a move.

Both hands suddenly appeared in front of him filled with iron. His Colt .44s fired almost simultaneously, exploding with a deafening roar and belching flame and smoke from the barrels.

A slug from his right-hand gun took Tom Blakely in the neck, punching a hole through his Adam's apple, ripping out his windpipe. He dropped his shotgun and grabbed for his neck, as if he could somehow hold in the blood and air that was pumping out in a scarlet, frothy stream.

The slug from Smoke's left gun hit Joe high in the chest, spinning him halfway around in his saddle, his horse jumping and crow-hopping at the sudden noise. As the animal bucked, Joe, a bloody grin on his face exposing teeth stained red, raised the rifle again.

At the same time, the short man in the duster ran a few steps out into the street, drawing his pistol.

As Smoke fired both his Colts again, two holes appeared in Joe's head, one under each eye, shattering his cheekbones and blowing the back of his head off.

He and his brother hit the dirt at about the same time, both dead as stones.

Mickey O'Donnel got off two quick shots, one passing over Smoke's head, the other burning a grove in his right thigh.

Monte dove onto his stomach, his shotgun out in front of him. He fired both barrels, hoping to distract Mickey from shooting at Smoke.

One barrel missed, but the other load of .00-buckshot hit Mickey just above his right knee, tearing his leg completely off and spinning him around to fall in a heap, screaming in pain.

Smoke jerked his bandanna off and held it against his leg as he hobbled over toward the fallen men. He knew at a glance Tom and Joe were done for, so he continued over to Mickey.

He and Monte arrived at the same time. Monte knelt and put his hands on Mickey's shoulders, trying to hold him still as he writhed on the ground, moaning and crying in pain.

"Dear Lord, save me! Help me, Jesus!" the man cried, using the holy names for probably the first time in his adult life.

Blood was spurting from his leg in a thick, crimson stream as if from a pump, and Smoke knew he had only moments to live.

"Who sent you?" he hollered, trying to get the man's attention.

After a couple of seconds, the man quieted, futilely holding his leg as if he could hold in the blood that was leaving his body and taking his life with it.

His eyes cleared momentarily, and he looked up at Smoke. "Count your days, Jensen. Cain is coming. . . ."

Then his eyes clouded and there was no life behind them as the man went limp and the blood coming from his leg slowed to a trickle, stopping completely as he died.

Another man, hidden in an alley across the street, quietly holstered his pistol. *Damn,* he thought, *I never even saw Jensen draw his pistols 'fore he was blowin' Tom an' Joe to hell an' gone.*

He watched as Smoke and Monte stood over Mickey while he bled to death. *It's too late fer them,* he thought. *I'd do better to ride on back to Fontana and tell Cain what happened.*

He slipped back through the alley to where he had his horse tied up and jumped into the saddle, spurring the animal toward Fontana as fast as he could ride.

When he got there, he wasted no time in rushing into the saloon.

Cain was at his usual table, and he looked up as the man burst through the batwings.

"Ah, Jimmy," he said, calling to the man. "How did it go in Big Rock?"

Jimmy, sweating profusely from both his ride and from having to face Cain and tell him they failed, walked to his table.

"You ain't gonna believe this, Mr. Cain, but Jensen got Mickey an' Tom and Joe. They's all deader'n stones."

"What? How did that happen?" Cain asked, his face turning beet red.

"It was somethin' to see. There Tom an' Joe was, they rifles and shotguns in they hands, pointin' 'em at Jensen, when suddenly his hands were full of six-guns an' he blasted 'em outta they saddles 'fore they could pull the triggers."

"You're tellin' me they had the drop on Jensen an' he was still able to draw an' fire before they could shoot?"

"Yes sir! That Jensen's quicker'n a rattlesnake, an' twice as mean."

"What about Mickey?"

"He was able to get off a couple'a shots—one of 'em hit Jensen in the leg—'fore the sheriff blowed his leg clean off with a shotgun. He bled to death right there in the street with Jensen and the sheriff watchin' him die."

Cain shook his head. "And you, what did you do to help?"

Jimmy's face flushed scarlet. "There weren't nothin' I could do, boss. It all happened so fast, it was over 'fore I could draw an' fire."

In a lightning motion, Cain reached out and slapped Jimmy across the face, almost knocking the man off his feet.

"Get your gear and clear out of here, Jimmy. I don't allow no cowards to ride with me!"

"But Mr. Cain . . ."

Cain let his hand fall onto the butt of his pistol. "One more word, an' I'll shoot you down right where you stand."

Thirteen

George Hampton glanced over at Johnny North riding next to him as they approached the outskirts of Fontana. "I don't know as how this is such a great idea, Johnny," he said, sleeving fear-sweat off his forehead.

Johnny returned his stare, "Don't worry about it, George. We're just a couple'a cowboys ridin' through town. They don't need to know why we're here."

"What if your idea is right, and this Lazarus Cain Smoke was askin' 'bout and his gang are holed up here?"

Johnny shrugged. "Then we'll have a sociable drink an' be on our way. They won't know we're gonna tell Smoke where they're hidin'."

The first thing both men noted as they entered the city limits was the amount of horse droppings in the street and their apparent freshness. This didn't look like the virtual ghost town it had become after the Tilden Franklin affair of a few years back.

"Uh oh, Johnny, looky there," George said as they rode past the rundown livery stable barn. It was full of horses, with not a single stall unoccupied. "Looks like there's quite a few men here."

Johnny's eyes narrowed as he looked around the town, seeing a number of men lounging on the boardwalks or pitching horseshoes in the alleyways. "Smoke said he thought Lazarus was ridin' with about fifteen or twenty men. Seems to me to be more like forty or fifty hanging around here from the number of hosses I can count."

At the saloon there wasn't room to tie up their horses, the double hitching rail in front already being full, so they walked down a few yards and tied up in front of the general store.

"Look in there," George said. "Them shelves is plumb full'a goods an' things."

"Don't exactly appear as if these gents're passin' through, does it?" Johnny remarked. "Matter of fact, it looks like they is plannin' on settin' up home here."

Johnny led the way through the batwings of the saloon, trying not to show any surprise at the number of men sitting around at the tables drinking and playing cards. About the only thing the place lacked was a piano player in the corner to bang away on the yellowed, stained keys.

When Johnny got to the bar, he ordered beer for himself and Hampton.

As the bartender placed foaming glasses in front of them he stared at Johnny for a moment, a puzzled expression on his face.

"You look a mite familiar, friend," Bob Blanchard said. "Do I know you?"

Johnny snorted and took a deep swig of his beer. "Partner, I don't know who in the hell you are, or who you know," Johnny said in a harsh voice. Then he leaned forward and added, "And you know what else, mister? I don't really give a damn, either."

Blanchard's face paled at the implied threat, and he took a step back, his hands held out in front of him. In the West, it was sometimes a fatal mistake to show too much interest in who a man might be or where he hailed from, and it was certainly considered impolite to ask unless the information was volunteered.

"I'm sorry, mister. Didn't mean no disrespect," Blanchard stammered, sweat forming on his brow.

"None taken," Johnny muttered, and he turned to lean his back against the bar and survey the other patrons.

He immediately saw the man Cal said had shot him. He was sitting at a corner table that was full of hard-looking men who were drinking whiskey like there was no tomorrow.

The tall, skinny, mean-looking man glanced up and his eyes met Johnny's for a second before Johnny looked away.

Out of the corner of his eye he noticed the man Smoke said was named Cain get to his feet and amble toward him at the bar.

Cain took a position next to Johnny and held out his hand to Blanchard, who quickly put a glass of whiskey in it.

"Howdy, stranger," Cain said, leaning on the bar as he stared at Johnny.

Johnny gave him a look, his face blank. "Howdy."

"What brings you and your friend to Fontana?" Cain asked casually, as if the answer didn't really matter all that much to him.

Johnny turned until he was facing Cain. "What's it to you, mister?"

Cain shrugged. "Well, I'm kind'a the head man around here, an' we don't particularly cotton to strangers hangin' around."

Johnny gave him a cold half-smile. "We're not exactly hangin' around. My friend and I are on our way north, and stopped off to water our mounts an' wash the trail dust outta our mouths. Is there any law agin that in these parts?"

Cain wagged his head. "Not if that's all you're plannin' on doin'."

"Good," Johnny said and turned back to the bar, ignoring Cain.

"I didn't catch your name, mister," Cain said, his voice harder, as if he wasn't used to being ignored.

Johnny emptied his glass and held it out to the bartender for a refill. "That's 'cause I didn't throw it," he replied, forcing boredom into his tone.

Cain made a slight motion with his head and a man with a heavy growth of whiskers stepped from a nearby table and squared off facing Johnny, his hands hanging next to his pistols.

"Mr. Cain asked you what your name is, mister. You'd better be tellin' him or I'm gonna have to make you."

Johnny looked back over his shoulder at the gunny. "First of all, I don't take orders from nobody, not even your Mr. Cain," Johnny growled as he turned to face the man. "And second, if you even twitch toward that hogleg on your hip, you'll be dead before you clear leather."

"You talk awful big, stranger," the man answered.

"If you think it's only talk, jerk that smokewagon and go to work, sonny boy," Johnny said in a hoarse whisper, unhooking the leather hammerthong on his Colt.

The man's face turned red, and he grabbed for his gun.

In a flash, Johnny's hand appeared before him filled with iron, the pistol making a harsh click as he eared back the hammer, the barrel inches from the astonished gunman's face.

"Now, this can go one of two ways," Johnny snarled. "You can unhand that gun and go sit back down to your card game, or I can scatter what little brains you have all over the saloon floor." He gave a tiny shrug with his shoulders. "Your call, sonny boy."

Cain quickly stepped between the two men, smiling, his hands out as if to make peace.

"Whoa, mister. I can see you're pretty handy with that sixkiller. My name's Lazarus Cain, an' I'm askin' you nicely what yours is."

Johnny holstered his Colt. "Johnny North."

Cain frowned. "Johnny North? I thought you were dead."

Johnny smirked. "Not likely."

Cain turned to the crowd in the saloon who were watching the action intently. "Men," he said in a loud voice. "This here is Johnny North, one of the most famous gunfighters of a few years back."

He put his hand out and Johnny took it. "Pleased to meet you, Johnny. I've heard a great deal about you, though not in recent times," Cain said in a friendly tone.

Johnny picked up his beer and took a deep swallow. That had been a close call, but he was glad to see he hadn't lost any of his quickness. It had been some time since he'd drawn on anyone.

"Times have been slow. I worked the Lincoln County war a few months back, but there hasn't been much call for my services since then," he said, referring to when he and Smoke had intervened with John Chisum in New Mexico.

Cain nodded. "I heard about that little fracas. Unfortunately, I was busy elsewhere an' didn't get to see it."

Johnny gave a half-smile. "It was interestin' for a while, then it just got boring. Chisum didn't have the stomach to really clear out the opposition, and he made peace a little too soon for my taste."

Cain laughed. "Well, Chisum is a businessman, and they often have goals that are different from men like us."

Johnny didn't answer, but continued to stare at Cain, waiting for him to get to the point.

Cain pursed his lips, as if considering what to say next. After a moment, he said, "I've got a little operation goin' on here that you might be interested in, Johnny."

"Yeah? What's that?" Johnny asked.

"Before I say any more, why don't you introduce me to your companion?"

"This here is George Hampton, from down Texas way," Johnny said.

George nodded at Cain, then turned back to his beer as if ignoring their conversation.

"Is he . . . in the business?" Cain asked.

Johnny smirked. "In a small way, but it's just a sideline for him. He's got a small spread down near Del Rio, an' he's just makin' some spare cash to buy a herd. His got wiped out by tick fever from some stock he . . . appropriated across the border."

Cain laughed. "Appropriated stock will sometimes do that, especially Mexican steers."

Hampton nodded without looking up. "Yeah, an' there ain't no one to go to for a refund, neither."

Cain laughed again.

"Well, if you boys are lookin' for work I may be able to oblige you. Like I say, I've got a deal workin' here that may pay off handsomely."

Johnny shook his head. "Maybe in a couple of weeks. We're on our way over to Pueblo to see a man about something else. If you're still around here when we finish up with that job, we'll stop by on our way back south."

A suspicious look crossed Cain's face. "And just who are you goin' to see in Pueblo?"

"A man name of Wells, Joey Wells," Johnny answered. "He's an old friend of George's, an' he asked us to help him with a little problem he's having with some U.S. Marshals up that way."

"Joey Wells is in Pueblo?" Cain asked.

"Yeah."

"I heard he killed more'n a hundred men durin' the big war."

"More like two hundred, I reckon," George said.

"I rode for a while with Bill Quantrill's raiders, an' we would've given a lot to have him with us," Cain said.

Johnny smiled. "Joey had retired across the border, 'til a bunch of *bandidos* shot his wife an' son. That's what brought him up here, to make 'em pay for that."

Cain nodded. "I wouldn't want Wells on my backtrail."

"Neither would I," Johnny said. "That's why I don't aim to disappoint him after sayin' I'd help out."

"I can see your point," Cain said. "Well, tell Joey that there's some work waitin' for him here if he's so inclined. Meanwhile, enjoy your journey and stop back by on your way south. We may still have need of your services."

"Thanks, we'll do that," Johnny said, flipping a gold coin on the bar for their drinks. Cain reached over and picked up the coin and handed it back to Johnny. "Your money's no good here, Johnny. The drinks are on me."

"Thanks," Johnny said.

Cain grinned. "No problem. It's not every day I get to meet a legend like Johnny North."

Fourteen

After Johnny and George left the saloon, Cain held his glass out for a refill.

"Bob," he said, as he took a sip of the alcohol, "you don't see many like that anymore. The old gunfighters had class, something sorely lackin' in these new young punks that seem so prevalent nowadays."

"Yes sir," Bob said, wiping down the bar with a rag that looked as if it'd seen better days. "Only—"

Catching the hesitation in his voice, Cain looked up at him. "Only what, Bob?"

"It's just that I seem to remember somethin' 'bout Johnny North, somethin' 'bout him hangin' up his guns a while back."

Cain's eyes narrowed. "Oh? Well if that were true, why wouldn't he've just said so?"

"I don't know, Mr. Cain. Maybe he found he didn't much care for retirement an' went back to gunnin' fer a livin'."

"Yeah, maybe . . . only, if North lied about one thing, maybe he lied about other things, too. If he comes back, we'll have to keep a special eye on Mr. Johnny North."

Smoke was on his front porch having a cup of coffee and a cigarette when Johnny North and George Hampton rode up.

"Light and set, boys," Smoke said, giving the old mountain man greeting to his friends.

While they dismounted, Smoke stuck his head in the cabin door and asked Sally if she'd make some more coffee for their company.

Within ten minutes, they were all sitting on the porch, coffee in one hand and some of Sally's pastries in the other.

"Smoke," Johnny said, "we rode out to Fontana and found that Lazarus Cain you been lookin' for camped out there with all his men."

"What made you think to look in Fontana?" Smoke asked. "I thought it wasn't much more than a ghost town."

"It were Johnny's idea, Mr. Jensen," George said around a mouthful of *pan dulce*.

"Yeah. I got to thinkin' after your visit when you tole me Cain'd disappeared without nobody havin' laid eyes on him," Johnny said. "There was only one place I knowed where that many men could hunker down an' not be noticed."

Smoke nodded. "It was a good thought, Johnny. No one would see them there because no one around here ever goes to Fontana anymore."

"Did you talk to him?" asked Sally, who was standing behind Smoke's chair with her hands on his shoulders.

"Tell 'em, Johnny," George said, reaching for another piece of Mexican sweet bread. "Tell 'em how you walked right into that den of rattlesnakes and chatted 'em up as pretty as you please."

"Well, I noticed on the way into town that there were quite a few more men than Smoke had thought. First off, there were at least fifty to sixty hosses on the street and in the livery, an' I could count more'n twenty men sittin' around the boardwalks an' gabbin'."

Smoke frowned. "You mean to tell me Cain has over fifty men with him in Fontana?"

Both George and Johnny nodded.

"At least that many," Johnny continued. "Anyway, we went into the saloon, that bein' the best place I know to pick up any gossip or to see what's happenin' in a town."

"You were very brave to do that, Johnny," Sally said.

"Dumb is more like it," George said, his eyes wide. "I never been more scared in my entire life."

"It wasn't all that bad, Miss Sally," Johnny said. "The saloon was filled to the brim with hard-lookin' men. Smoke, you know the kind I'm talkin' 'bout."

Smoke gave a half-grin. "Yeah, Johnny. Men who look like us. Men whose eyes tell you they're on the prod, looking for trouble, and not afraid of it when it comes."

Johnny nodded. "Right. Well, as I'm havin' my drink I notice this tall, skinny dude over in the corner who looks like the man you described as the one shot Cal. Sure enough, after a minute or two, he saunters over an' starts askin' me questions—"

"You should'a seen it, Mr. Smoke," George interrupted. "Johnny changed, right 'fore my eyes, into another man. He got this look on his face . . . like he was meaner'n a snake with a sore tail."

Johnny cut his eyes toward Sally. "That's my gunfighter face, Miss Sally."

Sally smiled. "Yes, I know the one. Every now and then, when something happens, like to Cal, I see Smoke change the same way. All the softness and gentleness leaves, and a shell comes down that's hard as the granite in those mountain peaks."

"Yes, ma'am," Johnny said. "Anyhow, one thing leads to another an' he offers me a job, a gunhand type of job. Says he's got somethin' in the works that's gonna make 'em all rich, only he needs all the guns he can find."

"He say what it was?" Smoke asked.

"No, but I made up some story 'bout goin' over to Pueblo to see Joey Wells, just to get us outta there, an' he 'bout wet his pants. He said he'd heard of Wells, an' shore wished he'd come to ride with his gang. I tole him it'd be a couple of weeks or more 'fore we could get back, an' he acted like they'd probably still be here then."

Smoke got quiet as he thought, refilling his coffee cup and building himself another cigarette. As he smoked, he went over the possibilities in his mind.

"What do you think he has in mind, Johnny? Did he give you any idea at all?" Smoke asked, tilting his head as smoke trailed from his nostrils.

"Nope, none a'tall."

"Well, it can't be a bank robbery. There isn't a bank in the territory that would warrant using fifty men, or that would make more than a few rich."

"Heck, Smoke, if'n he robbed the entire town of Big Rock of everything in it, it wouldn't be worth enough for that many men," George said.

"Likewise," Sally said, a thoughtful look on her face, "it can't be cattle or land. And there's no big army around here with a large payroll to rob."

Smoke shook his head. "We need to get someone on the inside to see what Cain has in mind. Did he seem to trust you, Johnny?"

"Yeah. He thinks I'm still on the owlhoot trail, sellin' my gun to the highest bidder."

"Wait a minute, Johnny," George said, a frightened look on his face. "Yore forgittin' 'bout Bob Blanchard."

"Who?" Smoke asked.

"Yeah, you're right, George," Johnny said. Then to Smoke, "Bob Blanchard is the bartender over at Fontana, an' seemed right friendly with Cain an' his men."

"Who is he?"

"He's a man who was on the fringes of the Tilden Franklin thing a few year ago. He wasn't directly involved, but when you shot up Fontana an' ran off or kilt all the gunnies, he sort'a stayed around. Word is he's lived almost like a hermit up there ever since."

"So?"

"Well, if'n he was in the know 'bout what happened then, George thinks sooner or later he's gonna remember that you an' I sort'a became friends, an' that I settled down up here an' hung up my guns. If he does, then Cain'll know I ain't no friend of his."

"George is right, Smoke," Sally said. "It's much too dangerous to ask Johnny to go back to Fontana. If those men even suspected he wasn't what he claimed, they'd kill him without a second thought."

"You're right, Sally. It is too dangerous to even think about sending Johnny back there. We've got to find someone else that they won't suspect."

"Trouble is, Smoke, too many of the folks around here were mixed up in that Franklin fracas," Johnny said. "Blanchard'd be sure to recognize most of 'em."

"Yes. We need someone from out of town, and they need to be handy with a gun to fit in with that group."

"How 'bout Joey Wells, Smoke?" George asked. "You think he'd do it if'n you asked him to?"

Smoke nodded slowly, thoughtfully. "That's not a bad idea, George, not a bad idea at all."

"Smoke, you can't ask Joey to do that," said Sally. "He's settled down now, and I got a wire not too long ago from Betty saying they'd had another baby."

Smoke turned in his chair to look up at her. "I know it's risky, Sally. But think of the damage fifty hard men under the leadership of a crazy man can do to this county. Think of how many innocent people may get killed if we don't find out what they're up to."

"Why not just call in the army?" she asked. "Monte says he's a wanted man, and probably most of those with him are, too. The army could just come in and arrest them all."

Johnny North shook his head. "It won't work, Miss Sally. Cain is an old rebel raider. He's gonna have pickets posted all around that town who'll warn him if any threat is comin'. The army'd never even get close to him."

"Johnny's right, Sally. It's going to take just one man, the right man, to do the job."

"Poor Betty," Sally said, a wistful look in her eyes. "Just when she thinks her man is settling down for good, something like this has to happen."

"Then you think he'll come?" Smoke asked her.

She gave him a look, her eyes soft. "Yes, Smoke, because he's just like you. You two are cut from the same bolt of cloth. If a friend needs you, no matter how dangerous it is, you're going to go. Same with Joey. If you ask, he'll come."

Smoke nodded. "I'll wire him in the morning. See if he'll come for a visit so I can explain what's happening and see what he thinks."

"You'd better mention for him to steer clear of Fontana on his way down here," Johnny said. "It wouldn't do for Cain to talk to him 'fore you get a chance to explain things."

"Right. I'll ask him to come the back way and not to let anyone see him."

"That ought'a be easy for him, since the entire Union Army looked for him for over two years an' couldn't find him," Johnny said, with a grin.

Fifteen

A week later, Cal was giving Smoke and everyone else around him fits. The young man was tired of being confined to bed and wanted to get out and about.

Cal looked up from trying to pull his boots on to see Sally Jensen standing in the doorway to the bunkhouse, hands on hips, a frown on her pretty face.

"Uh oh," he muttered.

"Uh oh is right, young man!" Sally said through gritted teeth. "How many times do I and Dr. Spalding have to tell you to stay in bed? If that lung wound gets infected, you'll die. Do you want that?"

Cal pulled his foot out of his boot and swung his legs back up under the covers on the bed. "No ma'am," he said in a low, dispirited voice. "It's just that I'm 'bout to go crazy if'n I don't get outta this room. The walls're closing in on me an' I feel all cramped up, kind'a like I cain't hardly breathe."

Sally's voice softened as she approached the bed. "I know how hard it is for you, Cal, but it's for your own good."

Suddenly, she snapped her fingers. "I know! I'll fix up a chair with a footrest on the porch of our cabin. That way you can get some fresh air and look out over the Sugarloaf and watch Pearlie and the other hands working cattle."

Cal's face brightened. "That'd be great, Miz Sally. Not as good as gettin' back in the saddle, but almost."

Sally smiled and walked back to the cabin she shared with Smoke. As she was piling some sheets and blankets on a chair on the porch, getting it ready for Cal, Smoke rode up to the front of the cabin.

He dismounted and tied Joker's reins to the hitching rail. When he got to the porch, he wrapped his big arms around Sally and gave her a gentle kiss.

"Um-m-m," she said in a low voice. "What was that for?"

He shrugged and smiled. "Nothing. Just a hello kiss."

She reached up and pulled his face back down and kissed him again. "Hello," she said.

He glanced at the chair she was fussing over. "What's that for?"

"So Cal can sit out here and get some fresh air. He says he's going crazy staying in bed for so long."

Smoke nodded. "I don't blame him. That's one of the hardest things about being wounded, the recovery time."

"What did you find out in Big Rock? Any news of the gang of bandits?"

"No. Monte says no one's come into Big Rock from Fontana way since Johnny told us they were holed up there."

"Did he contact the U.S. Marshals or the army?"

"Yes. They said they'd get here eventually, 'cause Cain and some of the men riding with him are wanted, but the marshals are way up in the northern part of the territory and won't be available for some time."

"What about the army?"

He shook his head. "The commanding officer of the nearest fort wired back they could only intervene if the governor requested it due to the gang causing massive civil disturbance, which they're not."

"So, what you're telling me is that we're on our own to deal with them."

"That's about the size of it."

"You look pleased," she said, staring into his eyes. "You really didn't want the marshals or the army to come here, did you?"

"Nope. This is our problem, and it was our friend they shot down in cold blood on our ranch. I'd just as soon take care of the snakes myself."

"But Smoke, there are more than fifty men in that gang."

He nodded. "I know. I didn't say I was going to do it all by myself. There are plenty of men around here who will be glad to help rid the county of that pond scum over in Fontana."

"Speaking of help, when do you expect Joey Wells?"

"I don't know. I haven't had an answer to my wire, but it's only been a few days."

"Do you think he'll come?"

"It all depends on how civilized his wife has made him. Sometimes, settling down raising a family changes a man, takes all the spirit out of him. He may not even consider picking up his guns again."

She laid her hand on his cheek, a wistful expression on her face. "It didn't change you, Smoke."

"Aren't you glad?" he asked with a grin. "You're not the kind of lady who wants a lapdog for a husband."

"You're right," she said with a sigh. "Life with you is many things, but boring is definitely not one of them."

She finished fixing the chair, adjusting the ottoman so Cal could stretch out in a semi-reclining position.

"Smoke, would you go get Cal and help him over here? I'll fix a fresh pot of coffee while you do that."

Smoke walked over to the bunkhouse and through the door.

"Hey, Smoke," Cal said, his face lighting up to have company.

"Get your boots on, boy. We're taking you for a trip over to the cabin."

After Cal struggled into his boots, refusing to let Smoke do it for him, he got shakily to his feet.

Smoke stood next to him. "Here, Cal, put your arm around my shoulders."

"I can do it on my own," Cal said.

Smoke looked at him. "Listen, Cal, I know you can, but Sally told me to help you over to the cabin. Do you want to go out there and tell her you don't need any help?"

"Uh . . . not really."

"Neither do I, so make it easy on both of us and just kind'a throw your arm around me so's she'll think we're both doing what she says."

With some effort they finally made it across the yard and onto the porch. Cal realized he really needed Smoke's help, the bedrest and wound having made him weaker than he thought.

He eased into the chair, sweat on his forehead from the effort to walk, and pulled the blankets up to his waist.

"How's that, Cal?" Sally asked.

"Great. I got me a good view of the whole Sugarloaf from here."

"Would you like some coffee? I made a fresh pot."

"Sure."

While she was gone, Smoke built himself a cigarette.

"Could I have one of those?" Cal asked.

Smoke frowned, but pitched the cloth packet of Bull Durham to Cal, along with his papers.

After they both had their cigarettes lighted, Sally appeared on the porch with two cups of steaming, aromatic coffee.

"Just what do you think you're doing, Cal?" she asked, looking at the cigarette in his hand.

"Uh—"

"You know you shouldn't be smoking with that lung wound."

"Sally," Smoke said gently, "quit babying him. If he's old

enough to get shot trying to defend our ranch, he's old enough to decide if he wants a smoke."

"But it's not good for him."

"Life out here is dangerous, dear. In the greater scheme of things, smoking is low risk compared to most of what we do."

She shook her head and whirled around to disappear back in the cabin.

As they smoked and drank their coffee, both men looked out over the rolling hills and green pastures of the Sugarloaf, enjoying the view and the day.

Sixteen

The next morning Cal was in his chair on Smoke's front porch as soon as breakfast was over.

Pearlie, on his way to do the day's chores, stopped by to chat.

"Well, how do it feel to be the king of the ranch, lazy-bones?" Pearlie asked in his soft drawl.

"Actually, not so good," Cal answered, his face serious. "I just know that without me out there to make sure things get done right, I'm gonna have to do 'em all over again once I'm back on my feet."

"Oh, is that so? By the looks of things, by the time you're back on your feet it'll be smack in the middle of winter, an' there won't be all that much left to do."

Cal started to answer. When, out of the corner of his eye, he spotted something on the horizon.

"Uh oh," he muttered. "Smoke, you better get out here. Looks like company comin'," he hollered.

When Smoke and Sally walked out onto the porch, Cal pointed off in the distance. A lone figure could be seen riding toward the cabin, taking his time, keeping his horse in a ground-covering lope.

"Who do you think that is?" Cal asked.

Smoke's lips curled in a smile. "Unless I miss my guess, that's Joey Wells."

"Mr. Wells?" Cal asked, his voice rising in excitement. Since Cal's first meeting with the man he'd read about in hundreds of dime novels, Joey had been a hero to him.

"Yeah. I guess he decided to just show up instead of wiring me back."

Sally turned and started back into the cabin. "I guess I'd better cook up another batch of eggs and some bacon. He's going to be mighty hungry after riding all the way here from Pueblo."

As the figure slowly got larger, Smoke thought back to the day Joey arrived at Longmont's Saloon, looking for him. . . .

The batwings were thrown wide and a man entered slowly, stepping to the side when he got inside so that his back was to a wall. He stood there, letting his eyes adjust to the darkened interior of the saloon. Louis recognized the actions of an experienced pistoleer, saw how the man's eyes scanned the room, flicking back and forth before he proceeded to the bar. The cowboy was short, about five feet nine inches, Louis figured, and was covered with a fine coat of trail dust. He had a nasty looking scar on his right cheek, running from the corner of his eye to disappear in the edge of his handlebar mustache. The scar had contracted as it healed, shortening and drawing his lip up in a perpetual sneer. His small gray eyes were as cold and deadly as a snake's, and he wore a brace of Colt .44s on his hips, tied down low, and carried a Colt Navy .36 in a shoulder holster. Louis, an experienced gunfighter himself, speculated he had never seen a more dangerous hombre in all his years. *He looks as tough as a just-woke grizzly,* he thought.

As hair on the back of his neck prickled and stirred, Louis shifted slightly in his seat, straightening his right leg and reaching down to loosen the rawhide thong on his Colt, just in case.

The stranger flipped a gold Double-Eagle on the bar, took possession of a bottle of whiskey, and spoke a few words in a low tone to the bartender. After a moment, the barman inclined his head toward Louis, then busied himself wiping the counter with a rag, casting worried glances at Louis out of the corner of his eye.

The newcomer turned, leaning his back against the bar, and stared at Louis. His eyes flicked up and down, noting the way Louis had shifted his position and how his right hand was resting on his thigh near the handle of his Colt. His expression softened and his lips moved slightly, turning up in what might have been a smile in any other face. He evidently recognized Louis as a man of his own kind, a brother predator in a world of prey.

Louis watched the gunman's eyes, thinking, *This man has stared death in the face on many occasions, and has never known fear.* With a slow deliberate motion, his gaze never straying, Louis picked up his china coffee cup with his left hand and drained it to moisten his suddenly dry mouth, wondering just what the stranger had in mind, and whether he had finally met the man who was going to beat him to the draw and put him in the ground.

The pistoleer grabbed his whiskey with his left hand and began to saunter toward Louis, his right hand hanging at his side. As he passed one of the poker tables, a puncher threw his playing cards down and jumped up from the table with a snort of anger. "Goddamned cards just won't fall for me today," he said, as he turned abruptly toward the bar, colliding with the stranger.

The cowboy, too much into his whiskey to recognize his danger, peered at the newcomer through bleary, red-rimmed eyes, spoiling for a fight. "Why don't you watch where yer goin', shorty?" he growled.

The gunman's expression never changed, though Louis thought he detected a kind of weary acceptance in his eyes, as if he had been there many times before. In a voice smooth with soft consonants of the South in it, he replied, "I believe ya' need a lesson in manners, sir."

The drunken cowboy sneered, "And you think yore man enough to give me that lesson, asshole?"

In less time than it took Louis to blink, the pistoleer's Colt was drawn and cocked, and the barrel was pressed under the puncher's chin, pushing his head back. "Unless ya' want yore brains decoratin' the ceiling I'd suggest ya' apologize to the people here fer yore poor upbringin', and fer yore Mamma not never teachin' ya' any better than to jaw at yore betters."

The room became deathly quiet. One of the other men at the table moved slightly and the stranger said without looking at him, "Friend, 'less ya' want that arm blown plumb off, I'd haul in yore horns 'til I'm through with this'n."

Fear-sweat poured off the cowboy's face and his eyes rolled, trying to see the gun stuck in his throat. "I'm . . . I'm right sorry, sir. It was my fault, and I . . . I apologize fer my remarks."

The gunman stepped back, holstered his Colt, and glanced at a wet spot on the front of the drunk's trousers. "Apology accepted, sir." His eyes cut to the man at the table who had frozen in position, afraid to move a muscle. "Ya' made a wise choice not ta' buy chips in this game, friend. It's a hard life ta' go through with only one hand." Without another word, he ambled over to stand next to Louis's table, his back to the wall where he could observe the room as he talked.

"Ya' be Mr. Longmont?"

Louis nodded, eyebrows raised. "Yes sir, I am. And to whom do I have the pleasure of speaking?"

"I be Joseph Wells, 'though most calls me Joey."

At the mention of his name, the men at the poker table got hastily to their feet and grabbed their friend by his arm and hustled him out the door, looking back over their shoulders at the living legend who had almost curled him up.

Louis didn't offer his hand, but smiled at Wells. "Pleased to make your acquaintance, Mr. Wells." He nodded at an empty chair across the table from him. "Would you care to take a seat and have some food?"

Wells scanned the room again with his snake eyes before he pulled a chair around and sat, his back still to a wall. "Don't mind if'n I do, thank ye kindly."

Louis waved a hand and a young black waiter came to his table. "Jeremiah, Mr. Wells would like to order."

"Yes sir," the boy replied as he looked inquiringly at Wells.

"I'll have a beefsteak cooked jest long enough ta' keep it from crawling off'n my plate, four hen's eggs scrambled, an' some tomaters if'n ya' have any."

The boy nodded rapidly and turned to leave.

"An' some *cafécito*, hot, black, and strong enough to float a horseshoe," Wells added.

Louis grinned. "I like to see a man with a healthy appetite." He glanced at a thick layer of trail dust on Wells's buckskin coat. "You have the look of a man a long time on the trail."

"That's a fact. All the way from Mexico. Pretty near a month, now."

The waiter appeared and placed a coffee mug on the table, filled it with steaming black coffee from a silver server, and added some to Louis's cup before setting the pot on the table. Wells pulled a cork from his whiskey bottle and poured a dollop of amber liquid into his coffee. He offered the bottle to Louis, who shook his head.

Wells shrugged, blew on his coffee to cool it, and drank the entire cup down in one long draught. He leaned back and took his fixings out and built himself a cigarette. Striking a lucifer on his boot, he lit the cigarette and stuck it in the corner of his mouth. He left it there while he spoke, squinting one eye against the smoke. "That's mighty good coffee." He refilled his cup and again topped it off with a touch of whiskey. "Shore beats that mesquite bean coffee I been drinking fer the last month."

Louis nodded, reviewing in his mind what he had heard about the famous Joey Wells. Wells had been born in the foothills of Missouri. He was barely in his teens when he fought in the Civil War for the Confederate Army. Riding with a group called The Missouri Volunteers, he became a fearless, vicious killer, eagerly absorbing every trick of guerilla warfare known from the mountain men and hillbillies he fought with. After Lee's surrender at Appomattox, Wells's group attempted to turn themselves in. They reported to a Union Army outpost and handed over their weapons, expecting to be sent home, as other Confederate soldiers had been. Instead, the entire group was assassinated—all except Wells and a few others who were late getting to the surrender site. From a hill nearby, they watched their unarmed comrades being gunned down. Under the code of the Missouri Feud, they vowed to fight the Union to the death.

After Joey and his men perpetrated several raids upon unsuspecting Union soldiers and camps—killing viciously to fulfill their vow of vengeance—a group of hired killers and thugs known as the Kansas Redlegs were assigned to hunt down the remaining Missouri Volunteers. After several years of raids and counter-raids, Joey was the last surviving member of his renegade group. It took him another year and a half, using every trick he had learned, to track down and kill all of the remaining Redlegs, over a hundred and fifty men. Along the way, he became a legend, a figure mothers used to scare their children into doing their chores, a figure men whispered about around campfires at night. With each telling his legend grew, magnified by penny dreadfuls and dime novels, until there was no place left in America for him to run to.

After the last Redleg lay dead at his feet, Joey was said to have gone to Mexico and set up a ranch there. Rumor had it Texas Rangers had struck a bargain with him, vowing to leave him in peace if he stayed south of the border.

Louis fired up another cigar, sipped his coffee, and wondered what had happened to cause Wells to break his truce and head north to Colorado. Of course, he didn't ask. In the West, sticking your nose in another's business was an invitation to have someone shoot it off.

After his food was served, Wells leaned forward and ate with a single-minded concentration, not speaking again until his plate was bare. He filled his empty coffee cup with whiskey, built another cigarette, and leaned back with a contented sigh. Smoke floated from the butt in his mouth and caused him to squint as he stared at Louis from under his hat brim. "A while back, I met some fellahs down Chihuahua way tole me 'bout a couple 'a friends of theirs in Colorado. One was named Longmont."

Louis motioned to the waiter to bring him some brandy, then nodded, waiting for Wells to continue. "Yep. Said this Longmont dressed like a dandy and talked real fancy, but not to let that fool me. This Longmont was a real bad pistoleer and knew his way around a Colt, and was maybe the second fastest man with a short gun they'd ever seen."

Louis dipped the butt of his stogie in his brandy, then stuck it in his mouth and puffed, sending a cloud of blue smoke toward the ceiling. "These men say anything else?" he asked, eyebrows raised.

"Uh huh. Said this Longmont would do ta' ride the river with, and if'n he was yore friend he'd stand toe-ta'-toe with ya' against the devil hisself if need be."

Louis threw back his head and laughed. "Well, excusing your friends for engaging in a small amount of hyperbole, I suppose their assessment of my character is basically correct."

Wells's lips curled in a small smile. "Like they said, ya' talk real purty."

"And who was the other man your friends mentioned?"

"*Hombre* named Smoke Jensen. They said Jensen was so fast he could snatch a Double-Eagle off'n a rattler's head and leave change 'fore the snake could strike."

Louis drowned his quiet smile in coffee. "Your friends have quite a way with words, themselves. Might I ask what their names are?"

"'Couple'a Mex's named Louis Carbone and Al Martine. Got 'em a little *rancho* down near Chihuahua." Wells dropped his cigarette on the floor and ground it out with his boot. "They be pretty fair with short guns theyselves, fer Mex's."

Louis nodded, remembering the last time he had seen Carbone and Martine. The pair had hired out their guns to a rotten, no good back-shooter named Lee Slater. Slater bit off more than he could chew when he and his men rode through Big Rock, shooting up the town and raising hell. Problem was, they also wounded and almost killed Sally Jensen, Smoke's wife. Smoke went after them, and in the end he faced down the gang in the very streets of Big Rock where it all started. . . .

Lee Slater stepped out of the shadows, his hands wrapped around the butts of Colts, as were Smoke's. "I'm gonna kill you, Jensen!" he screamed.

A rifle barked, the slug striking Lee in the middle of his back and exiting out the front. The outlaw gang leader lay dead on the hot dusty street.

Sally Jensen stepped back into Louis's gambling hall and jacked another round into her carbine.

Smoke smiled at her and walked down the boardwalk.

"Looking for me, *amigo?*" Al Martine spoke from the shadows of a doorway. His guns were in leather.

"Not really. Ride on, Al."

"Why would you make such an offer to me? I am an outlaw, a killer. I hunted you in the mountains."

"You have a family, Al?"

"*Sí.* A father and mother, brothers and sister, all down in Mexico."

"Why don't you go pay them a visit? Hang up your guns for a time?"

The Mexican smiled and finished rolling a cigarette. He lit it and held it to Smoke's lips.

"Thanks, Al."

"Thank you, Smoke. I shall be in Chihuahua. If you ever need me, send word. Everybody knows where to find me. I will come very quickly."

"I might do that."

"*Adios, compadre.*" Al stepped off the boardwalk and was gone. A few moments later, Sheriff Silva and a posse rode up in a cloud of dust.

"That's it, Smoke," the sheriff announced. "It's all over. You're a free man, and all these other yahoos are gonna be behind bars."

"Suits me," Smoke said, and holstered his guns.

"No it ain't over!" The scream came from up the street.

Everybody looked. Pecos stood there, his hands over the butts of his fancy engraved .45s.

"Oh crap!" Smoke said.

"Don't do it, kid!" Louis Carbone called from the boardwalk. "It's over. He'll kill you, boy."

"Hell with you, you greasy son of a bitch!" Pecos yelled.

Carbone stiffened. Cut his eyes to Smoke.

"Man sure shouldn't have to take a cut like that, Carbone," Smoke told him.

Carbone stepped out into the street, his big silver spurs jingling. "Kid, you can insult me all day. But you cannot insult my mother."

Pecos laughed and told him what he thought about Carbone's sister, too.

Carbone shot him before the kid could even clear leather.

The Pecos Kid died in the dusty street of a town that would be gone in ten years. He was buried in an unmarked grave.

"If you hurry, Carbone," Smoke called, "I think you can catch up with Martine. Me and him smoked a cigarette together a few minutes ago, and he told me he was going back to Chihuahua to visit his folks."

Carbone grinned and saluted Smoke. A minute later he was riding out of town, heading south. . . .*

Louis grinned at the memory. Carbone and Martine had been killers who had been given a second chance at life through the generosity of Smoke Jensen. He hoped they had taken advantage of it. "How are Carbone and Martine doing?"

Wells shrugged. "Pretty fair. Ain't much fer ranchin', though. Spend most of their time drinkin' tequila and shaggin' every *señorita* within a hundred miles—most of the *señoras*, too, I s'pect."

Louis laughed again. "That would certainly be like Al and Louis, all right."

"They said they owed you and Jensen a debt of honor fer how you all helped them out a while back." Wells reached into a leather pouch slung over his shoulder on a rawhide thong.

Louis tensed, his hand moving toward his Colt. Wells noticed the motion and shook his head slightly. "Don't you worry none, Mr. Longmont. I ain't here to do you or your'n any harm. I'm jest deliverin' somethin' fer Carbone and Martine. A token a' their 'preciation, they called it."

He opened his pouch and took out a set of silver spurs, with large, pointed star-rowels and hand-tooled leather straps, and a large, shiny Bowie knife with a handle inlaid with silver and turquoise. "The knife's fer Jensen, the spurs are fer you."†

*Code of the Mountain Man
†Honor of the Mountain Man

When Smoke arrived at the saloon a few moments later, he and Joey had taken to each other as if they'd known each other for years. They had shared so many common experiences, it would have been unusual for them not to become close friends.

Seventeen

As Joey dismounted, Pearlie whispered under his breath, "Boy, that's 'bout the most dangerous-lookin' man I ever did see."

Smoke nodded, taking in the scar on the right cheek, the brace of Colt .44s in twin holsters on his hips, and the ever-present Colt Navy .36 in his shoulder holster. Smoke realized Joey hadn't changed a bit in the couple of years since he'd seen him.

"Hey, old friend," Smoke said as they shook hands. "Having a passel of babies and becoming a rancher don't seem to have tamed you any."

"Not enough so's you can tell it," Joey replied with a smile. "Cal, Pearlie," he said, nodding in greeting.

"Howdy, Mr. Wells," Cal said, his hero worship showing in his eyes.

"Naw, it's still just Joey to my friends, Cal. What happened to you to get you all bundled up in that chair?"

"That's what I want to talk to you about, Joey," Smoke said. "Come on into the house and tell Sally hello. I suspect she's got breakfast all ready for you by now."

"Good. My wife said to tell her hello, and to say she was right. The second young'un's a whole lot easier to raise than the first."

Later, Smoke and Cal and Pearlie and Joey sat on the porch, drinking after-breakfast coffee and smoking.

"Now that we got the eatin' an' helloin' behind us, why don't you tell me what's stuck in your craw, Smoke?"

Smoke went on to tell Joey about Lazarus Cain and his gang, how they'd shot Cal and were holed up in Fontana, sitting and waiting.

"What do you think they're waitin' fer?" Joey asked.

Smoke shook his head. "God only knows, but one thing's for sure, they're up to no good."

"You can make bet on that," Joey said. "I heared 'bout Cain whilst I was still fightin' the Redlegs. He was a bastard clear through then, an' I'm bettin' he ain't changed enough so's you can tell it."

"That's what I need your help for, Joey. I need someone Cain will trust to ride on over to Fontana, stay a while, and see if they can find out what his plans are."

Joey's lips curved up in a half-sneer and half-smile. "I think I know someone who'll be glad to do that fer you, Smoke."

"It'll be dangerous. He might talk to someone who'll know we rode together a few years back."

Joey shrugged. "So what? I've rode with plenty of men I've later had to kill. How'll he know it'd matter to me one way or t'other?"

"You may have to prove yourself to him," Smoke said.

Another shrug. "No matter. I've been doin' that since I was knee-high to a toad."

Smoke leaned forward, his elbows on his knees. "Since it'd be too dangerous for you to come here to report, here's how we'll handle it . . ."

Joey rode into Fontana just before dusk, after circling around to enter from the north instead of the south.

The town was already jumping, with music and shouting and hollering coming from the only saloon in town.

Smoke was right, he thought as he looked in the batwings. There had to be at least forty or fifty hard cases sitting around the place, drinking as if the bartender was giving it away free.

He hitched up his holsters and walked into the room, pausing a moment as he always did to size up the place and get his bearings in case of sudden trouble.

After a moment, the room quieted as the men inside noticed him standing there. One, a six-and-a-half-foot-tall man who'd had too much to drink to sense the danger in Joey's eyes, walked over to him.

"Hey, mister. We don' much like strangers 'round here," the man slurred, his voice thick with too much whiskey.

Joey started to brush past him, saying, "Sit down before I plant you, bigmouth."

The man grabbed Joey by the shoulder and whirled him around, pulling his arm back with his fingers curled into a fist.

Before anyone could blink, both Joey's hands were filled with iron. Without a moment's hesitation, he brought the barrel of one of his big Army .44s crashing down on the man's skull, dropping him like a sack of flour.

In another second, both pistol hammers were eared back, and Joey faced the room, as calm as if he were alone.

"Anybody else got somethin' to say?" he asked in a harsh voice.

From the corner of the table, a tall, lean, hawk-faced man stood up. "Well, I'll be damned," he said, a broad smile on his face. "I do believe that's Joey Wells who just joined us, boys."

A low murmur swept the room. There wasn't anyone living west of the Mississippi who hadn't heard of the feats of Joey Wells, and to those south of the Mason-Dixon line he was more than a hero—he was a living legend.

"A couple of you boys drag Max out and put his head in

a horse trough, an' you can tell him how lucky he is to be alive after bracin' Joey Wells," Cain called.

After two men grabbed the fallen man by his boots and shoulders and half-carried, half-dragged him out the front door, Cain turned to Joey and held out his hand.

Joey hesitated just a second or two, looking Cain in the eye to show he wasn't intimidated, then took the hand.

"My name's Lazarus Cain, Joey. I heard about you when I rode with Bill Quantrill's raiders after the war."

"Yeah? Well, we all did some ridin' after the war. Seemed like the thing to do at the time."

Joey turned his back on Cain and sauntered over to the bar. "Gimme a whiskey, an' use that bottle with the label on it in the corner there," he said, pointing.

Bob Blanchard quickly grabbed the bottle Joey pointed at, jerked the cork out, and placed it and a clean glass on the bar in front of him.

As Joey filled the glass, Cain sidled up next to him. "I heard you had some marshal trouble over near Pueblo."

Joey downed his drink and poured another. He glanced at Cain out of the corner of his eyes. "Johnny North tole me he'd been by here. He's not bad with a gun, but he's got a big mouth."

"He tell you I have some work you might be interested in?"

Joey sipped this drink instead of bolting it, and turned to face Cain. "I heared about you when you rode with Quantrill, Cain. I heared you was crazy, always spoutin' off 'bout God an' the Bible an' such. Are you crazy, Cain? 'Cause I don't much cotton to workin' fer a crazy man, no matter how good he is with a gun."

Lazarus's cheeks burned, and his eyes narrowed at being called crazy. He stood there a moment, muscles rigid, fists clenched, thinking on what Joey had said. Then, suddenly, he burst out laughing. "You know, Joey, I probably was a little crazy back then. The war did that to some people, all the killin' an' dyin' an' knowin' that if we'd had more guns an' ammunition, the blue-bellies wouldn't've had a chance against us."

Joey nodded slowly. Cain was right about that. The war was crazy, and it made everyone who survived it just as crazy as it was. But this man was more than that. His eyes were burning with an inner fire, and it was clear if you studied him, as Joey did people, that he was filled with inner demons of some sort. He was plain off-kilter. Joey had no doubt about that. He would have to be careful, 'cause this man might just do anything, for any reason whatsoever.

"So, if I decide to work with you, what's the job and what's my cut liable to be?"

Lazarus stared at Joey for a moment with those insane eyes, then held out his hand to Blanchard, who stuck a whiskey glass in it. Lazarus held it out, and Joey poured it full from his bottle.

"There's a local rancher whose land is plumb covered with gold. The man has no interest in it, but won't let anyone else try to mine it. We"—he pointed over his shoulder at the men in the room—"plan to kill him and his hands and take the gold for ourselves."

"What's this rancher's name that don't have no interest in gold? He sounds even crazier than you, Cain."

Lazarus smiled. It was refreshing to have someone around who didn't walk on eggshells with him . . . who would speak his mind in front of him. Wells was proving to be every bit as interesting as he'd heard he was.

"His name's Smoke Jensen."

Joey let his eyes widen a bit in mock surprise. "Jensen, huh? I rode with him a few years back. He helped me . . . take care of some *bandidos* who shot up my family."

Lazarus's face turned suspicious. "You rode with Jensen? What'd you think of him?"

"Fastest man with a six-gun I've ever seed, 'ceptin' fer me, of course."

"So you and he were friends?"

Joey's eyes turned hard and cold as stone, though his expression didn't change. "Let me git this straight, Cain. I don't have no friends, an' that includes you. Just 'cause I ride with a man don't give him no claim on my friendship later. If'n I decide to ride with you, I'll do what I'm paid to do. But, when the job's over don't make the mistake of thinkin' I owe you anythin' else, 'cause you might be my next job—understand?"

"You're a man after my own heart, Joey. Hard as nails and tough as a just-woke grizzly bear."

Joey let his lips curl in a half-smile. "So I've been told."

"What do you think of the job offer?"

"I'll have to do some thinkin' on it. Jensen is mighty tough, an' he's got lots of friends in Big Rock. How do you plan to handle them?"

Lazarus held up his hand. "I'll tell you the details after you decide whether you're gonna ride with us or not."

Joey emptied his glass. "Well, then, how 'bout some grub? You got anythin' worth eatin' in this dump?"

"Only if you like enchiladas an' beans," Lazarus said with a smirk.

He inclined his head at Blanchard, who yelled at the Mexican cook in the kitchen to get another plate ready.

Joey picked up his bottle and glass and walked to the nearest table against a wall. The three men sitting there looked up from their drinks, scowls on their faces.

"Whatta you want, Wells?" one asked.

"I need yore table. I'm fixin' to sit down an' eat."

"You can kiss my butt, runt," the other man snarled. "We ain't afraid of you, or your reputation."

Joey turned and handed the glass and bottle to Lazarus, and when he turned back around, a long knife was in his left hand. Quick as a wink the blade was against the snarling man's throat and a tiny trickle of blood was running down his neck. The cowboy's eyes were wide and frightened.

"Excuse me. I don't hear so well," Joey whispered. "Just what was it you said to me?"

At a movement from one of the other men at the table, Joey filled his right hand with iron before the other man could get his pistol half out of its holster.

"Do you really want to ante up in this game, mister?" Joey asked, eyebrows raised.

"Uh . . . no . . . I was just gittin' up to leave the table," the man said, his voice harsh with fear.

Both the other occupants of the table scraped back their chairs and hurried out the batwings. Joey looked back into the eyes of the scared man with the knife against his throat.

"I'm sorry, but I didn't hear you answer my question. You said somethin' 'bout not bein' afraid of me—isn't that right?"

"No . . . no . . . I was just kiddin'. You can have the table if'n you want it, Mr. Wells," said the man, his voice breaking from fear.

"Why, thank ye kindly," Joey said in a low voice. "That's right neighborly of you."

He pulled the knife back, wiped the blood off its blade on the man's cheek, then slipped it in a scabbard on the back of his belt as the man bolted from the saloon.

By the time Joey sat down, he could hear the man's horse galloping out of town.

He glanced up at Lazarus, who was smiling down at him. "Looks like you lost a man."

"It wasn't any great loss. I don't need any cowards ridin' with me."

Joey shook his head. "That man wasn't a coward. He just knew his limitations. I don't call that yellow. I call it smart."

"Well, smart or yellow, he's gone," Lazarus said, "and good riddance to him."

"You got any peppers fer these enchiladas?" Joey asked. "They're a mite bland."

Eighteen

Lazarus Cain sat at the table and drank as Joey ate. "Say, Joey, what happened to those *bandidos* Jensen helped you go after?"

Without looking up Joey replied, "They died."

"You mind tellin' me about it?" Lazarus asked.

"Why?"

"Because I've been stuck here in this one-horse town for nigh onto three weeks waitin' for enough men to show up to take down Jensen and maybe even the town of Big Rock, an' I ain't had nobody with anything interestin' to say to talk to the entire time." He gave a small shrug of his shoulders. "I'll understand if'n you don't want to talk about it, but I'd be obliged if you would, just to pass the time."

Joey paused to slab a thick coat of butter onto a tortilla. After he rolled it up and bit off half of it, he sat back in his chair and pulled out his makin's. He built a cigarette, stuck it in the corner of his mouth, and lighted it.

He squinted one eye against the smoke curling up, and let the cigarette bob up and down as he talked in his soft, Southern accent, taking an occasional sip of whiskey without removing the butt from his mouth.

"The gang of *bandidos* had joined up with a man name of Murdock, an' Jensen and his men and me went to war with 'em. We'd managed to kill or wound most of 'em when the leader of the *bandidos*, a man called *El Machete*, 'cause of his habit of choppin' people to death with one, and Murdock ran off to Murdock's ranch. I'd taken some lead in the shoulder, but me an' Jensen took off after 'em. . . ."

Smoke put a hand on Joey's arm and helped him climb up on Red, then he stepped into the saddle on Horse. They rode off toward the Lazy M and Murdock and Vasquez at an easy canter.

After a few miles, Smoke noticed fresh blood on Joey's shoulder and a tight grimace of pain on his lips.

"This ride too much for your wound, Joey? If it is, we can go back and wait a few days for the stitches the doc put in to knit together."

Joey shook his head, looking straight ahead. "I want to end this business, Smoke. All my life it seems I've been livin' with hate—first during the war, then after, when I was chasin' Redlegs." He took a deep breath. "The only time I've been at peace was with Betty, and then when little Tom came I thought my life was complete and all that anger was behind me."

He pulled a plug of Bull Durham out and bit off the end. As he chewed, he talked. "Since Vasquez and his men rode into my life, I've found all that hate and more back in my heart." He looked over at Smoke. "At first, I thought I'd missed all the excitement of the chase, an' the killin'. But I've found that the hate festers inside of ya', an' I'm afraid if I don't git shut of it soon I won't be fit ta' go back to Betty. She's just too fine a woman ta' have to live with a man all eat up inside with hate and bitterness."

Smoke smiled gently. "I don't think you have to worry about that, Joey. You've just been doing what any man would do, fighting to protect your family and your home." He slowed Horse and bent his head to light a cigar. When he had it going good, he caught up with Joey. "When you see the end of Vasquez and Murdock, things'll go back like they were. The only hate I can see inside you is anger at the men who hurt your loved ones, and that's a good thing. A man who won't stand up for his family is no good."

Joey gave a tight grin. "You ought to be a preaching' man, Smoke. You sure know the right things ta' say."

Smoke laughed until he choked on his cigar smoke. After he finished coughing, he said, "Now that's a picture to think on—Smoke Jensen, holding Sunday-go-to-meeting revivals."

They stopped at the riverbed and watered their mounts in one of the small pools. "What are you going to do about the river, once this is over?" Joey asked.

Smoke gave him a look he didn't quite understand and said, "Oh, I think I'll leave that to the new ramrod of the Rocking C. It'll be his decision to make."

Another hour of easy riding brought them to the outskirts of the Lazy M. They could see two horses in the distance, tied up to a hitching rail near the corral, away from the house. Smoke pulled Puma Buck's Sharps .52 from his saddle boot and began to walk toward a group of trees about a hundred yards from the house, keeping the trees between him and the house so Murdock and Vasquez wouldn't be able to see him coming.

Joey walked alongside, carrying a Henry repeating rifle in his right hand, hammer thong loose on his Colt.

Murdock was in his study, down on hands and knees in front of his safe, shoveling wads of currency into a large leather valise.

He and Vasquez had arrived back at his ranch at three in the morning and had taken a nap, planning to leave the territory early the next morning. They had slept longer than intended, and were now hurrying to make up for lost time.

Vasquez was sitting at Murdock's desk, his feet up on the leather surface, a bottle of Murdock's bourbon in one hand and one of his hand-rolled cigars in the other.

"What you do now, *Señor* Murdock? Where you go?"

Murdock looked back over his shoulder, his hands full of cash. "I plan to head up into Montana. There's still plenty of wild country up there, a place where a man with plenty of money, and the right help, can still carve out a good ranch."

"What about Emilio?" Vasquez asked, his right hand inching toward his *machete*. He was looking at the amount of cash in the safe, thinking it would last a long time in Mexico. He could change his name, maybe grow a beard, and live like a king for the rest of his life.

Murdock noticed the way Vasquez was eyeing his money, so he pulled a Colt out of the safe and pointed it at the Mexican. "Just keep your hands where I can see 'em, Emilio. I was planning on taking you with me. I can always use a man like you." He raised his eyebrows. "But now I'm not so sure that's a good idea. I don't want to have to sleep with one eye open all the way to Montana to keep you from killing me and taking my money."

Vasquez smiled, showing all his teeth, "But *señor,* you have nothings to fear from Emilio. I work for you always."

Murdock had opened his mouth to answer when he heard a booming explosion from in front of his house and a .52 caliber slug plowed through his front wall, tore through a chest of drawers, and continued on to imbed itself in a rear wall.

Murdock and Vasquez threw themselves on the floor behind his desk, Vasquez spilling bourbon all over both of them in the process.

"Chinga . . ." Vasquez grunted.

"Jesus!" said Murdock.

Smoke hollered, "Murdock, Vasquez! Come out with your hands up and you can go on living . . . at least until the people of Pueblo hang you."

The two outlaws looked at each other under the desk. "What do you think?" Murdock asked.

Vasquez shrugged. "Not much choice, is it? I think I rather get shot than hang. You?"

Murdock nodded. "Maybe I can buy our way out."

Vasquez gave a short laugh. *"Señor,* you not know mens very well. Jensen and Wells not want money, they want our blood."

Murdock didn't believe him. Everyone wanted money. It was what made the world go round. "Jensen, Wells. I've got twenty thousand in here, in cash. It's yours if you turn your backs and let us ride out of here!" Murdock called.

His answer was another .52 caliber bullet tearing through the walls of his ranch house. It seemed nothing would stop the big Sharps slugs.

Murdock said, "I guess you're right."

Vasquez answered, "Besides, after they kill us they take moneys, anyway."

Murdock scrambled on hands and knees to the wall, where he took his Winchester '73 rifle down off a rack. He grabbed a Henry and pitched it across the room to Vasquez. "Here, let's start firing back. Maybe we'll get lucky."

Vasquez chuckled to hide the fear gnawing at his guts like a dog worrying a bone. "And maybe horse learn to talk. But I do not think so."

They crawled across the floor and peeked out the window. They could see nothing. Then a sheet of flame shot out of a small group of trees in front of the house and another bullet shattered the door frame, knocking the door half open and leaving it hanging on one hinge.

"Goddamn!" Murdock yelped. He rose and began to fire

the Winchester as fast as he could work the lever and pull the trigger. He didn't bother to aim, just poured a lot of lead out at the attackers.

"Vasquez," he whispered, "see if you can sneak out the back and circle around 'em. Maybe you can get them from behind."

"Hokay, *señor,*" the Mexican answered. He crawled through the house, praying to a God he had almost forgotten existed that he'd make it to his horse. He wasn't about to risk trying to sneak up on Jensen and Wells. If he got to his horse he was going to be long gone before they knew it.

He eased the back door open and stuck his head out. Good, there was no one in sight and no place to hide behind the cabin.

Crouching low, he ran in a wide circle to where he and Murdock had left their horses. He slipped between the rails on the far side of the corral and crawled on his belly across thirty yards of horseshit to get to his mount's reins. He reached up and untied the reins and stood up next to his bronc, his hand on the saddle horn, ready to leap into the saddle and be off.

"Howdy, *El Machete,*" he heard from behind him.

He stiffened, then relaxed. It was time to make his play. Maybe, as Murdock said, he would get lucky.

He grabbed iron and whirled. Before his pistol was out of its holster, Joey had drawn and fired, his bullet taking the Mexican in the right shoulder. The force of the slug spun Vasquez around, threw him back against his horse, then to the ground. He fumbled for his gun with his left hand, but couldn't get it out before Joey was standing over him.

"Okay, *Señor* Wells. I surrender."

Joey's eyes were terrible for the Mexican to behold. They were black as the pits of hell, and cold as those of a rattler ready to strike.

Joey leaned down and pulled Vasquez's machete from its scabbard on his back. "I don't think so, Vasquez."

He held the blade up and twisted it, so it gleamed and reflected sunlight on its razor-sharp edge. Joey looked at him and smiled. "Guess what, *El Machete?*"

Suddenly, Vasquez knew what the cowboy had in mind. "No . . . no . . . *por favor,* do not do this, *señor!*"

Joey pursed his lips, "Try as I might, Vasquez, I cain't think of a single reason I shouldn't."

With a move like a rattler's strike, Joey slashed with the machete, severing Vasquez's right arm at the elbow. The Mexican screamed and grabbed at his stump with his left hand.

"Remember Mr. Williams, *El Machete?*"

As Vasquez looked up through pain-clouded, terror-filled eyes, the machete flashed again, severing his left arm at the elbow.

Vasquez screamed again and thrashed around on the ground, trying to stanch the blood as it spurted from his ruined arms by sticking the stumps in the dirt. It didn't work.

Joey stood and watched as Vasquez bled to death, remembering his wife and son lying in their own blood because of this man.

Smoke continued peppering the house with the Sharps until one of the slugs tore open the potbellied stove, setting the house on fire.

As flames consumed the wooden structure, Murdock began to scream. Just before the roof caved in he came running out of the door, his clothes smoldering and smoking, holding a leather valise in one hand and a Colt in the other. He was cocking and firing wildly at Smoke, who stood calmly, ignoring the whine of the slugs around his head.

"This is for Puma Buck," he whispered, and put a slug between Murdock's eyes. His head exploded, and he dropped where he stood, dead and in hell before he hit the ground.

Smoke walked over and picked up the valise, looked in it, smiled, and hooked the handles on his saddle horn.

He helped Joey up on Red, climbed on Horse, and they headed home. . . .*

Joey'd had to replace his cigarette twice by the time he finished the story, but he had Lazarus's full attention.

"So, did you and Jensen split the money in the valise?" Lazarus asked.

Joey hesitated. Smoke had given him the money to help him build a new life in the Colorado territory, but he didn't feel he could tell Lazarus that.

"Actually, no. I took some to cover my expenses, but Jensen gave the rest to some ranchers who'd been burned out by Murdock an' his men."

"I guess what I've heard is right, that Jensen don't have no desire to get rich."

Joey shrugged his shoulders. "He feels he is rich, with his ranch an' wife an' friends. He just don't love money, or the gettin' of money, like the rest of us do."

"You two seemed to be awfully close friends in your story. Are you sure goin' after him won't cause you any second thoughts?"

"I done explained that to you, Cain. You got any second thoughts 'bout invitin' me in, I can leave any time. It's your call."

Lazarus shook his head. "No, I'll take your word for it, Joey. But," he paused and his eyes got hard, "make no mistake about it. I don't never forget if somebody crosses me, an' I don't rest until I've paid 'em back for their treachery."

*Honor of the Mountain Man

Joey opened his mouth in a prodigious yawn, as if Lazarus's words meant nothing to him. "Warnin' noted, Cain. Now, this town got anyplace a man can get some sleep? I been on the trail so long my feet're probably growed to my boots."

Lazarus got to his feet. "Come on, I'll take you over to the hotel. I can't promise you clean sheets, but at least they'll have a bed you can bunk in."

Joey gave a half-smile. "Hell, I'm so tired I could sleep standin' up leanin' again a wall."

Nineteen

It was just after three o'clock in the morning when Joey slipped out of his bed and pulled his boots on. He stepped to the window and glanced at the sky. The moon had set, and the night was as black as the bottom of a well.

Easing the window open, he slipped through it and out onto the balcony. He crawled over the rail and hung by his hands for a moment, then dropped the ten feet to the ground, landing with a soft thud in the dirt of the alleyway.

Slowly, looking over his shoulder as he went, he made his way to the livery stable. He knew from his years in the war that the hours between three and four in the morning were the hardest for sentries on guard duty. For some reason, the mind and body seem to shut down and not work well in those hours.

He peeked in the window of the livery office and saw a man sitting at a desk with his head on his arms, fast asleep. Of course, the empty whiskey bottle on the desk next to him explained his condition, as well as the hour.

Inside, Joey slipped a halter on Red but didn't bother with a saddle. He walked the big horse out the door and down the street a ways before he jumped up on his back. He continued to walk the mount until he was past the town limits, then he put the stud into a lope, using the stars as his guide through the inky blackness of the night.

Smoke had told him to ride straight east and he'd find the place he was to meet Pearlie.

Sure enough, after about an hour's ride he saw a huge rock sticking up out of the relatively flat land around it. On the side away from town, he could see some smoldering coals where a small campfire had been laid.

He slid to the ground and walked over to the figure lying in a blanket next to the fire. He reached out with his foot and gently nudged the form.

"Hold it right there, mister," called a voice from behind him.

Joey's hand went toward his pistol, then he recognized Pearlie's drawl.

He held his hands out and turned. "You wouldn't shoot an old friend, would you, Pearlie?" Joey said.

He heard the click of Pearlie earing down the hammer on his Colt as a shadow separated itself from the rock and moved toward him.

"Howdy, Joey. I couldn't tell for sure if'n it was you or not, so I figured better be safe than sorry."

"You did right, Pearlie. I was fixin' to jump your butt about sleepin' on the job when I saw that blanket next to the fire."

"You want some coffee? I believe it's still warm."

Joey squatted next to the bed of coals and held his hands out to warm them. The night was chilly, with the temperature almost down to the freezing level.

"Sure would hit the spot," he said.

He made a cigarette and stuck it in the corner of his mouth while he drank his coffee.

"What did you find out about Cain's plans?" Pearlie asked.

"Not much. He still doesn't trust me enough to give me the details. But I did find out he's plannin' to come after Smoke at the ranch."

Pearlie's voice rose a little in alarm. "When?"

Joey shook his head. "That I don't know. What I can't

figure out is why he's got so many men. It sure wouldn't take fifty men to raid the Sugarloaf if they weren't expectin' any trouble."

"Why does he want to come after Smoke?"

"For the gold on his land. He's heard there's enough there to make a lot of men very rich."

Pearlie nodded. He, like most of the people around the area, had forgotten all about the gold buried on the Sugarloaf. In the aftermath of the Tilden Franklin affair, a prospector had come out of the hills around Smoke's ranch loaded to the gills with fool's gold. Smoke had just let people believe that's what Franklin had found—fool's gold. Only a few people knew the truth, that the Sugarloaf was covered with the real stuff. Evidently, someone who knew the truth had been talking to Cain.

"Only thing I *can* figure," Joey continued, "is that after he takes out Smoke and the men on the ranch, he's gonna try and tree Big Rock to keep it under control while he gets the gold."

"That's crazy," Pearlie said. "Nobody's ever treed a Western town."

"I agree, but I don't believe Cain's playin' with a full deck of cards. The man seems to think he can't be beaten by anybody, no matter what the odds."

"And you don't have any idea when all this is gonna take place?"

"No, so you have to warn Smoke to be ready at any time. If'n I can, I'll try an' get away in time to warn you, but that may not be possible."

"All right. You ride with your guns loose, Joey. You're in a nest of snakes over there. Be sure you don't get bitten."

"*Adios,* partner," Joey said as he climbed up on Red. "Tell Smoke I'll see him soon, one way or another."

Joey turned to walk away, then snapped his fingers and

looked back over his shoulder. "Oh, an' tell Smoke to expect some visitors in the next couple'a days."

"Who's that?" Pearlie asked.

Joey gave a smirky grin. "Smoke'll know 'em when they git here. They is old acquaintances of his. When he wired me that he needed help, I figured if it was bad enough for Smoke to ask for me, it wouldn't do no harm to have a couple'a extra guns around . . . just in case."

Smoke nodded as Pearlie told him what Joey had said. "Damn, I wish there wasn't any gold on the Sugarloaf. Just the mention of the word is enough to drive men out of their minds with greed."

"He also said to expect some more help in the next few days. He wired some old friends of yours that you might need a couple of guns."

"I wonder who that could be?" Smoke said, a puzzled expression on his face.

"Well, I don't much care. If'n we're gonna be facin' fifty guns, we're gonna need all the help we can git," Pearlie said.

"I know. All right, here's what we'll do: They most probably won't hit us during the day, so I want you to have all the hands rest during daylight. Soon as night falls, they're all going to need to be on guard."

Pearlie looked worried. "Smoke, you know all the hands are loyal as can be, an' if'n you asked 'em they'd stick they hands in a fire for you, but I don't know just how much help they're gonna be in a real fight. Most of those men've never fired a gun in anger or at another person."

"I know. But it can't be helped. I want you to give all the men a choice. If they don't want to stay and help, I'll understand. They can stay in Big Rock until this is over and then come back to their jobs when it's done, no hard feelings."

"How about askin' Mr. Longmont or Sheriff Carson for some help?"

Smoke shook his head. "No. Out here, a man saddles his own horse and kills his own snakes. It's my home and my job to defend it."

"What else do you want me to do?"

"Head on into Big Rock. We're going to need plenty of supplies—some dynamite and gunpowder and lots of ammunition."

"Anything else?"

"Yeah. You need to tell Monte what Joey said, that Cain might try to attack Big Rock after he's done here."

Pearlie rode the buckboard into town, so he'd have a way to bring the supplies back to the Sugarloaf. In spite of some protestations from Sally, Cal rode with him. Smoke intervened and said it was time for Cal to get more active, or he'd turn to stone lying in the bed for so long.

"How're you feelin', Cal?" Pearlie asked when he noticed Cal's face screw up in pain whenever the buckboard bounced over a rock in the road.

"Not too bad, considerin' you've hit just 'bout every rock 'tween the Sugarloaf and town," Cal answered with a sideways glance at his friend.

Pearlie shook his head. "Well, it's your own damn fault. Drawin' down on that many men without ol' Pearlie to back you up."

Cal grunted. "You'd've done the same thing, Pearlie. Don't you go denyin' it, neither."

Pearlie gave a lopsided grin. "Yeah, but I'd've gotten more'n two of the bastards."

" 'Course, their bullets would've probably killed you, since you ain't had near the practice bein' shot as I have," Cal replied.

"That's the truth, boy, I'll admit it. You have been shot more times than I can shake a stick at." He looked at Cal out of the corner of his eye. "I guess you won't hardly be wearin' a shirt at all, this summer. You'll be paradin' around showin' that teensy scar to all the girls in Big Rock."

"Teensy scar?" Cal said with mock anger. "Hell, any bigger an' it'd cover my whole chest!"

As they pulled into Big Rock, Pearlie slowed the wagon and stood up, the reins in his hands.

"What're you doin'?" Cal asked.

"Just lookin' to make sure ain't nobody doin' any target practice. The way you attract lead, we're both liable to get shot by accident."

He pulled the wagon up before the general store and jumped down to the ground. "Let me take this list in to the store, an' then we'll mosey on over to Longmont's for a bite to eat while they get the supplies ready."

"Hell, Pearlie, you just ate lunch no more'n two hour ago. You hungry already?"

Pearlie got a pained expression on his face. "It ain't a matter of bein' hungry. It's a matter of eatin' when you get the chance. The way things been goin' 'round here lately, no tellin' when I'll next get to chow down."

He came out of the store a few minutes later and walked around the buckboard. When he reached up to help Cal climb down, Cal shook his head.

"Don't even think about it, Pearlie. I'm a growed man, an' I can do it on my own."

"You ain't all that growed up, pup. You just stubborn, is all."

Once Cal got down, they walked side by side up the street to Longmont's saloon. As they went through the batwings, Pearlie heard a voice with a strong Mexican accent growl, "Stick up those hands, *gringo!*"

As both boys crouched, their hands falling to their pistol

butts, Al Martine let out a loud guffaw, followed shortly by the staccato braying of Louis Carbone.

Cal and Pearlie straightened up, sheepish grins on their faces.

"Al, Louis, when did you two reprobates get into town?" Pearlie asked, walking over to shake their hands.

"On this morning's train, *compadre,*" Al answered.

"What are you doing up here?" Cal asked. "Last we heard you were down near Chihuahua chasin' the girls and pretendin' to be respectable ranchers."

Louis shrugged, holding his hands out and tilting his head in the Mexican manner. "*Señor* Joey wired us that Smoke might need some help, so we got on first train this way, an' here we are."

He threw his arm over Cal's shoulder, raising his eyebrows when Cal grunted in pain.

"What happen, little bronco?" he asked. "You sore?"

"It's nothin', Louis."

"Nothin', hell!" Pearlie said. "He took two bullets from a galoot named Lazarus Cain 'bout three weeks ago."

"Is that the trouble *Señor* Joey was talking about?" Al asked as they walked over to Louis Longmont's table and took their seats.

Pearlie nodded. "Yep. Seems this gent has got 'bout fifty or so men gathered up over at Fontana, an' he's plannin' on ridin' on the Sugarloaf in the next few days."

Longmont paused, a cigar halfway to his lips. "What was that, Pearlie? I hadn't heard that."

Pearlie told them about his meeting with Joey Wells out on the prairie near Fontana. "Joey says he don't know exactly when it's gonna take place, but he says they're comin' for Smoke for sure an' certain."

Al pulled a half-smoked, chewed up cigar butt out of his shirt pocket and stuck it in his mouth, leaning over to accept a light from Longmont. "Then it is settled. We ride today for Smoke's *ranchito*. He will need our help."

Louis Longmont stood up. "You boys eat all you want, on the house. I have a few very important errands to run, so I'll see you later."

Twenty

After getting the buckboard loaded up, Pearlie told Al and Louis to climb aboard and they headed for the Sugarloaf. Al sat on the front seat with Pearlie and Cal, while Louis propped his back up against a couple of bags of flour right behind them.

As they left the city limits, Al leaned back against the seat of the hurricane deck and lighted a long, smelly, black cigar. He glanced sideways at Pearlie, a sly grin on his lips. *"Señor* Pearlie, Louis and me, we hear the rumors of a *grande* fight from when *Señor* Joey was here before."

Pearlie looked at him. "You mean you heard 'bout that little fracas all the way down in Chihuahua?"

"Sí. El Machete was *muy famoso,* how you say . . . famous, in Mexico. Many of the *vaqueros* who visit speak of the time he was beaten by the outlaw Joey Wells and his *compadre,* Smoke Jensen."

Pearlie chuckled. "It was some how-de-do, let me tell you. First off, this rancher Murdock had hired himself a bunch of the most dangerous outlaws around, and he was set on bringing Smoke and Joey down. All we had to help us was a passel of men who barely knew which end of a gun the bullet comes out of, along with Louis Longmont, Monte Carson, and an old sheriff named Ben Tolson."

"Go on, Pearlie," Louis called from the back of the wagon, "only speak louder. The wheels they squeak *muy* loud."

"Well, we were holed up in this little ranch, an' Smoke had us prepare some surprises for Murdock an' his men, to kind'a even out the odds a mite. Smoke had set up some men in the cabin, an' others in some trees off to the left. Then he said he an' Louis an' Joey an' Cal an' me was gonna ride like cavalry, attackin' the raiders on hossback when they came ridin' in. . . ."

Smoke said, "Then let's shag our mounts, boys. I want to get a little ways away from the ranch house so we can ride and attack without getting shot by our own men."

Smoke and Louis and Joey waited while Cal and Pearlie mounted up and then rode toward Murdock's ranch at an easy trot. Smoke had Colts on both legs, a Henry Repeating rifle in one saddle boot, and a Greener 10-gauge scattergun in the other.

Louis rode with one pistol in a holster on his right leg and had two sawed-off American Arms 12-gauges in saddle boots on either side of his saddle horn. The two-shot derringer behind his belt would be useful only in very close quarters.

Joey had his Colt in his right hand holster, his Navy in his shoulder holster, and two short-barreled Winchester rifles, one in a saddle boot and one he carried across his saddle horn.

Cal had the twin Navy Colt .36 caliber pistols Smoke had given him that he'd used while riding with Preacher. He also carried a Henry Repeating rifle slung over his shoulder on a rawhide strap.

Pearlie had double-rigged Army Colt .44s and a Greener 12-gauge shotgun with a cut-down barrel for close-in work.

Joey glanced around at his compatriots and laughed. "Hell,

boys, if Lee'd had this much firepower at Appomattox he wouldn't have had to surrender."

The riders from the Lazy M came galloping toward Smoke's spread like an invading horde of wild men. They started shouting and hollering and firing their weapons toward the cabin while still well out of range.

Smoke, Joey, Louis, Cal, and Pearlie were bent low over their saddle horns behind a small rise in a group of pine trees, waiting for them to pass.

As they rode by, Joey cut a chunk of Bull Durham and stuck it in his mouth. He chewed a moment, then spat, a disgusted look on his face. "Guess those assholes are tryin' to scare us to death with all that yelping like Injuns."

Cal, whose heart had hammered when he saw the number of men who rode by, took a deep breath, praying he wouldn't disgrace himself or Smoke in the upcoming battle.

Pearlie glanced at him and saw the sweat beginning to bead his forehead in spite of the chilliness of the early evening air. He reached over and punched Cal in the shoulder. "Don't worry none, partner, we're gonna teach these galoots a lesson they'll never forget."

Cal nodded, relaxing a little bit, knowing he was among friends who would fight with him, side by side, against the devil himself if necessary.

When Smoke heard gunfire being returned from the area of the cabin, he put his reins in his teeth, took his Greener 10-gauge in his left hand and his Colt .44 in his right, and spurred Horse forward, guiding the big Palouse with his knees.

Joey looped his reins over his neck, took his short-barreled Winchester rifle in his hands, jacked the lever down to feed a shell into the chamber, and rode after Smoke.

Louis filled both his hands with his American Arms express guns, eared back the hammers on all four barrels, and leaned forward, urging his mount over the hill.

Pearlie winked at Cal as he grabbed his Greener cut-down shotgun in his left hand and drew his Colt with his right. Before he put the reins between his teeth, he said, "Come on cowboy, it's time to make some history of our own!"

Cal drew both his Navy .36s and took off after the others, teeth bared in a grin of both exhilaration and fear.

Murdock's men were in the trap Smoke had devised for them, caught with the shotgun brigade hidden among boulders at their rear, off to their left, hidden in the setting sun, the men with rifles, and to the front, the cabin with its contingent of men who, though not accurate with their weapons, were pouring lead into the outlaws at a furious rate, hitting some by mere chance.

Cal and Pearlie had scattered a series of twenty small piles of kerosene-soaked wood across the clearing where Murdock's men were trapped, and those were now lighted, making the area look like an army camp with its campfires.

Just before Smoke and his band arrived from the bandits' right side, completing their boxing-in maneuver, Monte Carson, leaning out of an upstairs window, did as he had been instructed.

He began to fire his Henry repeating rifle, fitted with a four power scope, at the base of the small fires. The wood had been piled by Cal and Pearlie over cans of black powder, put in burlap sacks with horseshoe nails packed around them.

When Monte's molten lead entered the cans of powder, they exploded, sending hundreds of projectile-like nails in all directions and spreading smoke and cordite in a dense cloud to blind and confuse the enemy.

Men and horses went down by the dozens. Those not killed outright were severely wounded by both explosions and nails.

Other traps began to become effective. Several trenches had been dug, with sharpened spikes stuck in the bottoms. As first horses, then men on foot, began to step into the trenches, horrible screams of pain from both men and animals began to ring out in the gathering darkness.

Curly Rogers and his group of bounty hunters were directly behind Vasquez and Murdock as they approached the cabin. Rogers was firing his Colts at the ranch house as he and his men passed the pile of boulders. A sudden explosion came from between two of the rocks, and Rogers felt as if someone had kicked him in the side. He was blown out of his saddle, three buckshot pellets in his hide. He bounced and quickly scrambled to his feet, barely managing to avoid being trampled by his fellow outlaws.

Rogers clamped his left arm to his side, pulled out another gun, and ran toward the cabin, hoping to find another horse. His feet went right through one of the deadfalls and his legs fell onto two sharpened spikes, sending agony racing through Rogers' body like a fire. He screamed, "Help me . . . oh dear God, somebody help me!" As he flopped on the ground, wooden stakes impaled his legs, and a bullet from the cabin, aimed at another rider, missed its intended target and severed his spine, ending his pain and leaving him lying paralyzed on the ground.

Cates, seeing the amount of resistance at the ranch, tried to veer his horse off to the left and escape. As he passed between two pine trees, the baling wire Cal had strung nine feet off the ground caught him just under the chin. Horse and rider rode on, but Cates's head stayed behind to fall bouncing on the ground like overripe fruit.

Trying to escape the withering fire from the cabin and the trees, the half-breeds Sam Silverwolf and Jed Beartooth whirled their horses and headed for the boulders, intending to take cover there among the rocks.

Tyler and Billy Joe, leaders of the shotgun brigade, saw them coming and stepped into the open, shotguns leveled. Silverwolf got off two shots with his pistol, taking Tyler in the chest and gut, doubling him over. Billy Joe, twenty-two years old and never having fired a gun in anger before, stood his ground as slugs from the two half-breed killers and rapists pocked stone and ricocheted around him. He sighted down the barrel, waited until they were in range, and pulled both triggers at the same time. The double blast from the shotgun exploded and kicked back, knocking Billy Joe on his butt.

When he scrambled to his feet, breaking the barrel open to shove two more shells in, he saw the breeds' riderless horses run past. He squinted and looked up ahead of him on the ground. What he saw made him turn his head and puke. Silverwolf and Beartooth had been literally shredded by the twin loads of buckshot. There wasn't much left of the two murderers that would ever be identified as human, just piles of blood and guts and limbs and brains lying in the dirt.

Juan Jimenez was jumping his horse over one of the small fires when Monte fired into it. Horse and rider were blown twenty feet into the air. Protected from most of the nails by his mount's body, Jimenez survived the blast, but both his legs were blown off below the knees, the stumps cauterized by the heat of the explosion. He landed hard, breaking his left arm in two places, white bone protruding from flesh.

When Jimenez looked down and saw both his legs gone, he screeched and yelled and began to tear at his hair, his mind gone. His agony ended moments later when Ben Tolson took pity on him and shot him from the doorway to the cabin.

The Silverado Kid, Blackie Bensen, and Jerry Lindy were riding next to each other. When the Kid realized the trap they were in, he yelled at his men to pull their mounts to the left. "Rush the trees over yonder—it's our only chance to get away!" he hollered.

The three men rode hard at the trees, guns blazing, lying low over saddle horns. Mike and Jimmy were lying behind a log, their Henrys resting on it as they fired. Jimmy drew a bead on Blackie Bensen and fired. His first shot took Blackie in the left shoulder, spinning him sideways in the saddle. This caused Jimmy's next shot to pierce Blackie's right shoulder blade, entering his back and boring through into his right lung. The ruptured artery there poured blood into Blackie's chest, causing him to drown before he had time to die from loss of blood.

The Silverado Kid fired his Colts over his horse's head, two shots hitting home—one in Mike's chest, killing him instantly, the second careening off a tree to imbed itself in Josh's thigh, throwing him to the ground.

Todd raised his Winchester '73 and pumped two slugs into Jerry Lindy, flinging the outlaw's arms wide before the twin hammer-blows catapulted him out of his saddle to fall under the driving hoofs of the Kid's mount, shattering his skull and putting out his lights forever.

Jimmy's next shot grooved the Kid's left chest, causing him to rethink his objective. The Kid jerked his reins to the side and pulled his horse's head around to head back into the melee around the cabin. He'd had enough of the rifle brigade.

Explosions were coming one on top of another. Billowing clouds of gunpowder and cordite hung over the area like groundfog on a winter morning. The screams of men hit hard and dying and those just wounded mingled to create a symphony of agony and despair.

Into this hell rode Smoke and his friends. Joey screamed his rebel yell at the top of his lungs—"Yee haw!"—striking fear into the hearts of men who knew it to be a call for a fight to the death.

Smoke answered with a yell of his own, and soon all five men charging the murderers and bandits were screaming and firing shotguns and pistols and rifles into the crowd as they closed ranks with them.

The mass of men broke and splintered as Smoke and Joey and Louis and Cal and Pearlie cut a swath of death through it with their blazing firepower and raw courage.

Smoke saw Horton and Max shooting at the cabin from

horseback, while Gooden, Boots, and Art South were nearby on foot, their broncs lying dead at their feet, pierced by hundreds of horseshoe nails.

Smoke glanced at Louis and yelled, "Remember them?" and pointed at the group of men. Louis nodded, his eyes flashing. "Damn right," he said. Louis had been one of the men who rode up into the mountains to stand with Smoke against the bounty hunters in the Lee Slater fracas.

Louis bared his teeth in a wide grin. "Let's do it!" he yelled, and rode hard and fast at the killers with Smoke at his side.

Horton and Max saw the two men coming, Colts blazing, and screamed in fear. "Oh Jesus," Horton shouted, "it's Jensen and that devil, Longmont." He whirled his horse and tried to run. A slug from Louis's Colt hit him between the shoulder blades, throwing him off his horse. It took him ten minutes to die, ten minutes of blazing pain.

Max, less a coward than Horton, turned his mount toward Smoke and Louis and charged them, firing his pistols with both hands. Smoke fired twice with the Colt in his right hand, missing both times. Then he triggered the 10-gauge Greener he held in his left hand. It slammed back, throwing Smoke's arm in the air, making him wonder momentarily if his wrist was broken.

The load of buckshot and nail heads met Max head on. The lead exploded his body into dozens of pieces, scattering blood and meat over a ten-square-yard area.

Smoke stuck the Greener in his saddle boot and pulled his left-hand Colt. He began to alternate, firing right, then left, then right again, as he continued his charge over Max's body toward Gooden, Boots, and Art South.

Gooden snap-shot at Louis and hit home, the slug tearing into the gambler's left thigh but missing the big artery there.

Louis returned the favor, punching a slug into Gooden's gut which doubled him over and knocked him to the ground.

"Oh, no," he screamed, "not the stomach again!" He lay there, trying to keep his intestines in his abdomen, but they kept spilling out. Finally, Gooden gave up and lay back and died.

Art South fired at Louis and missed, but nailed his horse in the right shoulder, knocking Louis tumbling to the ground. He rolled and sprang to his feet, left hand pushing his wounded left leg to keep him upright.

Art South stepped closer to Louis and extended his hand, pointing his Colt between Louis's eyes. "Any last words, Longmont?" South asked, grinning.

"No," Louis said, and he pulled his derringer out from behind his belt and shot both .44 barrels into South's chest, blowing him backward to land at Boots's feet.

Boots swung his pistol toward the now unarmed and defenseless Louis, who merely stared unflinchingly back at the outlaw.

Boots's lips curled up in a snarl, until they disappeared into the hole Smoke blew in his face with his .44s. The bullets entered on either side of Boots's nose, blowing his cheekbones out the back of his head.

Smoke grabbed the reins of a riderless horse while Louis bent and picked up the Colt Boots had dropped. Smoke reached down and picked Louis up with one arm and swung him into the saddle.

"Thanks, partner," Louis shouted.

Smoke just smiled and rode off, looking for other prey.

Cal and Pearlie had emptied their guns and were reloading, trying to keep their mounts from shying while they punched out empty brass casings and stuffed in new ones.

The Silverado Kid galloped over to where Bill Denver and Slim Watkins were riding, firing up into the cabin. Bill Denver shot into the second story window, his slug hitting Monte Carson in the side of the head and taking out a chunk of his scalp as it knocked him unconscious and blew him back out of sight. Two of the punchers in the room rolled Monte over and began dressing his wound while a third picked up his rifle and took his place at the window.

The Kid shouted, "Denver, Watkins, look over there!"

He pointed toward Cal and Pearlie, off to the side of the fracas, surrounded by dead gunnies they had killed. "There's only those two young'uns between us and freedom. Let's dust the trail on outta here, boys," he cried.

Denver and Watkins nodded and wheeled their mounts to follow the Kid's lead. The three desperadoes spurred their broncs into a gallop, right at Cal and Pearlie.

Cal shouted, "Look out, Pearlie, here they come!"

With no time to reload his pistols, Cal dropped them and swung the Henry repeating rifle off his back and jerked the lever, firing from the hip without bothering to aim.

Pearlie holstered his still empty pistols and shucked his Greener 12-gauge with the cut-down barrel from his saddle boot. He eared back the hammers and let 'em down as Cal began to fire.

The Silverado Kid, scourge and killer of women and children, the man too tough for Tombstone, took three .44 caliber slugs from Cal's rifle, two in the chest and one in the left eye. The entire left side of him disappeared as he back-flipped over his horse's rump to land spread-eagled and dead in the dust.

Denver and Watkins got off four shots with their pistols. The first shot took Cal in the right hip, above the joint, and punched out his right flank, blowing him out of the saddle.

The next shot missed, but the third and fourth both hit Pearlie, one burning a groove along his neck, and the other skimming his belly, tearing a chunk of fat off but not hitting meat.

Pearlie gave a double grunt and doubled over, then straightened up and let both his hammers down, one after the other. Denver took a full load of .00-buckshot in the face, losing his head in the bargain, and Watkins right arm and right chest were disintegrated in a hail of hot lead from Pearlie's express gun.

Both men were dead before they hit the ground.

Pearlie jumped out of his saddle and sat cradling Cal's unconscious body in his arms while he reloaded his pistols. No one else was going to hurt his friend as long as he was alive to prevent it.

Jerry Jackson, train robber from Kansas, rode his horse at the cabin, screaming curse words at the top of his lungs, a blazing torch in one hand and Colt in the other.

Ben Tolson stepped out of his doorway and onto the porch, his shotgun blasting back at Jackson.

Jackson was blown off his mount at the same time his .44 slug tore into Tolson's right chest, spinning him around and back through the door he gave his life to defend.

Joey, his pistols and both Winchester rifles empty, stood up in his stirrups, looking for Cal and Pearlie. He wanted to make sure they were all right.

He heard a yell from behind him and looked over his shoulder to see Colonel Waters riding at him, his sword held high above his head, blood streaming from a wound in his left shoulder.

"Wells, prepare to die, you bastard!" Waters screamed as he bore down on the ex-rebel.

Joey bared his teeth, let out his rebel yell again, and pulled his Arkansas Toothpick from its scabbard. He wheeled Red around and dug his spurs in, causing the big roan to rear and charge toward the Union man.

They passed, the sword flashing toward Joey's head. He ducked and parried with his long knife, deflecting Waters's blade, sending sparks flying in the darkness. Both horses were turned, and again raced toward each other. At the last minute, Joey nudged Red with his legs and the huge animal veered directly into Waters's smaller one, knocking both horse and rider to the ground.

Joey swung his leg over the saddle horn and bounded out of the saddle. He crouched, Arkansas Toothpick held waist-high in front of him and waited for Waters to get to his feet.

The Colonel stood, sleeving blood and sweat off his face. "You killed my men, every one, Wells, and now you are going to die."

Joey spit tobacco juice at Waters's feet. "Yore men, like you, Waters, were cowards who killed defenseless boys who'd given up their guns. They didn't deserve ta' live, an' neither do you."

Joey waved the blade back and forth. "Come an' taste my steel, coward!"

Waters lunged, his sword outstretched. Joey leaned to his right, taking the point of the sword in his left shoulder while striking underhanded at Waters.

Joey's blade drove into Waters's gut just under his ribs and angled upward to pierce the officer's heart. The two men, gladiators from a war long past, stood there chest to chest for a moment. Then light and hate faded from Waters's eyes and he fell dead before the last of The Missouri Volunteers.

Murdock saw they were losing the battle and shouted at Vasquez, "Emilio, let's get out of here!"

The two men, who had managed to stay on the periphery of the gunfight, wheeled their horses and galloped back toward the Lazy M. They were able to escape Smoke's trap only because of the heavy layer of smoke and dust in the air. By the time the men in the boulders saw them coming they were by and out of range of their shotguns.

The fracas lasted another twenty minutes before all of the gunnies were either dead or wounded enough to be out of commission.

It was full dark by now, and the punchers in the cabin lighted torches and joined with men from the trees and boulders and began to gather their wounded and dead. The injured who worked for Smoke were brought into the cabin and were attended to by Andre and the others. Their gunshot wounds were cleaned and dressed and they were given hot soup and coffee—those in pain, whiskey.

Smoke bent over Monte Carson, checking his bandages to make sure they were tight. Carson drifted in and out of consciousness, but Smoke was sure he would survive.

Andre fussed over Louis's leg wound, cleaning and recleaning it until finally Louis said, "Just put a dressing on it, Andre. There're others here who need you more than I do."

Smoke glanced at Louis, a worried look on his face. "Have you seen Cal or Pearlie or Joey, Louis?"

Louis looked up quickly, "Aren't they here?"

Smoke shook his head. "No."

Louis struggled to his feet, using a rifle as a cane. "Let's go. They may be lying out there wounded." He glanced at Smoke, naked fear in his eyes. "Or worse."

The two men walked among the dead and dying outlaws, ignoring cries for help and mercy as they looked for their friends. The outlaws deserved no mercy. They had taken money to kill others, and would now have to face the consequences of their actions. A harsh judgment, but a just one.

Finally, Smoke spied the horse Pearlie had been riding, standing over near a small creek that ran off to the side of the cabin. "Over here," he called to Louis and ran toward the animal, praying he would find the young man alive.

He stopped short at what he saw. Joey, his left shoulder wrapped in his bloodstained shirt, was trying to dress Pearlie's neck and stomach wounds, but Pearlie wouldn't let go of Cal to give him access. The young cowboy had one hand holding his wadded-up shirt against a hole in Cal's flank to stop the bleeding, while he held his Colt in the other, hammer back, protecting his young friend from anyone else who might try to harm him.

Smoke heard Joey say, "Come on, Pearlie, the fight's over. Let me take care of where ya' got shot. Then we kin git Cal over to the cabin fer treatment."

Pearlie shook his head. "I'm not movin' from here 'til I see Smoke. I promised him I was gonna watch over Cal, and I aim to do just that!"

Smoke chuckled as Louis hobbled up beside him. "Would you look at that, Louis. Like a mother hen with her chick."

Louis grinned. "If I ever find a woman who'll take care of me like that, I'll give up gambling and settle down."

"Pearlie, you've done a good job," Smoke said as he knelt by Cal. "Now let Joey fix you up while I take Cal to the cabin so Andre can patch his wounds."

Pearlie lifted fatigue-ridden eyes to stare at Smoke. "Smoke, you got him?"

Smoke lifted Cal in his arms. "Yes, Pearlie, I've got him."

Pearlie mumbled, "Good." Then he let his pistol fall to the dirt and passed out. . . .*

Al Martine shook his head as Pearlie finished recounting the events of that night two years ago. "I can see *es muy peligroso*—very dangerous—to ride with you, Pearlie. From what I hear, every time Cal does so he ends up shot."

"It's like I said, Al," Pearlie said, watching Cal as his cheeks burned red, "that boy draws lead like honey draws flies."

*Honor of the Mountain Man

Twenty-one

Lazarus Cain looked up as Joey Wells walked through the batwings of the Dog Hole Saloon in Fontana. When Joey walked straight to a table across the room and sat down by himself without so much as looking at Lazarus or saying hello, the bandits' leader leaned over to speak in a low tone to Blackie Jackson.

"Blackie, what do you think of Wells? Can he be trusted?"

The ex-blacksmith stared at Joey for a moment before answering. "I don't know, boss. He's a strange one, all right. Don't never enter into no conversation with the boys, nor join in with the whores in the back room." He shook his head. "I just don't have any clear idea of what's goin' on in his head most of the time."

Lazarus began to talk in the stilted manner he always used when quoting the Bible. "But let him ask in faith, with no doubting, for he who doubts is like a wave of the sea driven and tossed by the wind. If he is a double-minded man, unstable in all his ways, as a flower in the field he will pass away."

Blackie looked at Lazarus, his eyebrows raised. "What's that mean, boss?"

"That is from the Epistle of James, Blackie, an' it means if Joey is playin' both ends against the middle I'll cut him down like a weed."

"You got any reason to suspect he's gonna go agin us?"

"No . . . but then again, he ain't exactly acted overjoyed to be with us, either. I want you to keep a close eye on Wells, Blackie, an' let me know if he does anything outta line."

"Sure thing, boss. How about I get one of the boys to watch his room at night, an' make sure he don't leave without sayin' good-bye or nothin'?"

"That'll be just fine, Blackie."

Lazarus got to his feet and walked over to Joey's table, where he sat eating scrambled eggs and *chorizo.*

"Mornin', Joey."

Joey looked up and nodded, but continued to chew his food without speaking.

Lazarus pulled out a chair and sat down. "Some of the boys been complainin', Joey. They say you ain't actin' very friendly. Matter of fact, they say you been outright rude."

Joey cut his eyes at Lazarus, the cold deadliness of them making the hair on the back of the preacher's neck stand up. Since his days in the Civil War, Lazarus had never met a man who could make him taste the bitter flavor of fear, until Wells.

"Get to the point, Lazarus. I know you don't give a damn what the boys think or say," Joey growled around a mouthful of sausage and eggs.

"I've been kind'a wonderin' myself, Joey, if you're committed to this little enterprise I got planned, or if you're having second thoughts about it."

Joey swallowed and pushed his plate away, pulled out his Arkansas Toothpick, and shaved a sliver of wood off the edge of the table. He holstered his knife and used the piece of wood to pick bits of meat from between his teeth.

"Lazarus, if'n I decide not to go along with you on your plan, I'll pack my gear an' leave. I certainly won't hang around here, enjoyin' the . . . delightful company you've gathered together in this garden spot of a town."

Lazarus gave a short laugh at the wry tone of Joey's voice.

"They do leave something to be desired in a conversation, don't they?" he asked.

"Only if'n you want to talk 'bout somethin' other than whiskey, women, or who's killed the most men in their lives. I quit talkin' to 'em when the conversation always seemed to get around to who's fastest on the draw."

"Oh?"

"Yeah. I tried to tell the first couple'a men who brought it up that it ain't who's fastest that counts, it's who's left on his feet when the smoke clears. Any galoot can practice again' tin cans 'til he's fast as greased lightnin'. But when you're standing across from a man whose eyes tell you he's gonna kill you, and your bowels are turning to liquid and gurglin' in your stomach, it do make a difference in your perspective on the matter of gunfightin'."

Lazarus threw back his head and laughed out loud. "Joey, I couldn't've said it better myself. Speed with a gun is only one part of winning a duel. The willingness to go ahead, knowin' you're gonna take some lead an' maybe die, but knowin' also you're gonna drop that son of a bitch facin' you, is more important than speed."

Joey reached across and poured a couple of fingers of whiskey into his glass. He held up the glass and looked into the liquid, speaking as if to himself. "Hell, facin' death is easy, Lazarus. It's facin' life that's hard." As he finished speaking, he drank his glass empty and then stood up.

"If'n you're through askin' me questions, I'm gonna go take a walk."

"Sure, Joey. Go right ahead," Lazarus said, a wide smile on his face. "Go anywhere you want."

Joey glanced back at him with a smirk as he turned to leave. "I wasn't askin' your permission, Cain, I was just lettin' you know."

Lazarus's face turned a bright red as Joey sauntered out of the room. Damn, but that man could be infuriatingly smug.

After all this is over, Lazarus promised himself, *I'll wipe that smart alec expression off his face for good.*

As Joey strolled down the rotting boardwalks of Fontana, he noticed out of the corner of his eye that Blackie Jackson walked out of the batwings of the Dog Hole just after he did.

He decided to turn down a side street and see if the man was following him or if it was just a coincidence that he'd left at the same time.

After covering fifty yards, Joey stopped in front of an old storefront that still had a couple of panes of glass in the windows. He stood there, pretending to look inside, and watched the reflection in the glass.

Sure enough, he saw Blackie peek around the corner at the end of the street, evidently interested in just where Joey was going and what he was going to do.

Damn, Joey thought, *Cain must be suspicious to have sicced his trained dog on me like this. I'm gonna have to be careful when I go to meet Pearlie, that is if Cain ever lets it slip when he's planning on having his little party out at Smoke's place. It just won't do to have him dog my steps, so I'll just have to discourage his curiosity a mite.*

Joey put his hands in his pockets and continued to stroll the streets, as if he had nothing on his mind other than passing the time of day with a little exercise.

Eventually he came to the livery stable and entered. He walked over to where Red was stabled and took a bucket of oats and poured a generous helping into the bucket hung on a nail in front of his mount. Better let the big stud stock up on some grain, 'cause he was going to need all the stamina he could muster if push came to shove and Joey had to travel fast and far. Grass and hay were okay for general purposes with a horse, but nothing improved their bottom like grain, and plenty of it.

Twenty-two

Smoke came out on the porch when he heard the sound of the buckboard coming up the road to the cabin. He was surprised, and delighted to see the two Mexicans riding with Pearlie and Cal.

As they climbed down, he walked over and held out his hand. *"Compadres!"* he called. *"¡Buenos días!"*

"Señor Smoke," Al said as he took Smoke's hand. "Your Spanish has improved since our last meeting."

Smoke laughed. "Well, I haven't had much occasion to use it since you and your partner headed south, *amigo."*

"It has been most boring in Chihuahua, without you to liven up the lives of the occupants of our little town," Louis said, shaking Smoke's hand with both of his.

"I take it you two are the surprise Joey said he'd arranged for me?"

"Sí. Señor Joey said you might need some help, so we came as fast as the Union Pacific could bring us," Al said.

Sally stepped out on the porch and waved. "Hello, men," she said.

Both men bowed and took off their hats. *"Buenos días, Señora* Sally," they said in unison.

"I figure you've already eaten, but I've got some hot apple pie on the stove, if you're interested."

Al immediately turned and put his hand up against Pearlie's

chest. "Only if someone will restrain this man whose stomach is larger than the Grand Canyon. Otherwise, there will not be enough left for us to eat," Al teased.

"We'll put Pearlie at the end of the line," Smoke said.

"I think I should get first shot at that pie," Cal said, "since the doctor tole me I need to keep my strength up by eatin' as much as possible."

As he walked rapidly toward the cabin, Smoke laughed. "Seems to me you're pretty spry for someone who's supposed to be recovering from a gunshot wound."

He called back over his shoulder as he disappeared into the house, "Miss Sally's food has done wonders for my healin'."

Later, Al leaned back in his chair and eyed the empty pie tin on the table in front of the cowboys. "That was most wonderful, *Señora* Sally. I have not had such food in many months."

Sally brought the pot from the stove and refilled coffee cups all around, except for Cal, who was drinking fresh cow's milk.

"I'm glad you enjoyed it. Since you're going to be staying a while, I'll cook up some more, just in case you get hungry later."

Smoke took his cup and walked out onto the porch so he could smoke a cigarette. As he built one and lighted it, he said, "You boys know what you're getting into here?"

Both men nodded. *"Sí,"* said Louis. "Pearlie told us about the *bandido,* Cain, and his plans to attack your *rancho."*

"Are you aware of how much he's got us outnumbered?"

Al Martine shrugged. "Numbers, they do not matter so much, Smoke, as the men who make up the fight."

"Sí," Louis agreed. "It is what is inside a man, here," he said, pointing to his chest, "not how many guns he has in his hands."

Smoke nodded. "You're right. And with this group, I think Cain may have bitten off more than he can chew."

Pearlie, hearing the sound of hoofbeats in the distance, stood up and shaded his eyes with his hand as he peered out over the Sugarloaf.

"Company comin', Smoke," he said, resting his hand on the butt of his pistol.

Immediately the men on the porch got out of their chairs and drew guns, wondering if somehow Cain and his men were already coming.

After a moment, Pearlie relaxed. "You won't believe this, Smoke. It looks like Louis Longmont is bringin' us more reinforcements."

Sure enough, within minutes four riders came into view. Louis Longmont, accompanied by George Hampton, Johnny North, and Monte Carson rode toward the cabin.

They dismounted and tied their horses to the hitching rail nearby and walked to the porch.

Smoke shook his head, a tight smile on his face. "What have we here?" he asked as Longmont approached.

"Hello, Smoke, boys," he said.

"What's going on, Louis?"

"After talking with Pearlie and Al and Louis, I got to thinking that perhaps you might have need of some more fire-power, Smoke. So, I spoke to Monte, and then we rode out to North's place to see if he'd be willing to take a hand in this little poker game."

He spread his hands wide. "As you can see, you now have a few more guns available when Cain decides to make his move."

"Sally," Smoke called, "better put another pot on the stove. It seems there are some more men here who have more loyalty than brains."

Pearlie went into the cabin and brought out four additional

chairs and everyone sat down. Soon Sally brought cups and coffee for their guests.

"How do you want to play this, Smoke?" Johnny North asked. "You think it'd be better to set up an ambush here at the Sugarloaf, or plan on makin' our play somewheres else?"

Smoke glanced around at the terrain surrounding the cabin, slowly shaking his head. "If at all possible, if we have enough time, I don't think we ought to let them get this far. The area around the cabin is too difficult to defend. Too many trees and boulders that would give the attackers cover."

Monte Carson nodded in agreement. "You're right, Smoke. If they get this far, I don't know if eight of us, nine counting Joey, could stand 'em off without taking the chance of losing the cabin to fire or dynamite."

"Our best chance, when faced with as many men as Cain has riding for him, is to set up an ambush somewhere where we have the advantage of good cover or high ground," Louis Longmont said, pulling a cigar out of his pocket and firing it up.

Smoke agreed. "A lot will depend on how much time we have to prepare. Pearlie's supposed to meet with Joey tonight to see if he's heard anything definite about the time Cain plans to attack."

"Cicero, when writing about the campaigns of the Roman army, made mention of the fact that the best defense is a good offense," Longmont said. "We had good luck once before when faced with a similar situation by attacking the gunmen while they were still in Fontana."

"That is *un bueno* plan, *Señor* Longmont," Al Martine said. "That way, the *bandidos* will not be ready for the fight, which will give us an advantage."

"It'll also help keep the ranch safe. No tellin' how many head of cattle an' fences and things you'll lose if the battle takes place on the Sugarloaf," Johnny North added.

Smoke looked at Monte Carson. "We had a few more

men last time we took on Fontana. Do you think nine of us is enough to do the deed, Monte?"

Monte shrugged. "Better nine against fifty when they're not expectin' us an' fightin' in a town where there's plenty of cover, than tryin' to outfight 'em on horseback on the plains."

"Yeah, Smoke," Cal added. "If'n we can do it late at night, an' catch 'em whilst they're all asleep, they're liable to be shootin' each other in all the confusion, while we'll know where each other is."

"What do you mean *we,* Cal?" Pearlie asked. "You ain't in no shape for another fracas just yet."

Cal's eyes narrowed and his lips grew tight. "Just try an' stop me, Pearlie. I ain't about to miss a chance to get back at those men who shot me."

"Here's what I propose," Smoke said. "There's a hill overlooking Fontana, just to the south. I'll sneak up there and make a sketch of the town. When Pearlie meets with Joey, we'll have him try to find out where most of the gang is bunking down. Then we'll make a plan of attack to make the most out of the element of surprise."

Louis Longmont nodded. "With any luck, we'll be able to take out a significant portion of the gang with our initial attack, which will help even out the odds quite a bit."

"What if Pearlie is unable to talk to Joey?" Louis Carbone asked. "Perhaps Al an' me might go into the town to find out what you want to know."

Smoke wagged his head. "No, Louis, but thanks. That'd be much too dangerous. I suspect the nearer Cain gets to the attack the more suspicious of strangers he'll be, and we can't afford to lose your guns before the battle. We'll just have to hope Pearlie can meet with Joey and find out where the gang is staying in the town and the date of the attack."

Twenty-three

That night, Pearlie arrived at the place where he was supposed to meet with Joey and built a small fire. He made a pot of coffee and huddled there in the chilly blackness, waiting.

In Fontana, Joey eased out of his bed and began to slip his trousers on. As he glanced out of a window, he noticed a flare of light across the street from the hotel, followed by an intermittent glowing red spot.

Damn, he thought, *Cain has somebody watching the hotel. Probably makin' sure I don't go anywhere.*

He sat on the edge of his bed and thought for a few minutes. He really didn't have any news for Smoke, so risking his place with the outlaws just to have a meeting was foolish. He finally decided to go back to sleep and give it one more day trying to find out the date of the attack.

By five o'clock in the morning, Pearlie gave up any hope of seeing Joey. He kicked dirt over the smoldering coals of his fire and climbed wearily on Cold and began the long ride back to the Sugarloaf, hoping nothing had happened to his friend.

* * *

At breakfast the next morning Joey decided to force the issue with Lazarus. He finished his eggs and sausage, wiped his mouth on his sleeve, and stood up from the table.

Sauntering over to where Lazarus was sitting at his corner table with Blackie Jackson and Curly Joe Ventrillo, Joey flipped a twenty dollar gold piece onto the middle of the table.

Lazarus looked up, surprised. "What's that for, Joey?"

"Fer my room an' board the past week. I figger that'll 'bout cover it."

"What do you mean?"

"I'm leavin'. I'm bored sittin' 'round here doin' nothin' all day, with no prospects of any action in the near future."

"I told you, it won't be long now. Settle down and be patient," Lazarus said.

Joey leaned forward, his hands on the table. "That ain't all of it, Cain. I also ain't used to bein' treated like a hired hand, not bein' told what's goin' on an' expected to sit around waitin' fer my orders. I don't much like it."

Blackie Jackson glared at Joey. "Who cares what you like an' don't like, Wells? You'll wait for Mr. Cain's orders an' do like he says, just like everbody else."

Joey slowly turned his head to stare into Jackson's eyes, his gaze deadly as a rattler's just before it strikes.

"I don't recall addressin' your boy, Cain. But you better tell him 'fore he antes up in this hand, he'd best have enough chips to back up his big mouth."

As he finished talking, Joey straightened up and loosed the hammer thong on his Colt. He turned to face Jackson, his hands hanging limp at his sides, his eyes flat and cold.

"You want to try an' give me some more orders, boy?" he asked Jackson.

Blackie's face blanched white, and sweat began to bead on his forehead in spite of the coolness of the morning. He licked suddenly dry lips and glanced at Cain, his eyes begging for help.

The saloon became dead quiet as the men in it noticed what was happening. They all watched, wanting to see if Wells's deadly reputation was accurate.

Finally, Lazarus brought an end to it. "Men," he said, "take it easy. There's no need for this. Sit down, Joey, an' I'll tell you what you want to know."

Joey relaxed, the stiffness going out of his muscles and a small grin turning up the corners of his mouth. He turned away from Blackie, showing his contempt for the man in his manner.

"So, what the hell's goin' on? Are we gonna go after Smoke Jensen, or sit here until winter comes?"

Lazarus leaned forward and spoke in a low voice, so none of the others in the room could hear. "Give me two more days, Joey. I'm expecting the last wagonload of supplies in today or tomorrow. It's got the gunpowder for my cannons, an' enough ammunition to start our own war."

"And after we kill Jensen, what are your plans then?"

"I told you. We'll make a run on Big Rock an' shoot it to hell. Even if we don't destroy the town, we'll cause so much confusion no one will even notice that Jensen's ranch has been taken over. By the time anyone gets on to us, we'll all be rich from the gold we take out of his land."

Joey smiled coldly. "I must say, I do like the sound of that word rich, Cain." He reached over and picked up his twenty dollar gold piece and put it in his pocket. "I'll stick for two more days."

Lazarus nodded. "Good, Joey. You won't regret it."

Two of Cain's men riding sentry duty crested a small hill south of town. Mario Lopez, a man on the run from the Federales in Mexico for murder, rape, and cattle theft, noticed a glint of sun on metal just off to the left.

"Hey, Johnny, you see that?" he asked.

His riding partner, Johnny Crow, a half-breed Mescalero Apache, glanced over at him. Johnny's eyes were red-rimmed and swollen, showing he'd had a rough night the night before—as he did most nights, drinking enough whiskey for any two men.

"No, what'd you see?"

"Sunlight reflectin' off metal . . . right over there."

"It's probably nothin'," the Indian mumbled, wondering if his head was going to explode. He figured he must've gotten some bad whiskey, cause he'd never had a hangover like this one before.

"Let's go see, *muchacho,*" Mario said as he jerked his horse's head around and spurred it forward.

"Damn," Johnny said, fearing he was going to puke if he got his horse into a gallop.

As they crested the ridge, Mario saw something he couldn't understand. A tall man wearing buckskins was standing before a wooden framework, drawing on a large sheet of paper. He rode over to him, Johnny following.

"Hey mister, what you doin'?" Mario asked, his hand resting on the butt of his pistol.

Smoke Jensen looked up, showing no apparent concern at being seen. "Why, I'm drawing a sketch of Fontana."

"You what?" Mario asked again, not having any idea what a sketch was.

"Drawing a picture of Fontana," Smoke repeated. "Would you like to see it?"

"Why you do that?"

Smoke put his charcoal pencil down and turned to face the two men on horseback, a smile on his lips. "Because, there's a bunch of lowlifes staying in the town, and some friends of mine and me are going to ride in there soon and kill them."

Mario's eyes widened and he jerked at his pistol. Before he got his gun halfway out of his holster, Smoke's hand appeared in front of him, filled with iron. The Colt barked once, spitting a slug that took Mario full in the chest, shattering his breastbone and tearing a hole the size of a man's fist in his heart. He was blown backward off his horse, dead before he hit the dirt.

Having a couple of extra seconds, Johnny managed to get his gun clear of its holster, but never managed to raise the barrel before Smoke's second shot hit him in the forehead. The back of his head exploded, filling his hat with pieces of bone and brain as he tumbled off his horse to land facedown on the ground.

"That's two we won't have to worry about when we come calling," Smoke mumbled to himself.

Whistling a low tune, he gathered up his easel and drawing and packed them on Joker. After he was packed and ready to leave, he arranged the two bodies facing each other about three feet apart. He took a deck of cards from his saddlebag and scattered it between the two men, along with the few dollars he found in their pockets.

Joey was at the bar having a beer when one of the outlaws burst through the batwings. It was Boots Hemphill, so called because he wore expensive, knee-high leather boots which he spent hours each day keeping shiny.

"Boss . . . Mr. Cain . . . it's Johnny an' Mario! I found 'em dead off to the south."

Lazarus got quickly to his feet, motioning Blackie and Curly Joe to follow him as he went to the door.

"Mind if'n I tag along?" Joey asked, curious about what was happening.

"Suit yourself," Lazarus growled.

It took them about thirty minutes to find the bodies, laid out as Smoke had left them.

Lazarus got down off his horse and walked over to stand before them.

"It appears the fools were playing poker, an' one or the other got angry," he said, shaking his head.

Joey looked at the bodies and noticed something, but he kept his mouth shut. He knew it hadn't happened as Lazarus figured. The man named Mario was holding his pistol all right, but the hammer was still eared back. If he'd shot the half-breed, his gun wouldn't be cocked.

Joey had to turn his head to hide his smile. He recognized Smoke Jensen's handiwork, two bullets perfectly placed, two dead men who probably hadn't even gotten off a shot. He hoped Cain wouldn't think to check their pistols to see if they'd been fired.

Lazarus didn't. The men were low on his list of assets, so he just got on his horse and started to ride off.

"What about the bodies, Mr. Cain?" Boots asked.

"Take what you want, an' leave 'em for the buzzards an' wolves. Serves the bastards right for playin' cards while they were supposed to be on guard duty."

That evening, just after supper, Joey drank a glass of whiskey, then gave a wide yawn and started to walk out of the saloon.

Lazarus intercepted him just outside the batwings. "Where you goin', Joey?" he asked.

"Over to the hotel. It's been a long day. I think I'll turn in early tonight."

"Yeah, you do that. We got a big day tomorrow if that shipment gets here."

Joey nodded and touched the brim of his hat as he walked to his room.

Lazarus spoke over his shoulder to Blackie. "Have one of the boys watch him. I still got a funny feelin' about Mr. Joey Wells."

Joey gathered his few possessions together into his saddlebags, threw them over his shoulder, and slipped from his hotel room. Trying to stay close to buildings in shadows and out of the moonlight, he made his way to the livery stable.

He put a saddle on Red and cinched it down tight, flipped the saddlebags behind the saddle, and began to lead the big stud toward the door.

The sound of a pistol hammer being eared back stopped him in his tracks.

"Just where do you think you're goin', Wells?" came a voice from out of the darkness.

"I thought I'd take a little ride in the moonlight," Joey answered, his voice cool though his heart was racing.

Boots Hemphill walked out into the meager light streaming through a nearby window. "Mr. Cain told me to keep an eye on you. I guess it's a good thing he did."

Joey's eyes fell to the Colt Hemphill was holding in his right hand.

"Come on, let's go see what he has to say about your little moonlight ride," Hemphill said sarcastically.

"All right," Joey said. "Just let me get my saddlebags."

He turned and made to reach for the bags, but let his hand fall to his waist and grab the handle of his Arkansas Toothpick.

As he pulled the saddlebags off Red, he made a quick backhand motion. The knife turned over one and a half times before it imbedded itself in Boots's throat.

He dropped his pistol and grasped the knife's handle, gurgling and choking on his own blood.

Falling to his knees, he finally managed to get the knife

free, only to watch as his blood pumped out three feet in front of him from a severed carotid artery. He cast pleading eyes up at Joey for a few seconds, then he fell facedown in a pool of his own blood, dead.

Joey took his Arkansas Toothpick from the dead hands and wiped it on Boots's shirt, then slipped it back in his scabbard.

Figuring he might need the edge of a little getaway time, Joey bent over and grabbed Boots under the armpits and dragged him to a pile of hay in the corner of the livery. He used a pitchfork to dig a deep hole in the hay and rolled the dead man into it, covering him with a thick layer of straw.

Afterward, he used his boot to spread dirt over the thick pool of blood where the body had fallen, covering up all traces of the fight.

He led Red out the door of the livery and closed it behind him. As he climbed in the saddle, Joey sighed, thinking about the man he'd just killed. "A man should always know his own limitations," he whispered, walking his horse down the street and out of town.

Once clear of the town, he leaned forward in the saddle and urged the stud on, racing for the Sugarloaf to tell Smoke of the impending attack the next day.

He hoped Al and Louis had made it. They were going to need all the guns they could find to hold off Cain and his gang.

Twenty-four

Cal had insisted on riding with Pearlie out to where he was supposed to meet Joey, vowing that if their old friend didn't show up tonight he was going to ride into Fontana to make sure he was all right.

Pearlie just shook his head. "Ya cain't do that, boy. You wouldn't make it ten yards inside the town limits 'fore you'd be blown clear outta your saddle."

"I know, but that's what I want'a do."

Pearlie reined his horse to a stop next to the boulder. "Here, use up some of that energy makin' us a fire. It's gonna get plumb cold tonight 'fore long."

After Cal had the fire going and a pot of coffee cooking next to it, he settled down on his ground blanket and built himself a cigarette. Lighting it off a burning piece of wood, he squinted through the smoke at Pearlie sitting across from him.

"You remember the story Al and Louis told us 'bout how they met Smoke?"

Pearlie grinned. "Sure. It was just after Lee Slater an' his gang shot up Big Rock, an' some of the bullets hit Miss Sally."

Cal nodded, "Yeah, they signed on to fight with Slater agin' Smoke an' his friends."

"That's when they had that big shootout at the town of

Rio," Pearlie said. Leaning back against his saddle, his hands behind his head, he stared at the stars and thought about what it must have been like, and how much the next few days were going to be like it when they attacked Lazarus Cain in Fontana.

Cal handed him a cup of coffee and squatted next to him, his forearms on his thighs. "Al said Smoke had killed just about all the outlaws, an' Miss Sally put the final bullet in Lee Slater, when Al decided to make his move. . . ."

A man stepped out of the shadows. Lee Slater. His hands were wrapped around the butts of Colts, as were Smoke's hands. "I'm gonna kill you, Jensen!" he screamed.

A rifle barked, the slug striking Lee in the middle of his back and exiting out the front. The outlaw gang leader lay dead on the hot dusty street.

Sally Jensen stepped back into Louis's gambling hall and jacked another round into her carbine.

Smoke smiled at her and walked on down the boardwalk.

"Looking for me, *amigo?*" Al Martine spoke from the shadows of a doorway. His guns were in leather.

"Not really. Ride on, Al."

"Why would you make such an offer to me? I am an outlaw, a killer. I hunted you in the mountains."

"You have a family, Al?"

"*Sí.* A father and mother, brothers and sister, all down in Mexico."

"Why don't you go pay them a visit? Hang up your guns for a time?"

The Mexican smiled and finished rolling a cigarette. He lit it and held it to Smoke's lips.

"Thanks, Al."

"Thank you, Smoke. I shall be in Chihuahua. If you ever

need me, send word, everybody knows where to find me. I will come very quickly."

"I might do that."

"Adiós, compadre." Al stepped off the boardwalk and was gone.

Smoke finished the cigarette, grateful for the lift the tobacco gave him. His eyes never stopped moving, scanning the buildings, the alleyways, the street.

He caught movement on the second floor of the saloon, the hotel part. Sunlight off a rifle barrel. He lifted a .44 and triggered off two fast rounds. The rifle dropped to the awning, a man following it out. Zack fell through the awning and crashed to the boardwalk. He did not move.

Rich Coleman and Frankie stepped out of the saloon, throwing lead, and Smoke dived for the protection of a water trough.

"I got him!" Frankie yelled.

Smoke rose to one knee and changed Frankie's whole outlook on life—what little remained of it.

Rich turned to run back into the saloon and Smoke fired, the slug hitting him in the shoulder and knocking him through the batwings. He got to his boots and staggered back out, lifting a .45 and drilling a hole in the water trough as he screamed curses at Smoke.

Smoke finished it with one shot. Rich staggered forward, grabbing anything he could for support. He died with his arms around an awning post.

The thunder of hooves cut the afternoon air. Sheriff Silva and a huge posse rode up in a cloud of dust.

"That's it, Smoke," the sheriff announced. "It's over. You're a free man, and all these other yahoos are gonna be behind bars."

"Suits me," Smoke said, and holstered his guns.

Luttie Charles stepped out of the saloon, a gun in each hand, and shot the sheriff out of the saddle. The possemen filled Luttie so full of lead the undertaker had to hire another man to help tote the casket.

"Dammit!" Sheriff Silva said, getting to his boots. "I been shot twice in my life, and both times in the same damn arm!"

"No, it ain't over!" The scream came from up the street.

Everybody looked. Pecos stood there, his hands over the butts of his fancy engraved .45s.

"Oh, crap!" Smoke said.

"Don't do it, kid!" Carbone called from the boardwalk. "It's over. He'll kill you, boy."

"Hell with you, Carbone, you greasy son of a bitch!" Pecos yelled.

Carbone stiffened. Cut his eyes to Smoke.

"Man sure shouldn't have to take a cut like that, Carbone," Smoke told him.

Carbone stepped out into the street, his big silver spurs jingling. "Kid, you can insult me all day. But you cannot insult my mother."

Pecos laughed and told him what he thought about Carbone's sister, too.

Carbone shot him before the kid could even clear leather. The Pecos Kid died in the dusty streets of a town that would be gone in ten years. He was buried in an unmarked grave.

"If you hurry, Carbone," Smoke called, "I think you could catch up with Martine. Me and him smoked a cigarette together a few minutes ago, and he told me he was going back to Chihuahua to visit his folks."

Carbone grinned and saluted Smoke. A minute later he was riding out of town, heading south. . . .*

Cal finished retelling the story both he and Pearlie had heard several times, and Pearlie grinned.

*Code of the Mountain Man

"I can see why they both came so fast when Joey wired them Smoke needed help," Pearlie said. "He let them live when most men would have shot 'em down or at least put 'em in jail."

Cal nodded. "That's why Smoke has so many good friends. He don't judge a man as bad by his reputation, only by how he is to Smoke. If'n someone don't do him no harm, then Smoke'd just as soon let 'em be."

Their conversation was interrupted by the sound of hoof-beats coming toward them at a fast clip.

Pearlie jumped to his feet, his gun in his hand. "Sounds like somebody's comin' in a hurry. We better be ready for trouble, Cal."

Cal pulled his pistol and the men went to peer around the boulder, trying to make out who was approaching in the darkness.

"Yo, the camp," called a voice they recognized as belonging to Joey.

Pearlie and Cal holstered their weapons. "Come on in, Joey," Pearlie called.

He walked over to the fire and poured a fresh cup of coffee and handed it to Joey as he jumped down off Red.

"Thanks," Joey said, rolling the cup between his palms to warm them. "It's gettin' a mite chilly out there on the plain 'tween town an' here."

Cal nodded. "That's 'cause there's nothin' to break the wind comin' down off'n the peaks of the mountains over yonder."

Pearlie, impatient to find out what Joey knew, interrupted. "Did you learn when Cain's plannin' on attackin' the Sugarloaf?"

Joey grinned a sly grin. "Yeah. Tomorrow or the next day. He's waitin' fer a wagonload of dynamite an' gunpowder an' ammunition to come in. Then he's gonna make his play."

"That don't give us much time," Cal said.

"You got that right, boy," Joey answered.

"You headed back to Fontana?" Pearlie asked.

Joey wagged his head. "Nope. Done burnt my bridges there, boys. Cain must'a suspected somethin', 'cause he had me followed to make sure I didn't leave town."

"How'd you get away?" Cal asked.

Joey patted his Arkansas Toothpick. "I just showed the man my blade, up close like, an' then I got on Red an' rode on out."

"Do you need to rest, or can we head for the Sugarloaf now?" Pearlie asked.

Joey emptied his coffee cup. "Naw, I'm all right. Red is easy-gaited. Ridin' him's like sittin' on a porch in a rockin' chair. Let's shag our mounts, boys. We're burnin' time, an' we ain't exactly got a surplus of it to waste."

As Pearlie and Cal saddled their horses, Cal looked over his shoulder and said, "By the way, Al Martine and Louis Carbone arrived the other day."

Joey smiled. "Good. They once said if Smoke ever needed 'em they'd come runnin', but you never know if someone will really do it or not 'til you ask 'em."

"I don't think they thought twice about it," Pearlie said. "From the way they talked, they got on a train the same day they got your wire."

"It'll be good to see 'em again," Joey said. "Now, let's quit jawin' an' ride!"

Twenty-five

Lazarus Cain was enjoying his breakfast in the Dog Hole Saloon until Blackie Jackson approached his table.

"I can tell by the look on your face you got bad news for me," Lazarus said, spearing another piece of sausage and shoving it into his mouth.

"That's right, boss. I just got back from the hotel. Wells's room is empty. He must've cleared out during the night."

"What about Boots Hemphill? He was supposed to be watching Joey. Where is he?"

Before Jackson could answer, Lazarus pointed a finger at him. "If the bastard fell asleep and let Joey walk out of town, I'll crucify him."

Jackson shook his head. "Hemphill's missin' too, Lazarus. I can't find hide nor hair of him anywhere."

Lazarus washed down his food with a deep drink of coffee, then wiped his mouth with the back of his sleeve. He got to his feet, pulled out his Colt, and banged on the table with its butt until he had everyone's attention in the saloon.

"Listen up, everybody. I want all of you to comb the town. Boots Hemphill is missing, and so is Joey Wells. I don't have to tell you how much harder our job is gonna be if somebody tips Jensen off that we're comin' after him. Now, get lookin'!"

He glanced up at Jackson. "Blackie, did you look in Hemphill's hotel room?"

"Yep. All his clothes an' saddlebags an' gear is still there. If he left followin' Wells, or with him, he left all his belongings behind."

Lazarus rubbed his beard stubble for a minute, thinking. "That's an idea. I want you to go check out the livery, see if Hemphill's horse is still there. Seems there are only three possibilities of what happened."

"What're those, boss?"

"If Hemphill's horse is gone it means *he's* gone, either as Wells's partner, or followin' him like I asked. If Hemphill's horse is still there, then he's in town someplace, an' we need to find him and ask why he didn't stop Wells from leavin'."

"Yes sir."

After Blackie left, heading for the livery, Lazarus threw his coffee cup across the room in frustration. Nothing, absolutely nothing, was going right on this job. First, the wagon with the extra dynamite and ammunition was late in arriving, and now one of his best men had disappeared—either to warn Jensen, or just because he got impatient and wanted to be elsewhere. Lazarus knew it was crucial to his plans to find out why Joey had left. It would make a big difference in how he approached Jensen's ranch if he knew they were coming.

He walked over to the bar and poured himself a tall whiskey. To hell with coffee. The way things were going he needed something more substantial in his gut.

Blackie was back in less than an hour, the scowl on his face showing Lazarus the news wasn't going to be good.

"Well, is Hemphill's horse in the stable?"

"Yeah, an' so is Boots."

"What do you mean, so is Boots? Why didn't you bring him with you?"

" 'Cause I didn't want to drag him the whole way over here, that's why."

"You mean he's dead?"

"Deader than the cow that made his boots."

"How?"

"Looks like he took a knife, a big knife, in the throat. He was hid in the hay an' I'd never of found him 'cept the ground was muddy from all the blood he spilt."

"Damn!" Lazarus spit, slamming his hand palm down on the bar. "That means he must've caught Joey trying to leave, an' Joey killed him."

Blackie nodded. "Most likely the way it went down, all right."

Lazarus cut his eyes to Blackie. "If Joey wanted to leave bad enough to kill to get out quietly, he must be plannin' to tell Jensen what's goin' on."

"I'd bet my hoss on it."

"Call the men together. We've got to get movin' before Jensen has time to plan a defense against us. Even if Joey warns him this mornin' it'll take him a few days to round up enough men to cause us any problems. If we get the ammunition wagon today, we can hit him tonight!"

Blackie had the entire gang assembled in the saloon within thirty minutes. Lazarus had them sit at the tables, while he stood at the bar, addressing them.

He looked out over the crowd, thinking about the men he'd gotten involved in this.

At one table sat seven men, all bank robbers and members of assorted gangs that read like a Most Wanted list. The leader of this particular group was Three-fingers Sammy Torres. He was a tall, over six-foot Mexican with a large mustache and smallpox scars on his face. It was said he'd lost the two fingers of his left hand in a fight, when his opponent bit them off. Torres reportedly made the man swallow them, then cut his throat and gut and reclaimed the digits. He carried the mummified fingers in a small leather pouch hung on a strip of rawhide around his neck.

Two of his confederates, Dick Wheeler and Billy Baugh, were said to have ridden with the James gang until Jesse got mad 'cause they made eyes at his wife. It was a testament to their toughness that he didn't kill them but allowed them to leave the gang.

The remaining four men were from the Dalton gang. Having survived the shootout that broke up the gang in Coffeeville, Kansas, they'd headed north and joined up with Lazarus. They went by Jimmy, Jake, Sonny, and Clyde. He didn't know their last names, and didn't much care as long as they did what they were supposed to.

At the table next to them were four Mexicans in dirty clothes. They had come from somewhere down near Del Rio. They were called Pedro Gonzalez, Jaime Sanchez, Coronado Vallentine, and Perro Gutierrez. He hadn't asked how the man got the name Perro, which meant dog in English. They'd ridden with a local *bandido* on the Mexican border who'd just recently been strung up by the Texas Rangers—who they said had followed them over halfway here before heading back to Texas. The Mex's rarely bathed, and the other men didn't much like them in the saloon, saying the smell ruined their appetites. 'Course, it didn't seem to do much to lessen their thirst for whiskey. The Mexicans would be good cannon fodder if needed. He'd have them rush the ranch first to see how well defended it was.

Behind the Mex's were the Rebels, as they called themselves. Ex-Confederate soldiers, they still wore the tattered remains of their uniforms, as if it made any kind of difference at this late date. Bobby Barlow, Christopher Tucker, Riley Samuels, Danny Donnahue, and Willie Bodine were all from some backwoods place in Arkansas named Dogsnot, or some such hillbilly name. They weren't very intelligent, but Lazarus didn't plan to let them do any thinking. As long as they could ride and shoot and didn't turn yellow on him, he figured they'd do all right.

There were a couple of black men in the group. Ordinarily, Lazarus didn't have much use for men of darker color, but he figured they'd be useful, especially if there was much digging to be done for the gold. Nigras were good at digging. Whether they lasted until time came to divvy up the proceeds was another matter, entirely. Bartholomew Winter and Jedediah Jones were full-on black, and they rode with a man with a heavy reputation named Cherokee Bill, a half-black and half-Indian who'd been terrorizing the ranches up near the Indian Nations for some time. They'd joined up because the U.S. Marshals had finally gotten around to trying to roust them out of their mountain hideouts up there. Cherokee Bill said they planned to stay around until the marshals went back to Oklahoma Territory. Then they'd head back to the Nations. That is, Lazarus thought, if he decided to let them live that long. At least they seemed to know their place and never tried to sit with the white folks in the saloon.

Lazarus continued to review the men under his command in this manner for a few more minutes, then decided the time had come.

"Men," he called, raising his hands to stop the chatter and noise in the room so he could be heard. "There's a good chance we'll be ridin' on the Jensen ranch in the next day or so. I want you to go easy on the whiskey until this is over."

He scowled at the loud groan that arose from the men in the room, some of whom openly laughed at his suggestion.

He gave a cold smile. "All right, I realize temperance is something none of you are exactly used to. But know this—if any of you mess up because you're drunk or hungover, I'll personally put a bullet in your gut and leave you to rot to death on the trail. Have I made myself perfectly clear?"

The noise quieted down and some of the men dropped their eyes. He knew he had their full attention now.

"Jimmy, I want you and Jake and Sonny and Clyde to get to work puttin' fuses in the dynamite we've got stacked up over at the store. I know you Dalton riders liked to use explosives in your bank jobs, so I figure you're the ones who'd do the best at gettin' it ready to use."

Jimmy nodded his head after glancing at his companions. "No problem, boss. We'll get on it first thing in the morning."

Lazarus shook his head. "No, Jimmy. You'll get on it right now, as soon as I'm through talkin'.

"I want the rest of you to get on over to the store an' pick up as many boxes of shells for your guns as you think you'll need. Put 'em in your saddlebags an' have 'em ready to travel by tomorrow. When it comes time to leave, I want everything and everybody ready to go."

"Why the sudden rush, Cain? We been sittin' around here for two weeks or more, an' now you act like there's a fire in your britches," said Donny Donnahue, one of the rebel riders.

"We may have a slight problem. Joey Wells took off last night. I fear he may have gone to warn Jensen we're comin'."

As they all looked around at each other, Lazarus could see the fear this caused in some of the men.

"You mean we might not just be fightin' Smoke Jensen, one of the toughest hombres in the area, but may also have to go up agin' Joey Wells, *the* toughest hombre anywhere?" asked Three-fingers Sammy Torres.

"That's right, Three-fingers. You got a problem with that?" Lazarus asked.

Torres shrugged. "Not particularly. It will no doubt mean there will be less men left to share in the loot after we kill them," he answered with a laugh.

Lazarus nodded. "There is that to consider. Now you men get on over to the store and pick up your bullets and dynamite, like I told you."

He turned to Bob Blanchard. "Bob, the bar is closed for the rest of the day."

Lazarus ignored the groan from the men and walked over to his table, signaling his leaders to join him.

After the others had left, he looked around at Blackie Jackson, Tom Cartwright, Curly Joe, Pig Iron Carlton, Jeremy Britt, and King Johannson.

"Men, we're gonna stick together through all this. Let the other fools take the front of the charge and do the dangerous work. We'll hang back and finish off any survivors at the ranch after the others have broken through the defenses."

Jeremy Britt frowned. "I say, Lazarus, that doesn't sound very sporting."

Lazarus cut his eyes at Jeremy. "I don't think you realize who we're dealing with here, Jeremy. Wells and Jensen are two of the best men with guns we could pick to go up against. I only put our odds of beatin' 'em, even with a ten to one advantage in numbers, at about fifty-fifty. If for some reason they turn out to be too tough for this bunch, I want us to survive to fight another day."

Jeremy shrugged. "You're the boss, boss," he said with a smile. "But I want a piece of Joey Wells. I don't like traitors."

Lazarus's face grew cold as a gravedigger's shovel. "For that, my friend, you're gonna have to stand in line."

"Did you mean it, Lazarus, 'bout the bar bein' closed the rest of the day?" asked Curly Joe Ventrillo.

"Not for us, boys, only for the cannon fodder," Lazarus answered with a grin.

Tom "Behind the Deuces" Cartwright got to his feet and walked over to the bar.

"Bob, gimme that bottle of Kentucky bourbon over there and some clean glasses. We got a little more drinkin' to do 'fore the day's over."

Blanchard looked over at Lazarus, saw him nod, and handed Cartwright the bottle and glasses.

After he filled everyone's glass, Lazarus stood up and held his glass high. "Boys, a toast. To gold, and all the things it can buy!"

Twenty-six

After Lazarus and his men finished their drinks, he sent them after the others to make ready for the attack on Smoke Jensen's ranch.

He walked over to the bar and held out his glass for a refill.

Bob Blanchard poured more whiskey into the glass, a worried look on his face.

"What is it, Bob? You look like you got somethin' on your mind," Lazarus said.

"There's something I ought'a tell you, Mr. Cain. After all, you been awfully good to me, payin' me for the whiskey an' food an' such your men are usin'."

"Go on, Bob, I'm listenin'."

"I couldn't help but overhear you talkin' to your men just now, 'bout goin' on down the road an' tryin' somethin' else if the attack on Smoke Jensen don't work out."

"Yeah, so what?"

"How much do you really know about Smoke Jensen, Mr. Cain?"

"Just what everybody else does, that he's a famous shootist and ex-outlaw, and a mighty tough hombre."

Blanchard shook his head. "You don't know near enough, then. See, Jensen's an old mountain man, trained by the most famous mountain man of all, Preacher."

"So what? We ain't gonna be fightin' him up in the mountains, Bob."

"That's not it, Mr. Cain. The mountain men lived by a code, a code of vengeance. Once you done one of them wrong, he'd not never give up 'til he'd repaid you, double."

"I don't see what—"

"I'm just telling you this so you won't think you're gonna be able to ride away from this after it's over if Jensen is still alive."

Blanchard took down a glass and poured himself a drink and refilled Lazarus's.

"Let me tell you a story 'bout what happened to the men who kilt Smoke's dad, just after they got here to Colorado. . . .

"Smoke's dad, Emmett, came back from the War Between the States in the summer of eighteen sixty-five. Smoke, who was known as Kirby then, was only about fourteen or fifteen years old. Emmett sold their scratch-dirt farm in Missouri, packed up their belongin's, and they headed north by northwest. Long about Wichita, they met up with an old mountain man who called himself Preacher. For some reason, unknown even to the old-timer, he took them under his wing when he saw they was as green as new apples, and they traveled together for a spell.

"Soon they was set upon by a band of Pawnee Injuns, an' Smoke kilt his first couple of men. The story goes that Preacher couldn't hardly believe it when he saw him draw that old Navy Colt. Says he knew right off the boy was destined to become a legend—if he lived long enough, that is. That's when Preacher gave young Kirby Jensen his nickname—Smoke—from the smoke that came outta that Navy Colt, and from the color of his hair.

"Right after that, Emmett told Preacher that he had set out lookin' for three men who killed Smoke's brother and stole some Confederate gold. Their names were Wiley Potter, Josh

Richards, and Stratton—I don't remember his first name. Emmett went on to tell Preacher that he was goin' gunnin' for those polecats, and if'n he didn't come back he wanted Preacher to take care of Smoke until he was growed up enough to do it for himself. Preacher told Emmett he'd be proud to do that very thing.

"The next day Emmett took off and left the old cougar to watch after his young'un. They didn't hear nothin' for a couple of years, time Preacher spent teaching the young buck the ways of the West and how to survive where most men wouldn't. Preacher later told people that during that time, though Smoke was about as natural a fast draw and shot as he'd ever seen, the boy spent at least an hour ever day drawing and dry-firin' those Navy Colts he wore.

"About two years later, at Brown's Hole in Idaho, an old mountain man found Smoke and Preacher and told Smoke his daddy was dead, and that those men he went after'd killed him. Smoke packed up, an' he and Preacher went on the prod.

"They got to Pagosa Springs—that's Indian for healin' waters—just west of the Needle Mountains, and stopped to replenish their supplies. Then they rode into Rico, a rough-an'-tumble mining camp that back then was an outlaw hangout."

Blanchard halted in his tale to build himself a cigarette and stick it in his mouth, then continued telling Lazarus about the legend of Smoke Jensen's early years. . . .

Smoke and Preacher dismounted in front of the combination trading post and saloon. As was his custom, Smoke slipped the thongs from the hammers of his Colts as soon as his boots hit dirt.

They had bought their supplies and turned to leave when the hum of conversation suddenly died. Two rough-dressed and unshaven men, both wearing guns, blocked the door.

"Who owns that horse out there?" one demanded, a snarl

in his voice, trouble in his manner. "The one with the SJ brand?"

Smoke laid his purchases on the counter. "I do," he said quietly.

"Which way'd you ride in from?"

Preacher had slipped to his right, his left hand covering the hammer of his Henry, concealing the click as he thumbed it back.

Smoke faced the men, his right hand hanging loose by his side. His left hand was just inches from his left-hand gun. "Who wants to know—and why?"

No one in the dusty building moved or spoke.

"Pike's my name," said the bigger and uglier of the pair. "And I say you came through my diggin's yesterday and stole my dust."

"And I say you're a liar," Smoke told him.

Pike grinned nastily, his right hand hovering near the butt of his pistol. "Why . . . you little pup. I think I'll shoot your ears off."

"Why don't you try? I'm tired of hearing you shoot your mouth off."

Pike looked puzzled for a few seconds; bewilderment crossed his features. No one had ever talked to him in this manner. Pike was big, strong, and a bully. "I think I'll just kill you for that."

Pike and his partner reached for their guns.

Four shots boomed in the low-ceilinged room, four shots so closely spaced that they seemed as one thunderous roar. Dust and bird droppings fell from the ceiling. Pike and his friend were slammed out the open doorway. One fell off the rough porch, dying in the dirt street. Pike, with two holes in his chest, died with his back against a support pole, his eyes still open, unbelieving. Neither had managed to pull a pistol more than halfway out of leather.

All eyes in the black, powder-filled and dusty, smoky room

moved to the young man standing by the bar, a Colt in each hand. "Good God!" a man whispered in awe. "I never even seen him draw."

Preacher moved the muzzle of his Henry to cover the men at the tables. The bartender put his hands slowly on the bar, indicating he wanted no trouble.

"We'll be leaving now," Smoke said, holstering his Colts and picking up his purchases from the counter. He walked out the door slowly.

Smoke stepped over the sprawled, dead legs of Pike and walked past his dead partner in the shooting.

"What are we 'posed to do with the bodies?" a man asked Preacher.

"Bury 'em."

"What's the kid's name?"

"Smoke."

A few days later, in a nearby town, a friend of Preacher's told Smoke that two men, Haywood and Thompson, who claimed to be Pike's brother, had tracked him and Preacher and were in town waiting for Smoke.

Smoke walked down the rutted street an hour before sunset, the sun at his back—the way he had planned it. Thompson and Haywood were in a big tent at the end of the street, which served as saloon and café. Preacher had pointed them out earlier and asked if Smoke needed his help. Smoke said no. The refusal came as no surprise.

As he walked down the street a man glanced up, spotted him, then hurried quickly inside.

Smoke felt no animosity toward the men in the tent saloon—no anger, no hatred—but they'd come here after him. *So let the dance begin,* he thought.

Smoke stopped fifty feet from the tent. "Haywood! Thompson! You want to see me?"

The two men pushed back the tent flap and stepped out,

both angling to get a better look at the man they had tracked. "You the kid called Smoke?" one said.

"I am."

"Pike was my brother," said the heavier of the pair. "And Shorty was my pal."

"You should choose your friends more carefully," Smoke told him.

"They was just a-funnin' with you," Thompson said.

"You weren't there. You don't know what happened."

"You callin' me a liar?"

"If that's the way you want to take it."

Thompson's face colored with anger, his hand moving closer to the .44 in his belt. "You take that back, or make your play."

"There is no need for this," Smoke said.

The second man began cursing Smoke as he stood tensely, legs spread wide, body bent at the waist. "You're a damned thief. You stolt their gold, and then kilt 'em."

"I don't want to have to kill you," Smoke said.

"The kid's yellow!" Haywood yelled. Then he grabbed for his gun.

Haywood touched the butt of his gun just as two loud gunshots blasted in the dusty street. The .36 caliber balls struck Haywood in the chest, one nicking his heart. He dropped to the dirt, dying. Before he closed his eyes and death relieved him of the shocking pain by pulling him into a long sleep, two more shots thundered. He had a dark vision of Thompson spinning in the street. Then Haywood died.

Thompson was on one knee, his left hand holding his shattered right elbow. His leg was bloody. Smoke had knocked his gun from his hand, then shot him in the leg.

"Pike was your brother," Smoke told the man. "So I can understand why you came after me. But you were wrong. I'll let you live. But stay with mining. If I ever see you again, I'll kill you."

The young man turned, putting his back to the dead and bloody pair. He walked slowly up the street, his high-heeled Spanish riding boots pocking the air with dusty puddles.*

*The Last Mountain Man

Twenty-seven

Lazarus stopped Blanchard's story long enough to pull a cigar out of his pocket, light it, and get his glass refilled.

"How old was Jensen when this happened?" he asked the bartender.

"I don't know exactly. 'Bout eighteen or so, I guess."

Lazarus nodded, his eyes narrowed. "Go on, Bob."

"After Smoke shot and killed Pike, his friend, and Haywood, and then wounded Pike's brother, Thompson, he and Preacher went after the other men who kilt Smoke's brother and stole the Confederates' gold. They rode on over to *La Plaza de los Leones,* the plaza of the lions. It was there that they trapped a man named Casey in a line shack with some of his *compadres.* Smoke and Preacher burnt 'em out and captured Casey. Smoke took him to the outskirts of the town and hanged him."

Lazarus's eyebrows shot up. "Just hanged him? Without a trial or notifying the authorities?"

Blanchard flicked ash off his cigarette without taking it out of his mouth. "Yes sir. Smoke likes to take care of his enemies himself. Why, I'll bet that even if he knows you and your men are coming after him, he won't ask nobody else for any help."

Blanchard hesitated. Then, remembering where he left off, he continued. "Anyway, Jensen knew that town would never of hanged one of their own just on the word of Smoke Jensen."

Blanchard snorted. "Like as not they'd of hanged Smoke and Preacher instead. Anyway, after that the sheriff of that town put out a flyer on Smoke, accusing him of murder. Had a ten thousand dollar reward on it, too."

"Did Smoke and Preacher go into hiding?" Lazarus asked, figuring that's what he would have done.

"Nope. Seems Preacher advised it, but Smoke said he had one more call to make. They rode on over to Oreodelphia, lookin' for a man named Ackerman. They didn't go after him right at first. Smoke and Preacher sat around doin' a whole lot of nothin' for two or three days. Smoke wanted Ackerman to get plenty nervous. He did, and finally came gunnin' for Smoke with a bunch of men who rode for his brand. . . ."

At the edge of town, Ackerman, a bull of a man with small, mean eyes and a cruel slit for a mouth, slowed his horse to a walk. Ackerman and his hands rode down the street, six abreast.

Preacher and Smoke were on their feet. Preacher stuffed his mouth full of chewing tobacco. Both men had slipped the thongs from the hammers of their Colts. Preacher wore two Colt .44's—one in a holster, the other stuck behind his belt. Mountain man and the young gunfighter stood six feet apart on the boardwalk.

The sheriff closed his office door and walked into the empty cell area. He sat down and began a game of checkers with his deputy.

Ackerman and his men wheeled their horses to face the men on the boardwalk. "I hear tell you boys is lookin' for me. If so, here I am."

"News to me," Smoke said. "What's your name?"

"You know who I am, kid. Ackerman."

"Oh yeah!" Smoke grinned. "You're the man who helped kill my brother by shooting him in the back. Then you stole the gold he was guarding."

Inside the hotel, pressed against the wall, the desk clerk listened intently, his mouth open in anticipation of gunfire.

"You're a liar. I didn't shoot your brother. That was Potter and his bunch."

"You stood and watched it. Then you stole the gold."

"It was war, kid."

"But you were on the same side," Smoke said. "So that not only makes you a killer, it makes you a traitor and a coward."

"I'll kill you for sayin' that!"

"You'll burn in hell a long time before I'm dead," Smoke told him.

Ackerman grabbed for his pistol. The street exploded in gunfire and black powder fumes. Horses screamed and bucked in fear. One rider was thrown to the dust by his lunging mustang. Smoke took the men on the left, Preacher the men on the right side. The battle lasted no more than ten to twelve seconds. When the noise and the gunsmoke cleared, five men lay in the street, two of them dead. Two more would die from their wounds. One was shot in the side—he would live. Ackerman had been shot three times: once in the belly, once in the chest, and one ball had taken him in the side of the face as the muzzle of the .36 had lifted with each blast. Still Ackerman sat in his saddle, dead. The big man finally leaned to one side and toppled from his horse, one boot hung in the stirrup. The horse shied, then began waking down the dusty street, dragging Ackerman, leaving a bloody trail.

Preacher spat into the street. "Damn near swallowed my chaw."

"I never seen a draw that fast," a man spoke from his storefront. "It was a blur."

The editor of the paper walked up to stand by the sheriff.

He watched the old man and the young gunfighter walk down the street. He truly had seen it all. The old man had killed one man, wounded another. The young man had killed four men, as calmly as if picking his teeth.

"What's that young man's name?"

"Smoke Jensen. He's a devil."

"What did they do next, Bob?" Lazarus asked, sipping his whiskey slowly, considering what he was learning about the character of Smoke Jensen.

"Well, they both had some minor wounds, and there was a price on Smoke's head, so they took off to the mountains to lay up for a while and lick their wounds and let the heat die down."

Blanchard stubbed out his cigarette. "Except it didn't work out exactly that way. They chanced upon the remains of a wagon train that'd been burned out by Indians, and rescued a young woman. Nicole was her name. She was the lone survivor of the attack. There wasn't nothin' else they could do, so they took her up into the mountains with them, where they planned to winter.

"Smoke built them a cabin out of adobe and logs, and they spent two winters and a summer in that place, up in the high lonesome. After the first year, Smoke and Nicole had a kind of unofficial marrying, and by the second winter she had Smoke a son."

"I didn't know Jensen had a son."

Blanchard shook his head. "He doesn't, now. When the boy was about a year old, Smoke had to go lookin' for their milk cow that wandered off. When he came back, he found some bounty hunters had tracked him to the cabin and were in there with Nicole and the baby. . . ."

* * *

Some primitive sense of warning caused Smoke to pull up short of his home. He made a wide circle, staying in the timber back of the creek, and slipped up to the cabin.

Nicole was dead. The acts of the men had grown perverted, and in their haste her throat had been crushed.

Felter sat by the lean-to and watched the valley in front of him. He wondered where Smoke had hidden the gold.

Inside, Canning drew his skinning knife and scalped Nicole, tying her bloody hair to his belt. He then skinned a part of her, thinking he would tan the hide and make himself a nice tobacco pouch.

Kid Austin got sick to his stomach watching Canning's callousness, and went out the back door to puke on the ground. That moment of sickness saved his life—for the time being.

Grissom walked out the front door of the cabin. Smoke's tracks had indicated he had ridden off south, so he should probably return from that direction, but Grissom felt something was wrong. He sensed something, his years on the owlhoot back trails surfacing.

"Felter?" he called.

"Yeah?" He stepped from the lean-to.

"Something's wrong."

"I feel it. But what?"

"I don't know." Grissom spun as he sensed movement behind him. His right hand dipped for his pistol. Felter had stepped back into the lean-to. Grissom's palm touched the smooth wooden butt of his gun as his eyes saw the tall young man standing by the corner of the cabin, a Colt .36 in each hand. Lead from the .36s hit him in the center of the chest with numbing force. Just before his heart exploded, the outlaw said, "Smoke!" Then he fell to the ground.

Smoke jerked the gun belt and pistols from the dead man. Remington Army .44s.

A bounty hunter ran from the cabin, firing at the corner of the building. But Smoke was gone.

"Behind the house!" Felter yelled, running from the lean-to, his fists full of Colts. He slid to a halt and raced back to the water trough, diving behind it for protection.

A bounty hunter who had been dumping his bowels in the outhouse struggled to pull up his pants, at the same time pushing open the door with his shoulder. Smoke shot him twice in the belly and left him to scream on the outhouse floor.

Kid Austin, caught in the open behind the cabin, ran for the banks of the creek, panic driving his legs. He leaped for the protection of a sandy embankment, twisting in the air, just as Smoke took aim and fired. The ball hit Austin's right buttock and traveled through the left cheek of his butt, tearing out a sizable hunk of flesh. Kid Austin, the dreaming gun-hand, screamed and fainted from the pain in his ass.

Smoke ran for the protection of the woodpile and crouched there, recharging his Colts and checking the .44s. He listened to the sounds of men in panic, firing in all directions and hitting nothing.

Moments ticked past, the sound of silence finally overpowering gunfire. Smoke flicked away sweat from his face. He waited.

Something came sailing out the back door to bounce on the grass. Smoke felt hot bile build in his stomach. Someone had thrown his dead son outside. The boy had been dead for some time. Smoke fought back sickness.

"You wanna see what's left of your woman?" a taunting voice called from near the back door. "I got her hair on my belt and a piece of her hide to tan. We all took a time or two with her. I think she liked it."

Smoke felt rage charge through him, but he remained still, crouched behind the thick pile of wood until his anger cooled to controlled, venom-filled fury. He unslung the big Sharps buffalo rifle Preacher had carried for years. The rifle could drop a two thousand pound buffalo at six hundred yards. It could also punch through a small log.

The voice from the cabin continued to mock and taunt Smoke, but Preacher's training kept him cautious. To his rear lay a meadow, void of cover. To his left was a shed. He knew that was empty, for it was still barred from the outside. The man he'd plugged in the butt was to his right, but several fallen logs would protect him from that direction. The man in the outhouse was either dead or passed out. His screaming had ceased.

Through a chink in the logs, Smoke shoved the muzzle of the Sharps and lined up where he thought he had seen a man move, just to the left of the rear window, where Smoke had framed it out with rough pine planking. He gently squeezed the trigger, taking up slack. The weapon boomed, the planking shattered, and a man began screaming in pain.

Canning ran out the front of the cabin, to the lean-to, sliding down hard beside Felter behind the water trough. "This ain't workin' out," he panted. "Grissom, Austin, Poker, and now Evans is either dead or dying. The slug from that buffalo gun blowed his arm off. Let's get the hell outta here!"

Felter had been thinking the same thing. "What about Clark and Sam?"

"They growed men. They can join us or they can go to hell."

"Let's ride. They's always another day. We'll hide up in them mountains, see which way he rides out, then bushwhack him. Let's go." They raced for their horses, hidden in a bend of the creek, behind the bank. They kept the cabin between themselves and Smoke as much as possible, then bellied down in the meadow the rest of the way.

In the creek, in water red from the wounds in his butt, Kid Austin crawled upstream, crying in pain and humiliation. His Colts were forgotten—useless, anyway. The powder was wet—all he wanted was to get away.

The bounty hunters left in the house, Clark and Sam, looked at each other. "I'm gettin' out!" Sam said. "That ain't no pilgrim out there."

"The hell with that," Clark said. "I humped his woman, and I'll kill him and take the ten thousand."

"Your option." Sam slipped out the front and caught up with the others.

Kid Austin reached his horse first. Yelping as he hit the saddle, he galloped off toward the timber in the foothills.

"You wife don't look so good now," Clark called out to Smoke. "Not since she got a haircut and one titty skinned."

Deep silence had replaced the gunfire. The air stank of black powder, blood, and relaxed bladders and bowels, death-induced. Smoke had seen the men ride off into the foothills. He wondered how many were left in the cabin.

Smoke remained still. His eyes, burning with fury, touched the stiffening form of his son. If Clark could have read the man's thoughts, he would have stuck the muzzle of his .44 into his mouth and pulled the trigger, guaranteeing himself a quick death instead of what waited for him later on.

"Yes, sir," Clark taunted him. He went into profane detail about the rape of Nicole and the perverted acts that followed.

Smoke eased slowly backward, keeping the woodpile in front of him. He slipped down the side of the knoll and ran around to one wall of the cabin. He grinned. The bounty hunter was still talking to the woodpile, to the muzzle of the Sharps stuck through the logs.

Smoke eased around to the front of the cabin and looked in. He saw Nicole, saw the torture marks on her, saw the hideousness of the scalping and the skinning knife. He lifted his eyes to the back door, where Clark was crouching just to the right of the closed door.

Smoke raised his .36 and shot the pistol out of Clark's hand. The outlaw howled and grabbed his numbed and blood-ied hand.

Smoke stepped over Grissom's body, then glanced at the body of the armless bounty hunter, who had bled to death.

Clark looked up at the tall young man with the burning eyes. Cold slimy fear put a bony hand on his shoulder. For the first time in his evil life, Clark knew what death looked like.

"You gonna make it quick, ain't you?"

"Not likely," Smoke said, then kicked him on the side of the head, dropping Clark unconscious to the floor.

When Clark came to his senses, he began screaming. He was naked, staked out a mile from the cabin, on the plain. Rawhide held his wrists and ankles to thick stakes driven into the ground. A huge ant mound was just inches from him. And Smoke had poured honey all over him.

"I'm a white man," Clark screamed. "You can't do this to me." Slobber sprayed from his mouth. "What are you, half-Apache?"

Smoke looked at him, contempt in his eyes. "You will not die well, I believe."

He didn't.*

Lazarus shook his head, his brow furrowed with thought. "I see what you mean, Bob. If we fail in our attack, Jensen will hunt us down one by one until he's killed all of us or one of us kills him."

"That's about the size of it, Mr. Cain. I just didn't want you going up against him until you knew what kind of man he is."

"Thanks for the warning, Bob. I guess the only thing to do is make sure we kill Jensen when we get the chance."

Blanchard nodded. "It's that, or spend the rest of your life looking back over your shoulder, waitin' on him to show up."

*The Last Mountain Man

Twenty-eight

About five miles outside of Fontana, Smoke reined Joker to a halt. "If what I've heard about Cain is true, with his military background he's gonna have sentries posted around Fontana that'll warn him we're coming."

"What do you want to do, Smoke?" Louis Longmont asked.

"Since Joey and I have the most experience at this, we'll take out the sentries. I want the rest of you to ride in a wide circle around the town and try to intercept that wagon of dynamite and ammunition Cain's expecting to arrive today. It should be coming from the north, from Pueblo."

After the others rode off, Smoke pulled his Colts out and began to check his loads, while Joey did the same.

"It's gonna seem like old times ridin' with you, Smoke," Joey said.

Smoke grinned. "Yeah, let's hope it turns out as well this time as it did last time . . ."

Smoke and Joey began to ride a circuit around Fontana, keeping their eyes peeled for any approaching riders. It didn't take them long to attract a couple.

Two men rode up, each carrying Winchester rifles in their hands, the butts resting on their thighs as they reined up in front of Smoke and Joey.

One of the men, dark-skinned with several days' growth of beard, spoke up. "Where you gents headed?"

Smoke glanced at Joey, his lips curled in a lazy smile. "The man wants to know where we're headed, partner."

Joey, his face deadly serious, replied, "Yeah, I heard the nosy son of a bitch."

He looked directly at the man who'd spoken. "What's your name, mister?" he asked.

The dark-skinned man glanced at the man sitting on the horse next to him, then back at Joey. "What's it to you?"

Joey shrugged. "I just thought it'd be nice to have somethin' to carve on the cross over your grave, assumin' anybody cares enough 'bout your sorry butt to come out here and bury you."

"Why you . . ." the man growled and started to lower his rifle barrel.

Twin explosions erupted almost simultaneously from Smoke and Joey's hands, which were full of Colts. The two men were blown backward off their horses before they could ear back the hammers on their long guns.

The silent one struggled to get to his feet. Then a bullet from Smoke put him down for good.

Smoke cut his eyes to Joey. "I feel kind'a bad not offering them a chance to quit this madness and go on about their way."

Joey shook his head. "That kind of thinkin's gonna git you kilt, partner. There's not a one of the bunch ridin' with Cain who's worth two seconds of thought. They's all murderers an' thieves an' such, an' don't deserve the time of day, much less a chance to shoot us while they's decidin' whether to stay or leave."

"I guess you're right," Smoke said.

"Ain't I always?" Joey said, this time grinning.

* * *

The next two sentries, perhaps because they'd heard the shots or perhaps because they were just more ornery than the first pair, didn't bother to accost Smoke and Joey. They just started blasting away with long guns as soon as they saw them riding by.

Luckily for Smoke and Joey, the pair were abysmal shots, and the first volley of bullets whined by harmlessly, other than startling the two gunmen out of a year's growth.

"Damn!" Joey shouted even as he leaned far over Red's neck and spurred the big stud toward the distant men firing at them.

The two men, sitting on their horses, stopped shooting for a moment when they realized the men they were aiming at were doing something crazy. Instead of trying to get away from the hail of bullets, they were galloping at full speed *toward* them.

Pete Garcia looked at Julio Cardenez with disbelief. "Julio, the mens are *stupido!*"

Julio didn't bother to reply, since the men were getting closer by the second and he could see pistols in their hands.

Julio and Pete continued to fire, the explosions of their rifles making their horses jump and dance in fear, which did nothing to improve their already terrible aim.

Joey, who'd spent considerable years after the Civil War riding and shooting from horseback, was under no such handicap.

While he was still fifty yards from the attackers, his first slug whipped the bandit's hat off. The second took the man in the left chest, just above his heart. The force of the bullet twisted the man around in his saddle, but didn't knock him to the ground.

Julio Cardenez tried to put his rifle to his shoulder, but then he noticed his left arm wouldn't work right.

"Damn, Pete," Julio said, wonderment in his voice as if

he'd never expected something like this to happen. "I am hit!"

Pete glanced at Julio while levering his Winchester as fast as he could. When he turned his head to the left, a slug from Smoke's pistol entered the right side of his face and exited out the left, blowing his lower jaw completely off in a split second.

Pete tried to scream at the terrible pain, but could only gurgle as his blood poured down his throat and into his windpipe.

By the time Julio looked up from his useless left arm, Joey was twenty yards away, staring at him over the sights of a Colt Army .44 caliber pistol.

"No!" screamed Julio, holding out his good right arm as if that could shield him from Joey's bullets.

It didn't. The next one passed through the meat of Julio's forearm and hit him in the right eye, exploding his skull and killing him instantly.

Smoke, seeing the terrible mess his bullet had made of Pete's face, withheld his fire, watching the man strangle and drown in his own blood. Pete fell out of the saddle, his skin the color of night, gasping like a fish out of water as he died.

Smoke and Joey rested their broncs as they punched out empty cartridges and reloaded their pistols.

"How many left, do you think?" Smoke asked.

Joey pursed his lips for a moment, thinking. "If'n he's goin' by the rules the rebels used to follow, he's got eight sentries surroundin' his camp. Two on each point of the compass."

Smoke slipped his pistol into his holster. "That means we've got four more to deal with."

Joey nodded. "At least."

* * *

Louis Longmont was the first to spy the wagon. "There it is," he called to the others, pointing up the road.

A man could be seen driving a buckboard, a saddled horse following along behind on a dally rope.

Monte Carson was the first to speak as they signaled the wagon to a halt. "Howdy, mister. My name's Monte Carson, an' I'm the sheriff around here. What's in the back of your wagon?"

The driver looked worriedly around at the faces of the men surrounding him. "Uh, some supplies from Garrett's General Store over in Pueblo."

"What kind'a supplies?" Louis Longmont asked.

The man stared at Louis Carbone and Al Martine, who looked like Mexican *bandidos* with their large, silver spurs, crossed bandoliers of shells on their chests, and twin Colt pistols on their hips.

"What business is it of yours?" he asked.

Al drew his pistol and crossed his arms on his saddle horn, leaning forward, the barrel of the gun pointing down. *"Señor,* the man he asked you very nice. Why you not answer his question, *muy pronto?"*

"I'm carryin' dynamite, gunpowder, an' about two hundred boxes of shells, forty-fours, forty-fives, an' a few thirty-six caliber bullets."

Monte let his face look puzzled. "You figurin' on goin' to war, mister?"

"No. These are for a Mr. Cain, in the town of Fontana," the driver answered belligerently. "Now, why don't you just let me ride on into town and do what I'm bein' paid to do?"

"I can't do that," Monte said. "The town of Fontana is under quarantine."

"Quarantine?" the man asked.

"Yeah. Seems they's a disease in that town that's gonna kill everybody in it," said Pearlie, a smirk on his face.

"What is it? The pox?"

"No," answered Louis Longmont. "It is a disease called greed. It is being spread by Lazarus Cain, and it has infected everyone in the town."

"Greed ain't fatal," the driver persisted, not getting the joke.

Al Martine cocked his pistol with a loud metallic sound. "It is in this case, my friend," he growled.

"Uh, if you gentlemen will allow me, I'll just get on my horse and head on back to Pueblo."

"That'll be just fine," Monte said. He smiled, looking around at the group of men with him. "My friends and I will make sure Mr. Cain gets all of the bullets and dynamite in your wagon, one way or another." He hesitated and grinned at the others riding with him. "You have my word on it."

Nate Bridges and Will Calloway were riding sentry for Lazarus when Nate stopped his horse and pulled a small canvas sack out of his shirt pocket and began to build himself a cigarette. Will stopped his horse, too, and pulled out his canteen to get a drink of water.

As Nate dipped his head to lick the paper around his tobacco, there came a sudden sound from behind him, like a sledgehammer hitting a side of beef, and Nate back-flipped off his horse.

"What the hell?" Will said, glancing down at his partner as a booming sound echoed from across the valley.

He saw a spreading stain of crimson on the front of Nate's shirt, then looked back over his shoulder in time to see a puff of smoke come from a tiny figure on horseback over fifteen hundred yards away.

He jerked his reins and whirled his horse, saving his life as the bullet from Joey's Sharps Big Fifty hit him in the shoulder.

The force of the slug almost unseated Will, but he managed

to keep his balance and leaned over the neck of his mount and spurred it toward Fontana as fast as the animal could run.

"Damn! Missed the second one," Joey muttered as he reloaded the Sharps.

"That might not be so bad," Smoke said. "Let him tell Cain what happened, and when the other sentries don't show up and he realizes what happened to them, it'll cause him some confusion."

"Why is that good? I thought we wanted the element of surprise."

"We did. But that wasn't going to happen with us having to kill all the sentries. Sooner or later he was going to realize he was under attack, anyway. Now we'll let him stew on it a while, wondering just who and how many are after him."

"Well, if that's the plan, then we need to git those other two sentries pronto," Joey said.

After he put the Sharps in his saddle boot they rode north, the direction of the remaining two sentries.

Bill Boudreaux and Francois Tibbido, two friends on the run from New Orleans for killing five men in a riverboat gambling feud, were riding the northern sentry post.

"Say, Bill," drawled Francois, "here come two men." He pointed off to the west.

"Uh huh," Bill replied.

"What you want to do?"

"Let them come. Then when they get here we kill them, *mon ami,*" Bill said.

"Why not just tell them to leave?" Francois asked, his face glum.

" 'Cause Monsieur Cain, he be plenty mad if he find out. He say kill anyone who come, so we kill these two mens." Bill hesitated, then asked, "Unless you want to go to Monsieur Cain an' tell him you be too soft for this job?"

"No! I agree. They must die."

As soon as Smoke and Joey got within thirty yards of the two men they were approaching, they saw the men go for their guns.

Without hesitating, Smoke and Joey filled their hands with iron, firing on the two sentries before they could clear leather.

Smoke hit Bill Boudreaux in the heart and throat with two shots that sounded almost simultaneous. The bullets tore into Boudreaux, killing him before he had time to scream.

Joey's shots hit Francois in the stomach and left arm, doubling him over his saddle horn with a loud grunt.

After a few seconds, he toppled to the side to fall to the ground, moaning in pain and writhing in the dirt.

"Help me . . . oh dear God, help me . . ." he cried.

Joey rode over to look down at the dying man. "You got a gun. Help yourself," he said. Then he and Smoke rode off toward Fontana's town limits, where they were to meet with their friends.

Twenty-nine

Will Calloway made it to just in front of the Dog Hole Saloon in Fontana before impending shock from loss of blood caused him to faint and fall off his horse.

Donny Donnahue was just coming from the outhouse when he saw Will hit the dirt.

"Hey, everbody, come quick!" he yelled as he ran to help the fallen man.

When he got next to Will, Donny saw almost his entire shirt soaked with blood. "Jesus," he muttered, having never seen anyone lose that much blood and survive.

Several cowboys burst out of the batwings of the Dog Hole and ran to stand over Will. Finally, Three-fingers Sonny Torres, who had seen and treated more gunshot wounds than most doctors, knelt next to Will and pulled out a large knife. He stuck the blade in the front of Will's shirt and sliced it open.

After Torres peeled off the shirt, several of the men standing watching gave low whistles. There was a hole as big as a man's fist in the front of Will's shoulder. Most of the bleeding had stopped or at least slowed to a slow trickle, and there were no arterial spurters.

Sonny Torres rolled Will up on his side and looked at his back.

"Here's where the bullet enter," he said, pointing to a small hole just behind Will's shoulder, next to his shoulder blade.

He let him roll back. "And that is where she exit," he said, indicating the huge hole in the front of Will's chest.

"What the hell kind'a gun did that?" asked Donny.

Torres shrugged. "A large calibre, maybe a buff'lo gun of some sort, like a Sharps."

Lazarus Cain came striding through the crowd of men, parting them with his hands as if he were Moses parting the Red Sea.

"What the hell's goin' on here?" he asked.

" 'Pears one of our men went an' got hisself shot," answered Willie Bodine.

"Is that Will Calloway lyin' there?" Lazarus asked.

"Yes sir," answered Donny. "I's just comin' outta the shitter when I saw him fall off'n his horse."

Torres glanced up from where he still kneeled next to Will. "Looks like he was shot with a long gun of some kind, Mr. Cain. Prob'ly a Sharps or somethin' like it."

"Damn!" Lazarus stepped back and looked around the town. "Has anyone seen any of the other sentries? Who was ridin' with Will, anyway?"

"I believe it was Nate Bridges," Billy Baugh drawled in his low, Southern accent. "Leastways, I seen the two of 'em ridin' outta town together this mornin'."

Lazarus started pointing. "I need some men to ride out and check on the sentries. Wheeler, you ride north. Gonzalez, you take the south end. Tucker, you go east, and Samuels, I want you to ride to the west."

He hesitated. "Men, I don't know if this means anything or not, but ride with your guns loose and watch your backsides. We may have some problems comin' our way."

Within two hours, Lazarus had gotten the bad news and was having a meeting with his most trusted men in the Dog

Hole. They were seated at their favorite table in the corner, and several bottles of whiskey were being passed around.

Lazarus looked at his men. "We've got some trouble. The men I sent out found every one of our sentries dead, bodies scattered all over the countryside."

"Were all of 'em kilt with long guns?" asked Curly Joe Ventrillo.

Lazarus shook his head. "No. It appeared as if some were shot at close range with pistols."

"Did they find any other bodies, other than our chaps?" asked Jeremy Brett.

Lazarus shook his head slowly.

"That means whoever did this is good," said Blackie Jackson. "Those sentries were hard men. I don't see some pilgrims ridin' up an' killin' ever one without getting a least a little shot up."

"You're right, Blackie. Whoever is out there is a force to be reckoned with."

"Cain't hardly be the army, then," opined Pig Iron Carlton. "Them boys are so green they'd've probably shot one or two of their own men theyselves."

"No, I don't think this is the authorities," said Lazarus, a thoughtful expression on his face as he stared out the window. "If it was the army or marshals, we'd've heard from them by now."

He wagged his head. "This is something different."

"Well then, who could it be, boss?" asked Tom "Behind the Deuces."

"I don't know."

"Do you suspect it could be Smoke Jensen? Maybe Joey Wells warned him, after all," said King Johannson, absently fingering the handle of the machete hanging on his belt.

Lazarus frowned. "I doubt it. If Jensen knew we were comin' an' that we had over fifty men, why wouldn't he just notify the army or the territory marshals? There'd be no need for him to even get involved."

Jeremy Brett removed the Colt pistol from his shoulder holster and flipped open the loading gate as he began to check his loads. "I fear you may have underestimated this Jensen gentleman. From what I have heard and read, he is a man who does not suffer tribulation well."

"What's that supposed to mean, Jeremy?" asked Lazarus. "Speak English, will you?"

Jeremy smiled. "I believe we were on Mr. Jensen's ranch the day we arrived here."

"So?"

"Do you remember what happened that day?"

Lazarus thought a minute, then looked slowly up at Jeremy. "We shot some young ranchhand."

"It is merely my supposition that perhaps Mr. Smoke Jensen did not take kindly to us killing one of his men. Perhaps this is his way of telling us that."

"Do you really think a man of Jensen's reputation would go to war over losing one of his hired hands?" asked Lazarus.

"From what I've heard, though the stories are admittedly exaggerated, Jensen would go to war if you scuffed his boots."

Lazarus rubbed his chin whiskers as he thought. "If this is Jensen an' his men, it won't be so bad. As a matter of fact, it's probably better if he comes to us rather than us fightin' him on his own ground."

"What do you mean?" asked Curly Joe.

"This way there won't be no chance of us ridin' into no traps or ambushes."

"Wonder how many men he's got ridin' with him," said Blackie Jackson.

"It really doesn't matter, old chap," said Jeremy Brett. "Once they ride into town, they're all as good as dead."

"I want you men to get the boys scattered out all over

town," ordered Lazarus. "Have 'em get ready for an attack. Post some on roofs, some in high placed rooms where they have a good line of fire. You know the drill. Tell 'em to get ready. Smoke Jensen's coming to town, and we're gonna throw him a party."

Thirty

Smoke and Joey circled around Fontana until they found where their friends were waiting. They'd made a campfire and were cooking some beans and fatback and heating up some biscuits Sally had sent along in a paper sack.

Louis Longmont looked up from his coffee cup and smiled. "I see the sentries were no match for the team of Jensen and Wells."

"Not even close," Joey said. "Them boys just thought they knew how to fight 'til they ran into a twister called Smoke Jensen."

Smoke inclined his head at Pearlie, who was sitting on his haunches next to the fire, a plate piled high with food on his knees. "I might'a known you boys would be eating, since Pearlie's riding with you."

"Golly, Smoke," Pearlie mumbled around a mouthful of food, "ya just never know when you're gonna next git a chance to eat when you're fightin' outlaws an' such. I figgered it'd be best to eat while there weren't nothin' goin' on."

Smoke walked over to the kettle on the trestle over the fire and scooped out a helping for himself. "Don't worry, Pearlie, I was just funning with you. It is always a good idea to eat before a fight. You're right. There's no telling just how long we're going to be tied up in this little fracas."

Joey built himself a cigarette and stuck it in the side of

his mouth, then proceeded to drink coffee without disturbing the butt.

"We may have a little trouble, boys," he said.

"How's that, Joey?" Sheriff Monte Carson asked.

"One of the sentries got away. He was carryin' some of my lead in him, but we figure he might've made it back to Fontana to warn the others we're comin'."

"Damn!" said Louis Carbone. *"Es muy malo!"*

Longmont shrugged. "It's not all that bad, Louis. In fact, it really won't make a hell of a lot of difference. Even if they suspect someone has targeted them, they won't know who or how many, nor will they have much time to make preparations for our arrival."

Smoke nodded. "That's the way I figure it, Louis. In fact, it might be better if they have a little time to worry about just who's on their trail."

"Yeah," Monte Carson agreed. "Worried men don't always think as good as men without a lot on their mind." He smiled a grim smile. "I'd a lot rather trail a man who knows he's bein' trailed an' is spendin' a lot of his time lookin' back over his shoulder instead of thinkin' 'bout how he can get the drop on me."

Smoke walked over to the wagon and began to peer inside it. "What've we got here?"

Longmont stepped over to lean on the edge of the buckboard. "Looks like Cain was planning on going to war with you and the town of Big Rock, Smoke. He's got enough ammunition and gunpowder and dynamite in this wagon to cause quite a ruckus."

Cal added, "If he'd managed to get it, that is."

"You boys did a good job," Smoke said approvingly. "If Cain had been able to acquire this wagon we'd've had our hands full, all right."

"Now, our only problem," Monte said, "is to figure out how we can make the best use of this stuff ourselves."

Smoke's lips curled up in a wide grin. "Oh, I think I have some ideas on that subject, Monte."

He took his sketch of Fontana out of his saddlebag and spread it on top of the boxes in the buckboard. With a pencil, he pointed to various areas of the town as he talked, dividing up his forces as commanders had been doing before upcoming battles for centuries.

"Louis," he said, addressing Carbone, "you and Al are used to working as a team. I want you two to approach the town from the south. Take as much dynamite as you can carry, tied together two sticks at a time. When you begin your approach, light a cigar and keep it in your mouth to set the fuses off when you're ready to toss the dynamite."

"Cal, I want you and Pearlie to stay together. You're still not up to full strength, so I don't want you to try anything too strenuous. I'm gonna station you on the road out of town, in case some of the outlaws decide it's getting too hot in Fontana and try to make tracks for someplace cooler."

Cal's face fell. "You mean you're gonna keep me outta the action so I won't get shot again, don't ya?"

Pearlie turned to face Cal. "That's not it at all, Cal. Smoke's got to put each man where he can do the best for the team, 'cause we're so outnumbered."

"Pearlie's right, Cal. Your job is just as important as anyone else's. If any of the gunnys get away, they're liable to come back later and do us damage. Your job, and Pearlie's, is to make sure that doesn't happen."

Smoke turned to the remainder of the men. "Louis, I'd like you and Monte to attack from the north, and Johnny and George to come in from the east."

He hesitated. "Joey and I will go in first from the west, from the back of town."

"What do you mean, go in first?" Monte asked.

Smoke pointed to the tins of gunpowder lying in the buckboard. "We're gonna sneak in and plant a few of those where they'll do the most good. Your signal to attack will be when you see them go off."

"What if Cain's men manage to get you before that happens?" Johnny North asked.

Joey shrugged. "Then, you'll hear the gunshots. Either way, it'll be time for you to do your best to blow those bastards to hell and gone."

Thirty-one

Smoke took a tin of bootblack out of his saddlebag and scooped some out on his fingers before handing the can to Joey.

"Put some of that on your face, Joey. It'll help keep us from being seen while we skulk around tonight."

Smoke smeared boot polish around his eyes and mouth until his face was as black as the night. "If things go well," he said to the others, "Joey and I should have the gunpowder set up within about thirty minutes. Give us ten minutes more, just in case. If you haven't heard from us by then, come in with your guns blazing."

Joey finished applying the bootblack and looked up. "Just be careful. If'n you see a couple'a fellows with black faces, make sure you don't blast 'em 'til you see who they are."

Smoke turned to his saddle boot and removed his Greener 10-gauge sawed-off shotgun. He slipped the rawhide strap over his neck so that the gun hung down just under his right arm. He took out a box of shells and filled his buckskin jacket pockets.

While he was doing this, Joey did the same thing with his Winchester rifle, filling his pockets with shells, as well.

Finally, Smoke took two black dusters from his saddlebag. He threw one to Joey and put the other one on. As the two men stepped into their saddles, Pearlie touched the brim of his hat. "Luck, Smoke, Joey."

Joey smiled sarcastically. "Son, luck don't have nothin' to do with it . . . it's who's the meanest gonna survive. The others gonna be buzzard bait."

Smoke and Joey slipped off their horses and left them ground-reined fifty yards from the first buildings on the outskirts of Fontana. Smoke glanced at the sky. Luckily, though there was a half moon the fall weather had brought storm clouds scudding in from over the mountaintops which kept the moonlight to a minimum.

Smoke handed Joey one of the canvas bags full of tins of gunpowder, and he threw another over his shoulder. Stepping lightly and crouching over to minimize their outline against the horizon, they walked quickly into town. With their dark faces and the black dusters flaring out behind them, they looked like strange, malevolent shadows moving in the night.

Slipping down an alleyway, Smoke peered around a corner of the building he was behind and looked toward the Dog Hole Saloon.

"Uh oh," he whispered.

"What is it?" Joey asked.

"It's just past seven o'clock, and I don't see any activity at the saloon."

He could just make out Joey's head in the semi-darkness when he nodded. "That means they're expectin' us," Joey said. "Otherwise they'd all be in there gettin' liquored up."

Smoke took one of the tins of gunpowder out of his sack and placed it next to the corner of the building. While getting ready for this evening, he'd had Pearlie and Cal put blasting caps and fuses into the cans, and Louis Longmont had tied white strips of cloth to the tops of the cans so they'd be easily visible from a distance.

Easing out of the alley, keeping close to the buildings, Smoke and Joey went in separate directions, each planting tins of the black powder along the way.

Bobby Barlow turned to Christopher Tucker. "Hey, Chris. You got any tobaccy?"

The two men had been riding together since Manassas, and Bobby had been smoking Chris's tobacco since before then.

"You know we ain't supposed to smoke whilst we're on guard duty, Bobby."

"Guard duty, hell! There ain't nobody comin' tonight. It's all in Cain's head."

Chris passed over a small sack with his Bull Durham in it. The two were sitting in a darkened room that used to be the town doctor's office, watching out the front window. They'd been placed there by Blackie Jackson to keep an eye on the main street of Fontana.

Bobby struck a lucifer on his pants leg and lighted his cigarette. As he blew smoke out of his nostrils, he squinted and tapped Chris on the shoulder.

"Looky there, Chris. There goes one of those darkies, walkin' down the boardwalk as bold as brass."

Chris shrugged. "So?"

"So? Didn't Blackie Jackson tell us everbody was gonna be under cover tonight, waitin' fer the attack?"

"Yeah, he did."

Bobby got to his feet. "I'd better tell that dumb ass to get off'n the street, then."

He stepped to the door and called softly, "Hey, Bartholomew, it that you?" He figured it had to be Bartholomew Winter, who was the shortest of the three black men riding with them.

The black-faced figure turned his head and took two quick

steps toward Bobby, muttering something the man couldn't understand.

"What'd you say?"

Bobby saw something flash in the meager moonlight and then felt a horrible burning pain in his chest as twelve inches of Arkansas steel pierced his heart.

When Bobby grunted in surprise and pain, Chris called, "Anything wrong, Bobby?"

The short man stepped back from Bobby and let him fall to the floor. Before he hit the ground, Joey's Arkansas Toothpick was slicing across Christopher Tucker's throat, killing him without a sound.

He walked to the window and placed one of the tins of powder on the windowsill, where it could be seen from the street. Then he vanished silently into the darkness.

As Smoke straightened from placing his last tin of gunpowder next to a wall, a harsh voice came from the blackness behind him.

"What do you think you're doin', nigger?" asked Riley Samuels, smiling as he stood there next to Donny Donnahue in the doorway to the old dry goods store.

"Yeah," added Donnahue, "you boys too ignorant to know we supposed to be off the streets tonight?"

The two ex-Confederate soldiers were grinning, their teeth glowing white in the scant moonlight as they took out some of their frustration on what appeared to be one of the black men riding with Cain.

When the figure stood up, Riley's mouth dropped open. None of the Negro troops were this big. This man had to be well over six feet tall.

Donny pointed to the figure's midsection. "What you got there, boy?" he asked.

The black man's teeth gleamed in a wide smile. "It's called a Greener, *boy,*" Smoke answered, and let the hammers down.

The gun kicked back, turning him half around as a two-foot-long tongue of flame leapt out of the barrels toward the rednecks. Six ounces of molten lead spread out in a tight pattern, opening the men's chests and exploding their hearts into tiny pieces.

Before the echoes of the explosion of the shotgun had faded Smoke lit a cigar, touched it to a fuse sticking out of the can of gunpowder on the floor next to him, and calmly walked out of the room.

Willie Bodine, the last of the rebels with Cain, came running down the stairs from where he'd been keeping watch out of a second floor window.

"Donny, Riley, what the hell's goin' on down here?" he asked just as he noticed the burning fuse in the corner of the room next to the bodies of his friends.

"God!" he managed to get out as the gunpowder exploded, blowing his right arm and leg off and tearing his stomach open to expose his guts as he was thrown out the front window. What was left of Willie Bodine landed in the middle of the street, his blood pooling around his dead body in the dirt.

South of Fontana, Louis Carbone leaned over and lit the cigar sticking out of Al Martine's mouth when he heard the shotgun blast followed closely by the explosion of the gunpowder.

"Well, *amigo,* it is time to ride."

Al nodded. "Time to ride and kill, *compadre.*"

They leaned over the necks of their mounts and put spurs to their flanks, heading into hell.

In the north, Louis Longmont stuck out his hand to Monte Carson. "You ready, partner?" he asked.

Monte took his hand and nodded. "It'll be a pleasure to do battle with you, Mr. Longmont."

The two gunfighters rode toward the town at an easy canter, their hands filled with iron and their eyes flicking back and forth, looking for targets.

On the east side of town Johnny North looked at George Hampton as they moved their horses toward town. "George, don't you go gettin' yourself killed tonight. My daughter'd never forgive me if I let that happen."

George shook his head, smiling grimly. "Johnny, neither would I, neither would I."

Lazarus Cain jerked his head to the side when he heard the shotgun blast and the explosion of the gunpowder. "Damn! It's begun," he said to Blackie Jackson, who sat next to him in the saloon.

Blackie nodded and reached over to turn off the lantern hanging on the wall next to them, plunging the room into darkness.

The rest of Cain's personal team were scattered around the saloon and on the second floor and roof of the building, waiting for the attack.

As Al and Louis rode into town, Pedro Gonzalez and Jaime Sanchez rose up on the roof of a boardinghouse and began to fire down at them. Pedro's second shot hit Al's horse in the neck and he somersaulted, throwing Al to the ground.

Louis put the fuse on a bundle of dynamite to his cigar, and when it ignited he threw it onto the roof behind the shooters.

It exploded, sending the two gunmen catapulting off the roof as if they'd been shot out of a cannon. Jaime Sanchez landed on his head not five feet from where Al lay, snapping his neck and breaking his back in three places.

Al glanced back over his shoulder at Louis. "Careful, *amigo,* you almost landed him on top of me."

Pedro Gonzalez's headless body slammed into the ground twenty yards away, and still moved, writhing in the dirt, as if it were alive for several seconds.

Al scrambled on hands and knees, grabbed his sack of dynamite off his saddle horn, and then ran toward the nearest building, trying to get off the street.

Two black men stepped out of the building, guns in their hands.

"Hold it, mister," Bartholomew Winter said, in his soft Southern accent. "Drop that bag and raise your hands."

"Sure . . . sure . . . only, don't shoot me," Al begged as he complied with the man's orders.

When he saw their eyes follow the bag as he dropped it, his hands flashed to his pistols, drawing and firing before the two men saw him move.

His left-hand gun shot Bartholomew Winter in the throat, blowing out his spine and almost decapitating him. His right-hand gun shot Jedediah Jones in the middle of his chest, shattering his sternum and piercing his heart, killing him before his finger could tighten on the trigger.

Cherokee Bill, notorious outlaw, watched this happen from the building where he and Bartholomew and Jedediah had been stationed. He shook his head. *This ain't my fight,* he thought. He quietly slipped out the back door of the room and got on his horse. He spurred the animal into a gallop and headed south out of town as fast as he could ride back toward the Indian Nations in Oklahoma Territory. He didn't know it, but he was riding toward a date with a hangman's noose, in less than a year.

On the east side of town, Coronado Vallentine and Perro Gutierrez were holed up in a barn next to the livery stable with Dick Wheeler and Billy Baugh. They watched silently as buildings began to explode and burn all over town.

"Damn!" Dick Wheeler muttered, watching through his window as the flames leapt toward the sky.

"Hey, here comes two men ridin' down the street," said Billy Baugh, pointing his rifle out his window.

Wheeler was just about to tell the other men to hold their fire until they got closer when Perro Gutierrez snapped off a shot with his pistol.

The bullet took George Hampton in the right chest, spinning him around and knocking him to the ground.

Johnny North, fearing the worst, spurred his horse directly toward the barn as fast as he could ride. He rode into the building through the doors, both hands full of iron.

Perro Gutierrez whirled around, firing blindly.

Johnny shot him in the face, exploding his head and throwing him backward over a bale of hay.

Thumbing his hammers back and firing as fast as he could from the back of his rearing, screaming horse, Johnny was deadly accurate.

Dick Wheeler didn't get off a shot before he was hit in the neck and chest. Billy Baugh managed to fire twice, one of his bullets notching Johnny's left ear, before Johnny shot him in the gut, doubling him over and knocking him to his knees, where he knelt as if in some sort of grotesque prayer.

Coronado Vallentine aimed his shotgun at Johnny's back, earing back the hammers and grinning over the sights. Just before he pulled the trigger a shot rang out from behind him, and he felt a blow between his shoulder blades.

He whirled around in time to see George Hampton standing there, blood all over his shirtfront, looking at him over the barrel of a Colt .45 that was still smoking.

Vallentine coughed, spitting blood, and found he didn't have the strength to pull the triggers on his shotgun. He grinned, and died, falling facedown on the straw-covered floor.

Johnny jumped down off his horse and ran to grab George just as he began to fall.

"Thanks, George, you saved my life," Johnny said.

George smiled. "My future wife'd never forgive me if I let her daddy get killed," he said. Then he fainted.

Three-fingers Sammy Torres was holed up in the hotel building with the ex-Dalton gang members, Jimmy, Jake, Sonny, and Clyde. They were on the second floor, stationed at windows in various rooms where they had a good view of the street.

When Three-fingers Sammy saw two black-clad figures running across the street toward the saloon, he opened fire, pocking dirt around the running men but missing with all his shots.

Luckily, Monte and Louis Longmont saw the muzzle flash from his rifle and reined up their horses before they got to the hotel. Jumping to the ground, they pulled pistols and eased down an alley and around the corner and into the back door of the building.

Finding no one on the first floor, they began to climb the stairs, eyes staring upward for any sign of a hostile body.

They just reached the second floor landing when Jake stepped out of a doorway, checking his pistol to see if it was fully loaded. He looked up to find four barrels pointed at him.

He snapped his loading gate shut and started to raise his pistol. Two bullets, one each from Louis and Monte, took him in the chest, blowing him back into the room he'd just come out of so hard that he backpedaled and hit the window, shattering it, and fell out onto the street below.

When Sonny and Clyde burst out of their doors, Monte and Louis crouched and began to fire away. Monte blew Clyde to hell, but not before one of Clyde's slugs pierced his abdomen, exiting out his flank after burrowing through six inches of fat and muscle. Monte doubled over, pressing his elbow to the wound to slow the bleeding, but keeping his eyes open for more enemies.

Louis shot Sonny in the face, shattering his buckteeth and blowing them out the back of his head.

Jimmy peered around the edge of a doorway, trying to see through the smoke and haze before he ventured out. Monte snapped off a shot, grazing the boy's head and making him duck back out of sight behind the door. Monte put two more bullets through the door, and Jimmy slowly fell out into the hall, his eyes showing surprise at the events of the evening.

Three-fingers Sammy Torres walked out of his room, his hands held high.

"I give up. I surrender," he said, grinning cockily, as if he hadn't a care in the world.

Louis shook his head. "Uh uh, mister. It is not going to be that easy. You dealt yourself into this hand, so ante up, or die where you stand."

"You wouldn't shoot a man who surrendered, would you?" Torres asked.

Monte, from down the hall, grunted, "If he won't, I sure as hell will. Fill your hand, outlaw, or I'll shoot you down like a dog."

Torres scowled and grabbed for his pistol. He managed to get it half raised and fire a shot before Louis shot him between the eyes, snapping his head back and flinging him spread-eagled onto his back on the floor.

"I must be getting too old for this," Louis mumbled, looking down at his thigh, where a spreading pool of crimson was appearing.

"Yeah," Monte agreed, "me too," and he sat down with his back to a wall.

* * *

Cain peered out a front window of the saloon, watching as the town was destroyed around him. Al Martine and Louis Carbone were walking down the street, calmly throwing dynamite onto roofs and into windows, blowing men and pieces of men to hell and gone.

Johnny North, after dressing George Hampton's wound and making him lie down in the barn, was walking down the street from the other direction, using a rifle to fire into the tins of gunpowder Joey and Smoke had secreted along the boardwalk. Buildings on both sides of the street were exploding in flames, which were spreading, fueled by fall winds blowing in from the mountains.

Monte Carson and Louis Longmont, leaning on each other for support, managed to make it out onto the street before Al Martine shot into the gunpowder in the lobby, collapsing the building and throwing more dead men from the roof.

Floyd Devers, Walter Blackwell, Tad Younger, and Johnny Samson, all ex-members of Bloody Bill Anderson's gang, were hiding in one of the boardinghouses.

"Men, it don't look good out there. Half the damn town's burning already," Devers said.

"Yeah," answered Tad Younger. "Let's get the hell out of here."

"You got my vote," agreed Samson.

The four men ran out the back door and jumped on their horses and rode down a back road, out of town.

Joey and Smoke made their way toward the saloon, figuring that was where Cain and his cadre of picked men would hole up.

King Johannson and Pig Iron Carlton leaned over the parapet of the saloon roof, searching for someone to shoot.

Johannson leveled his rifle at Carbone, taking aim. A bullet plowed into the board he was resting his elbow on, sending a shower of splinters several inches long into his face.

He screamed and stood up, clawing at his right eye, which had a long piece of wood protruding from it. Joey levered another shell into his rifle and fired again, taking Johannson just under the hairline, the bullet blowing the top of his skull off and knocking him back out of sight.

Carlton leaned over and fired twice at Joey, his second slug gouging a chunk of meat from Joey's left shoulder before Smoke leveled his Greener and fired both barrels.

The buckshot took half the roof off as it tore through Carlton, shredding his left arm to bloody pulp and flinging him out off the roof. He landed on his back on a water trough, his spine snapping with an audible crack.

In the saloon, Blackie Jackson leaned over and whispered to Lazarus, "It don't look good, boss. Let's hightail it out of town and live to fight another day."

"Have you got the horses tied out back like I told you?" Jackson nodded.

Lazarus jumped to his feet and hurried toward the door. "Then let's make tracks."

Curly Joe Ventrillo, Tom "Behind the Deuces" Cartwright, and Jeremy Brett were left to face Smoke and Joey alone in the saloon.

Smoke and Joey slipped through the batwings and stepped to the side, each with their backs against the wall, letting their eyes adjust to the gloom in the room.

Ventrillo, Brett, and Cartwright walked out onto the second floor landing, looking down at Smoke and Joey over the railing.

"I don't suppose you chaps would allow us to ride out of here, would you?" Brett asked, a sardonic smile on his face.

"Not likely," Joey growled, his hands hanging next to his pistol.

Ventrillo spread his hands wide. "But, we have you out-numbered. You don't have a chance of killing all three of us before one of us gets you."

"You fellows called this dance, now someone's got to pay the band. Jerk that sixkiller and go to work."

The five men drew, Smoke and Joey's hands moving so fast it was almost a blur.

Four shots rang out before any of the outlaws on the landing cleared leather.

Smoke put one in Brett's chest and another in Carlton's neck. Joey put a slug in Ventrillo's face and another in Carlton's stomach.

As smoke billowed and the men fell to the floor, Smoke heard hoofbeats from the back of the saloon.

"Cain's getting away," he said.

Smoke and Joey ran toward the livery to get horses to follow the outlaw leader.

Thirty-two

Pearlie and Cal were watching the sky over Fontana turn orange and red in the reflected glow of burning buildings.

"Dammit, Pearlie," Cal said, "we oughta be there to help Smoke out."

"Yeah, I know, Cal, but I aim to do what Smoke said, as hard as it is to miss the action."

"Sh-h-h," Cal whispered. "I hear horses comin'."

The two men got down off the buckboard where they'd been sitting and slipped the hammer thongs off their pistols.

Four riders came galloping up, reining in when they saw the road blocked by the wagon, and the two men standing in front of it.

Walter Blackwell called out, "Get your wagon outta our way!"

Cal gave a low laugh. "You know who that galoot is, Pearlie?"

"No," Pearlie shook his head.

"It's the man who shot his friend, Bloody Bill Anderson, in the back, to save his own skin."

Pearlie nodded. "Looks like he's turning tail and runnin' from another fight, don't it, Cal?"

"Sure does," Cal answered.

Sweat began to form on Blackwell's forehead. "You men get out of our way or we'll be forced to gun you down!" he yelled.

Both Cal and Pearlie grinned. "Let's dance!" Pearlie said.

Six men went for their guns simultaneously.

Cal was a shade faster than Pearlie and got off the first shot, hitting Blackwell in the chest before he cleared leather.

Pearlie shot a fraction of a second later, his slug taking Johnny Samson in the left eye, blowing out the side of his skull and breaking his neck.

Floyd Devers fired once, just as Cal's second shot hit him in the stomach, doubling him over his saddle horn with a grunt of pain. Cal fired again, into his right ear, knocking him out of the saddle and onto the ground.

Tad Younger and Pearlie fired at the same time, Younger taking one in the neck and Pearlie taking one in the left shoulder.

As cordite and gunsmoke swirled in a thick cloud and echoes of gunfire reverberated off distant mountains, Pearlie and Cal looked at each other.

"Well, I'll be darned," Pearlie muttered, glancing down at his shoulder. "Looks like some of your natural attraction for lead has rubbed off onto me."

Cal removed his hat and stuck his finger through the hole Devers's bullet had left in it. "Yeah, thank goodness." He sighed.

Blackie Jackson and Lazarus Cain slowed their horses to a walk, letting them blow after their long ride from Fontana.

"You think any of the boys got out alive?" Jackson asked.

Lazarus shook his head. "Doubtful. Not if Jensen's as good as they say he is."

A voice came from the darkness behind them. "He is, and they didn't," Joey Wells said.

Jackson and Cain whirled around to find Smoke Jensen and Joey Wells sitting on horses just behind them.

"Well, well," Lazarus said. "So it comes down to this, huh?"

"That's right," Smoke said. "You came after me, and now you've found me. Let's settle this."

Blackie Jackson, thinking Smoke's attention was fixed on Lazarus, went for his pistol. Two shots rang out almost as one, both hitting Jackson in the chest an inch apart, right over his heart. When he hit the dirt his gun was still in its holster, untouched.

Lazarus eyed the tall figure dressed in buckskins as they faced each other across the mountain meadow. His hands tensed above the walnut grips of his holstered revolvers, pistols that had killed dozens of times before.

"You're no match for me, Jensen. I'll kill you before you can clear leather."

"That hasn't been decided yet," a stony voice replied, a cold stare fixed on Lazarus. "You reach for them guns, an' one of us is gonna die."

Something stirred inside Lazarus Cain, a chilly feeling he'd never known before, forming a knot in his belly. He looked down at Blackie Jackson, lying dead as a stone where Smoke Jensen and Joey Wells had killed him as casually as swatting a fly.

"You can't be that good," Lazarus spat at the mountain man. His mouth went dry as he said it, yet he refused to believe the taste on his tongue might be fear.

"Only one way to find out," Smoke Jensen replied evenly, no change in his tone or expression. "Go for your guns and we'll settle this. I'm tired of all this banter. You're wastin' a helluva lot of my time."

Lazarus gave Jensen a false grin, ready to make his play. "I never was one to let a feller back me down . . ."

As he grabbed for his gun he saw Jensen's hand move almost faster than his eye could follow.

His gun was half out of his holster when Lazarus heard

an explosion and felt as if he'd been kicked in the chest by a mule.

The next thing he knew, he was flat on his back looking up at stars and a moon half hidden behind scurrying clouds.

He reached into his coat pocket, over his heart, and took out the Bible his father had given him. Just above the bullet imbedded in it was a hole. He smiled grimly, then died.

On the way back to Fontana, Joey glanced over at Smoke. "We're gonna have to get together more often, Smoke," he drawled. "Life's been gettin' plumb dull without you around."

William W. Johnstone
The *Mountain Man* Series

**WILLIAM W. JOHNSTONE
has done it again . . .**

Introducing 2 New Series:

*THE LAST
GUNFIGHTER*

and

CODE NAME

THE LAST GUNFIGHTER:
THE DRIFTER
February 2000

CODE NAME: PAYBACK
March 2000